MW00658669

Magic Portals

To Bill,
when you need
to get away —
Jodi
Ruzzotto

Magic Portals

Enrapturing Tales is an imprint of:

Knight Writing Press
PMB # 162
13009 S. Parker Rd.
Parker CO 80134
knightwritingpress.com
KnightWritingPress@gmail.com

Additional Copyright Information can be found on page 301

Interior Book Design and eBook Design by Knight Writing Press

Editor Sam Knight

First Publication June 2022

Paperback ISBN-13: 978-1-62869-049-1
eBook ISBN-13: 978-1-62869-050-7

Dedicated to the
part of you that
always felt there
was something
more out there...

because there is.

Table of Contents

A Billion Specks of Light

by
James Rumpel

A Billion Specks of Light

I was working in the garden when I first noticed something peculiar. I'd spent most of the last week enjoying my early retirement and the peacefulness associated with the fact that my wife, Heather, was still working. Don't get me wrong, I loved Heather with all my heart. She meant everything to me. However, I was enjoying the opportunity to be alone with my thoughts.

I had the entire day to myself. I'd just dug up the sod and was starting to break up the topsoil on a new garden patch when I noticed a quiet humming sound. At first, I thought it was an insect, but I soon dismissed that idea. The sound seemed mechanical, unnatural. I looked in the direction of the noise, but all I saw was our three-acre plot of land with our two-story house sitting prominently in the background. I had mown the lawn the day before; the smell of the fresh clippings still lingered in the air.

The sound did not go away.

I am generally curious by nature, and since I had nothing that I needed to do, I set down my shovel and started walking around the area, searching for the noise's source. I must have passed it a half-dozen times before I saw it. A thin, black line floated vertically near a corner of my garden. I tried to grab the mysterious shape, but my hand pushed it aside. It separated slightly, as if I were spreading a curtain.

I probably should have left it alone, but I didn't. I used my two hands to open it even farther. It was an odd sensation to watch the darkness expand as I widened the gap between my hands. I could see some sort of dim light deep within the recesses of the space I had created. Looking back, I can't believe I had the guts to stick my head inside, but I did. I felt there was something important for me through that opening. What I saw was a dark corridor leading to an open doorway and a brightly lit room. Nudged onward by something greater than curiosity, I pulled the invisible curtain back farther and stepped inside.

The curtain shut behind me. Panicking, I probed with my fingers to try and find the slit that would lead me back to my yard.

I had made a drastic mistake. I was trapped. My heart raced as I fought back tears and resisted the urge to scream. There was no one in the yard to hear me, and I had no idea what my shouts would bring. I wished and prayed that this was all a dream. I wanted nothing more than to wake up and find myself in my hammock, having dozed off after lunch.

My prayers went unanswered. I gave up on the search for an opening and decided that there may be an answer in the corridor ahead, so I moved toward the light. The walls of the hall were dark and smooth, metallic to the touch. When I reached the doorway, I peered into a long, thin room. It was only a couple of feet wider than the corridor, but the two side walls must have been fifty feet tall and were at least that long. One of these walls was unlit and appeared to be made of the same material as the corridor. The other, however, was filled with specks of light, each the size of a pencil point. I couldn't begin to hazard a guess as to how many there were. They were spread about the surface in no discernible pattern.

Again, I found myself pulled forward. Was there some unnatural force compelling me into this bizarre world?

Inside the room, I checked for a doorway on the opposite wall but there wasn't one. I have no idea how long I stood there staring at the strange wall. It looked like a moonless night sky; the specks playing the roles of unblinking stars.

I nearly jumped out of my shoes when I heard a voice behind me.

"How did you get in here?"

I turned to see a man standing in the doorway. He looked to be in his early twenties. Shoulder-length hair framed his clean-shaven face. He wore a white robe that covered his entire body except for his head, his hands, and his bare feet.

I'm sure my confusion showed on my face. "I…I…don't really know. I saw this black line that turned out to be an opening…"

The young man smiled. "Don't worry. You did nothing wrong. I am sure it was a glitch in the system. They are extremely rare, but they do happen. With billions of people on Earth and billions of different timelines, something occasionally goes wrong even if the probability is zero. I know that sounds like a mathematical impossibility, but it isn't."

I wanted to ask all sorts of questions. Unfortunately, I just stood there with my mouth open like a fool.

The man approached me and placed his hand on my shoulder. "Just relax. I will explain everything to you, and we will find a solution to your problem."

Finally, I was able to speak. "What problem?"

"Before I can answer that, you need to know where you are," answered my host. He looked squarely into my eyes. "I am about to tell you some amazing things."

He pointed to the wall of lights. "You have found the way into your life display. Every human being on Earth has a room like this. It records every moment in your life when you make a decision that greatly alters your future. Each speck of light represents a significantly different outcome to your existence."

What he was describing seemed too fantastic to be true. The fact that I had just climbed through a floating hole in my garden made me more willing to accept what he was saying.

"Is this heaven? Are you an angel?" Now that I had regained enough composure to speak, the questions were coming like an avalanche of ignorance.

"You might call me an angel. When the Earth's population was smaller, we used to have more time and would sometimes make brief visits. That may be where the concept of angels came from. I am what is called a Guardian of the Lights. This is not heaven. It may well be your ticket there, however. When all of your possible life paths are complete, the totality of all your possible lives is used to determine your worth."

"So, everything on Earth isn't real? This is all some kind of computer simulation?" I was beginning to worry that my head might explode.

"No. It is very real. This is just another plane of existence. From here we watch."

"But you said there was a glitch. Doesn't that imply computers or machines?" I wasn't sure why I was fixating on that one aspect of the amazing situation. Maybe I was hoping that everything could be rebooted, and I could get back to my garden and my life.

This time the young man was the one who looked confused for a moment. "I guess I don't really know. It doesn't matter. It is what it is. My job is to monitor millions of lives and deal with rare occasions like this."

"Can you send me back?" I was more than ready to put this strange journey behind me. I would have been very happy to forget that it ever happened.

"Well," replied the Guardian after a brief pause. "That's the problem. By coming here, you stopped that particular path of your life. The light that represents that existence has gone out."

"You mean, I'm dead?" This was a turn I had not expected.

"Yes and no," was his cryptic reply. "You aren't dead. You're here. But your world is permanently gone."

I found myself shivering at the news. "You mean that Heather is going to come home from work and find that I have mysteriously disappeared. She won't know what happened to me. My family, my friends..."

My knees buckled. I would have collapsed to the floor had not the young man grabbed me and held me steady.

"I am so sorry," he said. "You cannot go back. Once a path reaches its conclusion, and the light goes out, there is no going back. But understand that your wife's path is still going on. In her room, the light that signifies the existence that the two of you shared is still glowing. The two of you are living together in that reality."

"My path just stopped? Wouldn't I disappear in her life?" The possibility of my head exploding was increasing rapidly.

"No, because that change was caused by one of your decisions, not one of hers."

Now that I was more stable, he released me and backed up a few steps.

"But if I can't go home, and I am not dead, what's going to happen to me?"

"We do have a contingency for occasions like this," explained the Guardian. "There are still millions of lights in the room. I can send you to one of them and you can continue living that life."

"Great. Send me to the one that is closest to what I just came from." Maybe this was going to work out.

"That's the problem," was his sobering reply. "We can't see what a life path is like until it ends. You are just going to be randomly sent into one of them."

"But what if it's a bad life. What if I never met Heather? What if I am poor or sick?"

He reached into his robe and pulled out a small black cube. On one side of the cube was a red button. "This failsafe will allow you to return here if you end up in an unsatisfying existence. It will only work three times, and you must use it within the first five minutes, or it will not send you back. The few other people I have encountered in your situation have always found a path where they remained. They must have been satisfied with the lives they jumped into. I expect your results will be the same."

"There has to be another way," I begged. "I can't believe my life ended just because I found that opening. It's not fair. I should get to live the life I created. I demand to speak with someone who can fix this."

Despite my escalating anger, my host remained calm. "There is no one else. Every other Guardian has the same duties and offers the same option that I do. You need to either select a light and go to that time-path, or I have to leave you here until your body perishes. I am sorry there are no other options."

"Ok," I found myself succumbing to the inevitable. If all the previous visitors had found acceptable lives, then I could too. "What do I do?"

"Pick a light and touch it."

"What if I want to pick a light that is by the ceiling?" I think I was just being difficult.

"Concentrate on it and it will move to within your reach. Good luck." He handed me the cube, and I placed it in my pocket.

I focused on a point of light about halfway up the wall and watched it slowly descend and stop in front of me. Tentatively, I reached out and touched it.

A deluge of memories flooded into my brain. I still remembered my life, but now there was a second life coexisting in my thoughts. The shock almost made me lose my balance. Luckily, I reacted with cat-like reflexes I didn't know I possessed. I found myself standing on the roof of a newly built two-story home.

I searched my new memories for as much information about this reality as I could find. To my disappointment, I was single. Heather and I had never crossed paths. I'd dropped out of college after a semester in which I'd picked good times over studies. The real me remembered being tempted to ignore my schoolwork. I didn't give in to those temptations. In this time-path I had.

I soon realized that on this path I lived a good but lonely life. I worked long, physical hours doing construction. This would not be a bad life, but it was not as good as the one I left. I pulled the button the Guardian had given me from my pocket. Was it worth the risk to try and find a better life? After a brief hesitation, I pushed the button.

"You decided that was not for you?" asked the robed young man.

I answered, "I can do better." I found that I could remember my thoughts from the few minutes I was on the rooftop though the new memories that had jumped into my brain were no longer present.

"You must choose again."

This time I selected a spot of light right next to me. I took a deep breath and reached out with my finger.

I was better prepared for this transition. For the second time, my mind was inundated with a different set of memories. I looked around and realized I was in my garden, but something was different. This garden was little more than a conglomeration of weeds. The grass in the yard was patchy and in need of mowing. I felt alone.

In this new life, I had been married to Heather, but we were no longer together. I'd driven her away. A series of selfish decisions had led to her leaving early in our marriage. Bitterness kept me from finding joy in the years that followed and my heart had darkened over time.

I considered the possibility that I could make amends with Heather. Perhaps I could fix all the things that I'd done wrong. My new memories told me that Heather had remarried and moved to the East Coast. I realized that this life's past was affecting my thoughts when I felt anger welling in my stomach. I couldn't let myself become this resentful husk of a man. I pulled out the button and pressed it once again.

"You only have one more use of the button," stated the Guardian, calmly.

"I know, but I just couldn't handle that life. Maybe I should have stayed with my first choice. Can I go back to that one?" I asked the question even though I already guessed the answer.

"Even if you could find the correct light you could not return." The young man appeared sadder than had earlier. Maybe I was just projecting my growing gloom onto him.

"I have to do better this time." I reached to my left and touched a speck of light.

I immediately knew something was terribly wrong. I was in a hospital bed, unable to move my arms or legs. The memory of a car accident jumped to my thoughts. I had been late to pick up Heather from work. I'd driven too fast.

Where was the button? How could I push it?

I tried to speak but found that I couldn't. My mind screamed but my body remained motionless. I was distinctly aware of the passage of time. I only had five minutes.

Somehow my new memories fought through the panic, and I remember that I could write messages on a computer screen by blowing through a straw. It had been a difficult skill to master but I could do it.

I hurriedly tried to spell out a message, "HELP ME BUTTON UNDER SHEET PUSH NOW." I could only hope that the button was lying near where it would have been if I had pockets.

Luckily, the computer beeped with each letter. Moments after I began my message, Heather appeared at my bedside. I battled against the urge to stop the message and stare at her beauty. I finally finished the message and gazed up at her confused face.

After what seemed like way too long of a pause, she put her hand by my hip and felt under the sheet. An expression of surprise joined the confusion. She pulled the sheet back and picked up the button. She held it in front of my eyes. "Is this the button you want me to push?"

I wanted to nod my head, but I could not. I remembered; blink once for yes. I blinked and then made sure that my eyes remained wide open.

With each second that passes, I became more certain it was too late. The horror of the remainder of this life was going to be this reality. Heather shrugged and pressed the button.

"I have never seen someone use all three pushes of the button. You will not be able to return from your next choice."

"I don't want to try again," I said. "I can't risk it. I only want my true life."

The young man cocked his head to the side as if listening to some sound that I was unable to hear. Eventually, he looked at me and nodded. "It turns out that there is another option. Since you could not find a new life-path and the glitch was not your fault, we are willing to offer you a position as a Guardian of the Lights. Frankly, we could use the help."

"You mean, I would do what you do?"

"Yes. If you accept, we can begin your training immediately."

I knew it was the best solution I was going to be offered. After my last experience, I didn't want to jump into another life. "I accept," was all I said, though it felt like I should have said more.

"Very good," said the young man. "I am Barnabas. Come with me. We will start your training." He started walking toward the far end of the room. A doorway appeared where there had not been one earlier.

Out of the corner of my eye, I noticed the specks of light on the wall fading, one by one. My life was gone. I regretted not appreciating what I had. I thought of Heather and prayed that the billions of specks of light in her room each represented happy and complete lives. I would never see her again. I had a different life now; I was a Guardian of the Lights.

About the Author

James Rumpel is a retired high school math teacher who has greatly enjoyed spending his additional free time trying to turn some of the many odd ideas circling his brain into stories. He lives in Wisconsin with his wonderful wife, Mary.

Manna

by

Edward J. Knight

Manna

Going dry was no fun, but no one would give Winston any booze. He'd long abandoned his spot by the Golden Dream Hotel after the beating from the manager. The sheriff had said it'd served him right, bothering the guests. But they had the money, so where else was he supposed to sit?

Instead, he leaned his back against the rough pine of the General Store. The awning shaded him enough from the hot Nevada sun to keep his sweat from streaming down his face. He was mighty parched, but it was a scorching walk to the creek that he wasn't quite ready to take. Besides, Mrs. Abernathy, God bless her soul, had given him a heel of bread. If he chewed the grainy crust slowly, he could almost keep his mouth wet.

Maybe if he'd had a better hat, without the big tear in the seam, he'd be able to keep cooler. Or maybe if his old dungarees didn't need so much patching. The skin on his exposed knee had browned and cracked in the heat. If he died, he'd be tanned leather before they put him in the ground.

It was a long cry from New Jersey.

He sighed. How had it come to this?

But he knew. He couldn't forget. Those memories of Mary, her smile matching the sun. The memories of her words, in that final letter, that he'd tried to drown. At least they didn't hurt so much anymore.

Maybe Sheriff West had done him a blessing when he'd forbade the townsfolk from giving him booze. He still missed it. Longed for it. Could feel the memory of its burn in his throat. But he wasn't dead.

Yet.

True, he was a beanpole, but he hadn't lost all his strength. Something that ranch hand had learned the hard way. Sheriff West had just laughed at the kid's bloody nose and sent him on his way. Sheriff West had told Winston to be careful and maybe stay off the streets, but it was hard when you barely had a pot of beans to your name.

So he sat and he waited, his little tin cup by his side with two pennies he could rattle when the next townsfolk came by. With two more coins, he could get some soup without raiding his stash. And maybe Reverend Stillwater would let him have an egg or two before church.

But speaking of the reverend…

The burly, bearded minister strode down the dusty road. In his black suit, he had to be sweating, but the reverend never let it show. His set jaw and hard eyes matched his purpose. He was gonna save the souls of Cave Creek if he had to drag them out of Hell with his own bare hands.

Winston expected the reverend to march on by. He was one of the few that treated Winston with charity, though even he most often had other tasks to do. But the reverend spotted him and altered his steps. A minute later, he stood in front of Winston, his fists on his hips.

"Winston," he said, his deep voice booming, "I am in need of some assistance. I will feed you supper, and you can sleep in the church tonight if you'll help."

Winston scrambled to his feet before he even thought to answer yes. Widow Gallagher fixed the reverend cutlets and potatoes every Saturday night, and Winston could already smell the gravy.

Once Winston was on his feet, Reverend Stillwater turned and headed back down the way he'd come. He glanced back once to make sure Winston was keeping up, but he didn't slow. After some quick stepping, Winston managed to even up, so they could walk side by side.

"Thought you were going back to New Jersey," Reverend Stillwater said.

"Still saving for the coach," Winston replied. He actually *was*, but it was hard. Money flowed through his fingers like placer water, and both were far too scarce out here. He was a fool to leave New Jersey, but it was a foolishness that was hard to correct. At least he'd saved some, since no one would sell him a whiskey no more.

They stopped at the stables at the edge of town. Reverend Stillwater told Winston to wait outside while he secured a wagon for the day. Winston scratched his forehead but noticed the trough for the horses wasn't too brackish. Using his hands for a cup, he drank deep, and then splashed some more on his face.

Ahh.

The reverend noticed his wet shirt when he returned, but only quirked one eyebrow.

"Can you drive a team?" he asked.

"I did all the time, back in Jersey," Winston said. "Coaches. Deliveries. I had a regular job takin' boxes from the railroad to the factories and laboratories."

Until he'd decided to chase after a fortune in gold. A foolish, foolish choice. Not all the booze in the world could make him forget how stupid he'd been. Mary had told him not to, pleaded with him not to, but he'd been too puffed up. A mockingbird full of pride.

"Good," Reverend Stillwater said. "You drive." He gestured for Winston to follow him around to the back.

The wagon and the team weren't nothing special. They'd do for the reverend, just like Winston would. In due time, they were on the road toward the hills. Winston didn't ask where. He'd learn, soon enough.

They didn't go as far as he'd expected. Just outside of town, they left the road and went through a small twisty canyon barely wide enough for the wagon. Then they crossed the rough to the first hill and went around to its far side. The ground was lumpy and uneven, but the wagon managed the bumps. When they finally wormed their way around the last little rise, Winston's jaw dropped.

Ahead sat the strangest trash dump he'd ever seen.

The rotten, rancid smell hit him at once. He wrinkled his nose and fought back the desire to pinch it. Still, he stopped the wagon and stared.

The dump wasn't as large as he'd first thought. It was more a mound, really, peaked in the middle and rolling off to the sides. All in all, it was probably not much taller than a man on a horse, and not much wider at the base than one of the streets in town. But what a mess it was.

Winston spotted metal bits and bones and rotten vegetables. The edges were half-dried sludge baked hard in the desert heat.

Small steel boxes and rods poked out here and there and at the top—

Winston swallowed hard and tried to keep his belly under control. Thank the Lord he hadn't eaten much today for he surely would've lost it.

For on top of the garbage dump sat a human head, flesh and hair and all.

"What is this place?" Winston asked.

"The Devil's trash." Reverend Stillwater started to climb off the wagon. "Come, Winston, let us retrieve the body and give it a Christian burial."

Shaking, Winston tied off the reins and dismounted. The horses tugged and shifted in their tethers, which made the wagon rock. Winston managed to keep his feet, just barely, as he climbed to the ground.

"Whoever butchered this poor soul," Reverend Stillwater pointed to the head, "will have done so in large sections, thank the Lord."

"There have been others?" Winston's heart raced with the thought.

"Yes." Reverend Stillwater's expression was grim. "More than I wish to count." He gestured at the trash heap. "Let us make haste. The sooner we have him, the sooner we can leave this evil place."

Winston wasn't sure how evil it was. He carefully picked his way through the outer edges of the mound. Most of it was just regular trash. He stepped over a desiccated turkey carcass covered with flies and around some old tin cans. He furrowed his brow at a little yellow bottle with a nozzle and a label with writing on it. Alas, he'd never learned his letters so he couldn't read the words. The bottle looked like it was made of rubber, which made no sense.

But then he saw the severed arm. So maybe the reverend was right. Evil lurked here.

Thank the Lord, the body parts were all on top. Even more blessedly, they didn't bleed or ooze. They didn't have clothes either, which made them more like just meat. So, like handling old steaks, Winston gathered up what he found and returned it to the wagon, where he placed it on a filthy sheet the reverend had spread out. He barely noticed that his stomach had settled with the new familiarity with this place.

"Look out!" Reverend Stillwater pointed skyward where an object now plummeted down.

At the wagon, Winston was nowhere close to where it smashed into the pile and then bounced down the side. It tumbled toward him instead of the reverend. When it came to rest, his eyes went wide.

It was a gun.

Winston scrambled off the wagon and hurried over to it. The reverend gave him a glance, but then turned back to his own tasks. Winston reached the gun and picked it up.

It was a strange one. With the barrel and grip, it had to be a pistol, but there was no rotating barrel for the bullets. He tucked it into his waistband under his shirt to examine later.

After another dozen minutes, they had the remains of the poor soul all laid out in the wagon. Reverend Stillwater gave a short prayer and then pulled a second sheet over the naked corpse. He then had Winston drive them to the cemetery.

Inside the low wire fence, Winston let out a sigh. Mason, the gravedigger, leaned on his shovel next to a freshly dug hole. The wiry little man had dust and dirt all over his pants and shirt and beard, but he stood straight as the wagon approached and helped them lower the body from the wagon.

"Gotta name?" Mason asked.

"Not this time," Reverend Stillwater said. When he saw Winston's confusion he added, "Sometimes we find a funny little playing card in their clothes with a photograph and a name, but not this time."

Winston furrowed his brow. Photographs were so expensive and rare; he could not imagine one on a playing card. But the reverend had no reason to lie.

They lowered the body, wrapped in the sheets, into the grave. Then the reverend asked them to bow their heads and began the funeral service. Winston fought to avoid shuffling. The gun poked against his belly, warm and hard. His thirst had returned, and he wondered if the reverend carried a canteen. Part of him itched for booze, but he fought it, and fought it hard. He needed water. Not another night of waking up in the dirt.

After the service, Winston helped Mason fill the grave. Reverend Stillwater erected the wooden cross and simply wrote "Unknown" on it in charcoal. Then Reverend Stillwater slipped Mason a coin as Winston turned the wagon around. They rode back to the stables in quiet. After they'd returned the wagon, Reverend Stillwater invited Winston to follow him to the church.

The reverend kept a small room at the rear of the simple building. With a cot, a small round pine table, a desk, and a small bookcase with a dozen volumes, there was little room for Winston and the reverend to both sit at the same time. A large ceramic carafe sat on the table, and the reverend poured water into nearby glasses. Winston took his and drank greedily.

"You did well out there, Winston," the reverend said. "Mason won't assist me any longer. He says the place is cursed."

Winston shrugged. He didn't believe in curses. That trash heap had been made by men. Evil men, given the bodies, but men nonetheless. How was beyond his reckoning. But why was clear. They sent things to the pile that the did not wish to ever return.

"I was wondering...," the reverend continued, "would you be willing to help in the future? It is difficult for me to keep an eye on that...place...while also attending to the flock here in town."

"Can I sleep here?" Winston's eyes fell on the cot.

"In the nave, yes. As long as your bedroll is gone from the church before service."

Winston smiled. That would be easy. He didn't have a bedroll.

But that night, as he stretched out on a pew, he pulled out the gun to examine. The barrel glinted in the low light from the candles on the altar. It was unscratched and shinier than any steel he'd seen before. He still didn't see how it worked. He pulled the trigger and it clicked. He did it again to the same effect.

It took him several minutes to figure out how to pop the bottom of the handle out. The hollow chamber was clearly designed for bullets but was also empty. He held the gun up. He'd never seen anything at all like it.

The next day, Winston walked out to the dump again. Reverend Stillwater had loaned him a canteen, and he'd brought his old haversack, that he'd kept hidden behind a feed barrel out back of the general store. One of the straps was broken, but as long as he didn't take much weight, one strap would do.

The sun scorched down as bad as the day before. He tucked an old, ragged bandanna over his nose this time. It didn't help the smell much, but anything was a blessing. He wished for gloves, but good gloves were well beyond his means. At least for now.

He started on the shady side of the trash pile. Food scraps and sludge and bones he just pushed aside. Anything strange, he set off to one side, beside his pack. The yellow bottle was first. Then what looked like an old tin pan, crusted with food. Except the tin was thinner and shinier than any he'd ever seen.

The more he sorted, the more he figured out what most of it was. He had plates made out of a funny stiff paper stained with sauce. There were boxes that felt like they were coated in thin wax and had pictures of noodles or cut up vegetables and meat. It was like some amazing kitchen with all these miraculous things existed high in the sky above him.

Back in New Jersey, he'd once taken a delivery to a grand hotel, seven stories tall. They'd had a chute near the stairs with a big garbage bin at the bottom. It saved the guests, and more importantly the maids, from carrying the trash down the long flights of stairs.

This was the bottom of such a chute, he realized. Though who would throw away such miracles as these, he'd never understand.

In early afternoon, with his usual hunger from a missed meal pushed aside, he found his treasure. The black cylinder was about the length of his hand. Made up of the stiff but slick stuff he'd dubbed "not-metal," it had a switch on the side and a glass covering on the front. Behind that glass was something he knew. Something miraculous.

It was one of Mr. Edison's artificial lights.

All the memories of the demonstration back in Menlo Park flooded back into Winston's mind. How Mr. Edison had lit up the night with the flick of a switch. How everyone had oohed and aahed.

Mary's face, bright in the night.

Mr. Edison had promised a new world, an amazing world of science and technology. He promised a future filled with wonders, and filled with riches for those who could invest.

Winston had seen the advertisement in the newspaper touting gold strikes in the Sierra Nevada the very next day. Mary had said he was a fool, and that she wouldn't wait. He'd promised to be back in a year. She'd said he'd never make it.

She was right. But it no longer hurt the way it had. The gold mines had been tapped out before he'd arrived, and then his funds had run dry. He decided he would've made it with better luck. And losing to bad luck didn't hurt so bad.

He pushed the switch on the light. Nothin' happened. But still. The light bulb inside was smaller than any Mr. Edison had even dreamed of.

And someone had thrown it away. Tossed it in the trash with the dead man that had arrived the day before.

He stiffened at the thought of people so evil as to do that. And of people so rich they could make things like what he held in his hand.

A loud splat startled him. He looked up just in time to see chicken bones smack into the top of the trash.

Perhaps it was time to leave. If another corpse came through—he shuddered. Far better to not be here when it did.

He tucked his treasures into his haversack and returned to the church.

That night, as he mopped up the last of the gravy on his plate with the soft bread, Reverend Stillwater asked him about his day.

"I explored the garbage," Winston said. "I think there are people who make it. I think it's the bottom of a garbage chute." He described the one in New Jersey. "Judging from the trash, most of the guests are normal folks, but some of them are murderers. They sent that body down so it couldn't be found."

"We've decided as much," Reverend Stillwater replied. "Me and the sheriff. And it galls me that we cannot bring justice for those poor butchered souls, God bless them. But we tried, and could no more find traces of the victims than the murderers. Just the bodies. A decent burial is the best we can do."

"I suppose," Winston agreed, "but I was wondering—what do you do with the rest of the trash?"

"What would you do?"

Winston shrugged. Best to not be too obvious.

"I know a man," he eventually said, "who might be interested. I thought I might send him some pieces."

"Go right ahead. I don't have the time, as the souls of the living in Cave Creek are my true duty, but I'd like to see any other bodies you find laid properly to rest."

Winston nodded, and for the first time in a long while, a spark of hope lit in his heart. These strange trinkets. These broken things. Mr. Edison would pay for them, and Mr. Edison would pay well.

His mind flitted to the whiskey he could buy, but then he caught himself. Could he do without the booze? Do something better? Perhaps instead…he could buy a ticket East?

Yes, yes he could.

He could buy a fancy suit, one of those ones with the silver cufflinks, and hire a proper team to drive him to Mary's—

No. Her letter had made it clear. As much as it panged his heart, he knew she'd have found another by now.

He moistened his lips, already tasting the whiskey, but caught himself again. The reverend often preached that drink was the road to ruin, and in Winston's case, he'd been right.

But maybe now his luck had changed.

The next morning, Winston returned to the dump with a bandanna over his nose, his haversack in hand, and a shovel he'd borrowed from Mason at the graveyard. He carefully dug through the near edge of the trash, looking for anything with wires or switches or other parts he knew Mr. Edison would desire. Those he found, he dusted off and tucked into his haversack. He could wash them in the creek before he shipped them. Maybe he'd set up a placer box to clean his new "gold."

That made him smile.

Then about an hour before noon, another trickle of trash fell from the sky. He watched as the kitchen scraps and empty tins bounced down the side. At the end, what looked like a coffee pot with a cord dropped down. After he'd retrieved it, Winston stared up at the empty blue above.

The trash wasn't going to stop coming, he realized. The gold mines in the area had tapped out. This…this wouldn't.

All daydreams of a coach East vanished. Edison wasn't the only inventor who'd buy his treasures. He could set up right here. He could build a mansion that rivaled the finest in New Jersey. Mary and her new beau could read about him in the papers. With a lot of work and some cleverness, he could live like a king.

He felt a surge of hope. And determination. The mix was more intoxicating than any whiskey he'd had in a long, long time.

Winston put the coffee pot in his haversack. He wiped his brow and picked a new spot to dig.

About the Author

A fourth generation Coloradoan, Edward J. Knight only left the Denver area long enough to learn how to put a satellite into orbit. Four satellites (and counting) later, he's returned to both the mountains and writing fantastical fiction. Along the way, he met the love of his life and became the father of two amazingly curious kids. He's a huge fan of tightly constructed universes and smart plots. He hopes his own Mythic West stories hold up to those standards. More of his work can be found at www.edwardjknight.com.

Breach

by

Robinne Weiss

Breach

"Come on, girl. Don't you have a little more for me?" Mary worked the cow's teats for another minute but gained only a few drops of milk for her effort. She sighed and stood, stretching the kinks from her back. Opening the head bail, she patted the cow on the rump. "Off you go, Bess."

The cow made her leisurely way from the milking shed, rejoining her companions in the dusty brown paddock. Mary poured Bess' milk into the large stainless-steel jug, and then heaved the jug into the chiller. She wiped the sweat from her face with her shirt.

A drink. That's what she needed. A glass of water, and then she'd go to the south paddock and weed the millet. She stepped into the glaring sun and walked to the house. Dust rose up at each step, and the breeze sent it eddying around the yard. She touched the water tank as she passed it. The ritual reassured her but didn't alleviate her fears they would run out. In a month, they'd be drawing nothing but silt from the well, and the rainwater they'd stored during winter would have to get them through the hottest days of summer. It was always a struggle, but this year would be worse. Winter rain had been light, and the tank wasn't full.

When she reached the kitchen, she found Les already there. His face was streaked with dirt and sweat. She smiled and swiped at his face. "You look like a zebra."

"How was the milk this morning?" Les asked, pouring himself a glass of water from the pitcher they kept cool in the chiller.

Mary held out her glass for him to fill. "Not as much as yesterday." She sighed. "I think those N'Damas were a mistake. They're just not giving as much as the Sahiwals." She pulled out a chair from the battered kitchen table and sat down. It creaked under her weight, and she wondered how long it would be before she had to fix it again.

Les sat down across from her, leaning his elbows on the table. "Remember, those N'Damas are also giving us beef. Bess and Lily's calves sold for more than any of the others."

"I suppose. Still, their milk production is lousy. I think I'll cut some extra acacia for them today. Maybe I can boost their production with a little more feed." She frowned. Extra feed now meant extra need for water later.

Les leaned across the table and kissed Mary on the nose. "It'll be okay. We'll make it through this year." He shrugged. "A dry year is good for prices." He downed the last of his water and stood. "Speaking of prices, I should be going if I'm going to get to Port Geraldine and back today."

"It seems ridiculous we should have to take the milk all the way down there, and pay the agent, just to sell our milk on Banks Island."

"Yep, but since those rich bastards out on the Island raised the West Melton ferry fees, it's cheaper this way."

Mary grunted. "You know they only raised that ferry fee so they don't have to put up with us poor Mainlanders on their pristine streets." She stood, picking up both their glasses and carefully wiping them with a towel before replacing them in the cupboard.

Les put an arm around her shoulders and kissed her sweaty forehead. "We're doing okay, Mary. We're still getting good money for the milk." He pulled away and brushed a wisp of hair from her face. "Need anything from town while I'm there?"

"Here's a list." Mary picked up a scrap of paper from the benchtop and handed it to Les. She kissed him on the cheek. "I'd kill for some more of those Stewart Island cherries, too, if they're not too expensive this week."

"I'll see what I can do, though I'm not sure I'm willing to resort to murder." He winked and returned her kiss.

After Les was gone, Mary grabbed a hoe and headed to the south paddock. On her way, she stopped to scratch the cows' ears. She loved her 'girls,' as she called them. Her herd of fifteen was one of the larger in the region. Few farmers bothered with dairy cattle on the Canterbury Plains. The climate was simply too hot and dry for it to be profitable. For that matter, few farmers bothered with the Canterbury Plains at all. Only those who couldn't afford more forgiving land elsewhere. But Mary's family had been farming dairy in Canterbury for hundreds of years. Her father had always told her she had milk running through her veins. As a child, she was surprised to see beads of dark red blood whenever she cut herself.

Her herd was composed mostly of Sahiwals, well-adapted to the heat and drought. Bonnie, whose reddish-brown hump Mary now scratched, was the boss of them all. She insisted on first milking, first scratch, first feed. She was a good milker, too, and four of Mary's other cows were Bonnie's offspring. The pair of N'Damas had been a gamble. One Mary didn't think she'd repeat. Not only did they not produce as much milk, but they looked strange, with their grey pelts and flat backs. She gave a parting scratch to one of Bonnie's daughters, promising to return with food for them later.

Les still hadn't returned from Port Geraldine when Mary began the evening milking. She was dreaming of ripe cherries as she sat coaxing milk from one cow after another. The girls knew the routine; all Mary had to do was open the gate, and they'd file in one by one. The rhythm was relaxing, and Mary greeted each cow by name as she entered the milking shed. She finished with Bess, disappointed again with her production, and bent down to press the lid onto the milk bucket.

When she straightened, she let out an involuntary cry. A huge animal stepped up to the bail and poked its head into the feed trough. Black and white patterns over its hide gave it a bizarre look, and its sheer bulk was intimidating. It was a cow, no doubt about that, but it was like nothing Mary had ever seen before. Her eyes skimmed along its broad flat back and down to an udder bulging with milk.

She gave a nervous laugh. Where had this animal come from? Had Les brought it home? But, no, she hadn't heard the truck return. And where would he have gotten *that* thing from? She looked at the animal's udder again and began to calculate how much milk must be in there. It would well make up for the shortfall from Bess and Lily. And wherever the cow was from, she needed to be milked—that udder was taut. Warily, she closed the bail to keep the cow in place. She emptied Bess' milk into the jug, then sat down beside the giant cow.

Timid at first, not knowing how the beast might react, she began to milk. The cow munched placidly, ignoring Mary, and she relaxed into the rhythm of the job.

An hour later, when Les came home, Mary was leaning on the fence, watching the new cow grazing with the others. He came up beside her and slipped his arm around her waist. Then she felt him stiffen.

"What the hell is that?"

"A cow." Mary giggled.

"That's not a cow, that's a house. She's huge!"

"And she gave twice as much milk as the others. Twice. It just kept coming."

"You milked her?"

Mary nodded.

"Where did she come from?"

"I have no idea. She just showed up in the milking shed. Followed the others right in, came up all quiet-like to the bail and stood there to be milked."

"Do you think it's from the Parnhams' place? Have they gotten a new animal? I've never seen anything like that."

"I don't know."

"They're going to be pissed off you milked her."

"She was bursting, Les. What could I do?"

"Well, we'll have to ring them and see if they're missing an animal." He turned to go into the house.

The cow didn't belong to the Parnhams. It didn't belong to the McCormicks either. Or the Browns. It seemed to have materialised out of thin air in Les and Mary's paddock.

"Well, it has to have come from *somewhere*." Les was watching Mary milk the cow the following morning.

"Here, pour this into the jug." Mary handed Les her bucket. "There's still more coming," she added as she took the empty bucket back from him.

"What are we going to do with her?" Les asked.

"I say we keep her. We've asked the neighbours, and she doesn't belong to any of them. If someone's lost this animal, they'll surely come looking for her. Until then…" Mary shrugged. "It's a heck of a lot of milk."

Les frowned. "She'll need a lot of feed, too." But he didn't contradict her. The cows were Mary's responsibility. It was her decision. And she was probably right. Someone would come looking for the cow, and until then, well, who could blame them for taking advantage of the situation? Better than letting that milk go to waste and risk the cow getting mastitis.

Two weeks passed, and no one came for the cow. Mary vacillated between wishing someone would show up for her and hoping no one did. The cow ate so much food. Mary was cutting twice the amount of acacia from the alley cropping as usual, and she began to worry about having enough feed for the year. If they had to buy in feed, it would cancel out any benefit of having the extra milk.

And the extra milk seemed to be drying up, too. By the end of two weeks, the giant cow was only giving a little more than the others, and she seemed lethargic. Was she still not getting enough feed? Mary simply couldn't give her more and hope to have any left by the time the autumn rains started. The cow wasn't grazing much, either. She stood in the shade of the hedgerow most of the day, not venturing into the sun at all. The healthy fat layer she had on arrival had wasted away. Mary began to think that whoever had bought this cow had gotten a bad deal.

She hoped it wasn't sick. She didn't need a new disease to infect her herd.

And then, sixteen days after the cow arrived, it vanished again. No one came for it, no one rang. It just disappeared as mysteriously as it had arrived.

Mary wouldn't have minded much, except that Bonnie disappeared with it. When she asked around, none of the neighbours had seen either animal.

"She's my best milker. My breeding stock! What am I going to do? We can't afford to replace her right now."

Les sighed. "I don't know, Mary. Maybe wait a couple days. She might turn up again."

But she didn't. And two days later, Bess and Lily vanished.

"Someone's stealing them," Mary suggested at dinner that evening. She pushed her beans around her plate, too upset to eat much.

"But why take Bess and Lily? They're the worst animals in the herd."

"The thief doesn't know that. Not until they milk them."

"Have you contacted the police?"

Mary scoffed. "Like they'd do anything." She sighed. "But, yes, I filed a report, for all the good it will do." She set down her fork. "I'm going to spend the night in the paddock tonight."

Les nodded. "We can trade off nights." Les stood, his empty plate in his hand. "Take the gun with you." He kissed Mary on top of the head. "And eat. It won't do any good to starve yourself."

When Mary sat down in the paddock at dusk, the cows drifted over to her, curious and eager for scratches. After satisfying their curiosity and itches, they settled down next to her. Mary smiled, surrounded by the sound of chewing cud and the sweet, fermented smell of bovine breath. She leaned back against a fencepost, closing her eyes for a moment to savour the cool night air.

She woke with a start some time later. The cows were no longer arrayed around her. She squinted into the darkness and saw them grazing about fifty metres away. She counted. Twelve. She hadn't lost any more. But something had woken her, she was sure of it. She stilled herself, opening her senses to everything around her.

The smell. Something was different about the smell. Had it rained? No. That was ridiculous. It wouldn't rain until May. The sky was clear, and Mary was dry. Why, then, did the air smell so…so *green*? A cool breeze wafted over her, and she shivered. And why was it so cold? She stood and wrapped her thin jersey more closely around herself.

Three of the cows raised their heads, sniffing the air. So, they smelled it, too. Mary walked into the breeze. Two more cows raised their heads. She stepped cautiously, wishing she'd thought to pick up her torch. The smell seemed to grow the further she went. She closed her eyes for a moment and breathed deeply. It was the smell of moist soil and green grass. Entirely out of place, and so seductive she couldn't help but follow it.

Maybe she blinked, but she didn't think so. One moment she was walking on the hard, dry ground of home, and in the very next step, her foot came down on thick, springy grass. She cried out in surprise and peered down. It was hard to see in the dark. She bent and ran her hand across a carpet of plants. She grabbed a handful and pulled, bringing it to her nose and inhaling deeply. Grass. Lush and tall, and utterly impossible. She turned, looking back where she'd come from. She sucked in a sharp breath and dropped her handful of grass.

Her cows were gone.

Her paddock was gone.

Stretching away from her was a vast expanse of grass, dotted with enormous black and white cows like the one that had mysteriously appeared, then vanished. There were hundreds of them, their white patches glowing faintly in the starlight like wisps of fog.

Turning in a slow circle, Mary could see nothing but lush grass and enormous cows. Was she dreaming? Surely, she must be. She walked a few more steps into her dream. The smell of moist soil was intoxicating. One of the giant cows noticed her and lumbered toward her. A few others followed. Mary staggered back, intimidated. Then she spun at a noise behind her. More giant cows walked toward her. Feeling terribly small, she was beginning to think this dream was about to become a nightmare.

"Okay Mary, wake up," she said aloud. The cows stopped for a moment at the sound of her voice, and then continued to pace toward her. "Now."

But she couldn't wake. Maybe if she retraced her steps, she could find her way back to the beginning of her dream and out of this place. But the shifting livestock and her own spinning had confused her sense of direction. She had no idea which way she'd come from. And the cows were all around her now.

"Go away!" She waved her arms at the beasts, and they scattered like flies. Mary laughed nervously. "Well, that was easy. Too bad I can't wake up as easily." She would just have to wait it out. This strange dream couldn't last forever. She hoped it wouldn't keep her from waking, should someone arrive to steal her cows.

She sat cross-legged on the ground. The damp slowly seeped through the seat of her pants, and she wondered at her own ability to imagine sitting on wet ground when it was something she'd never felt before. She listened to the cows around her, their steady munching relaxing her.

But even the sound of grazing cows couldn't keep the panic from rising as the hours passed and Mary didn't wake. When the sky began to lighten, she had to acknowledge that she wasn't dreaming. Whatever this was, it was real.

The rising light revealed an alien landscape, greener than anything she'd ever seen. The grass seemed to stretch forever. It was a cow's paradise.

And now the cows were slowly making their way toward a low shed in the distance. The milking shed. It must be. And at the milking shed would be a person—she looked at the hundreds of animals around her—lots of people who could tell her where she was and perhaps explain what was going on.

She dusted off her trousers and followed the cows.

Her eyes grew wide as she neared the shed. It was more like an airplane hangar in size, and as noisy as the planes that flew overhead at home. In spite of the noise, the cows walked calmly into a narrow chute and up a slight ramp into the shed. Mary hung back. She wasn't going to go into that chute, to be crushed by giant cows. There must be another way into the shed. She clambered over a metal gate and skirted around the building.

One side was entirely open, and as she rounded the corner, Mary's jaw dropped. Dozens of cows stood shoulder to shoulder, head inward on a giant, raised, slowly rotating platform. Pulsing tubes were connected to their teats and milk flowed through the translucent tubing. At first, she saw not a single person. Then, as she scanned the vast space, she saw one man managing the cows as they entered and exited the shed. He let them into each stall on the platform as it turned and opened the gate for the ones who had gone all the way around so they could step off the platform.

Movement at ground level caught her eye and she watched a woman deftly pull the tubes off a cow who had gone around the circle. One after another she removed the tubes, and they retracted out of the way. She was in constant motion, only barely keeping up with the carousel of cows. Mary reasoned there must be another person putting the tubes on the cows on the other side, where they entered. Three people to milk maybe four hundred cows! Mary stood dumbfounded.

"Um… Can I help you?" The voice came from behind, and Mary jumped in surprise. She turned to see a burly man in coveralls. He was clean-shaven, and his short-cropped hair was mostly silver.

"I…um…well…" What could she say? She waved a hand toward the milking shed. "What is all this?"

The man frowned. "What do you mean? It's a milking parlour. This is a dairy farm. What did you expect to see?" He looked her up and down. "And who are you?"

Mary shook herself and held out a hand. "Mary McPherson. I live—" she waved a hand vaguely in the direction of the paddock "—nearby."

"Mary McPherson, huh?" The man didn't take her proffered hand.

"And you are?" Mary dropped her hand, feeling decidedly uncomfortable as the man scrutinised her.

"Ian. Ian McPherson." He let the name sink in for a moment. "I'm surprised that a Mary McPherson I've never seen or heard of lives nearby and has to ask what a milking parlour is. So, what do you do, Mary McPherson?"

"I...well... I'm a farmer. My husband and I have twenty hectares in dairy and millet."

"Millet? Who the hell grows millet in Canterbury?"

Mary frowned. "Well, what else *can* you grow?" She looked around at the green expanses of grass. "Obviously you've got some source of water here. And the money to pay for it."

"Look, I don't know who you are or where you're from, but I'm going to have to ask you to leave."

"But I'm not sure how to get home from here. I've...I've never seen this place before. I never knew this sort of place *existed.*"

Ian's manner changed. He looked at Mary for a moment, and then spoke slowly, as if explaining something to a child. "How about I take you inside? Do you have someone you can ring to come and get you? Someone who takes care of you?" He took Mary by the elbow and turned her around, steering her toward a large house nearby.

"Someone who takes care of me?" She pulled her elbow out of Ian's grasp. "I take care of myself, thank you very much. And I'll thank you to treat me as an adult." Then a gasp escaped her. "Bonnie!" She broke away from Ian and rushed to a small pen where Bonnie stood chewing her cud. The cow greeted her by stretching her neck over the fence for a scratch. "Oh! And there's Bess and Lily."

Mary greeted all three of her cows, and then turned back to Ian. "These are *my* cows. They were stolen over the past couple of days. Where did you get them?"

"Whoa!" Ian held up his hands. "I haven't stolen anything. Your cows appeared in my paddock. I think, before you accuse anyone of theft, you should check your fences." Then he made a face. "Why you'd care about such lousy stock, though, I don't know."

"Lousy? Bonnie is my best milker—fourteen litres a day." Mary paused. "The two N'Damas...well, they are pretty lousy. But for a dual-purpose breed, they're not bad." She glanced back at the milking shed, with the hundreds of giant cows, and barked a laugh. "I suppose, with that herd, my animals do look pathetic."

Ian nodded. "I get thirty-two litres a day from each of my cows."

"Yeah, the one that showed up at my place gave twice the milk Bonnie gives."

"The one that showed up at your place?"

Mary laughed. "Yeah. Maybe you need to check your fences, too."

Ian rubbed his chin and frowned. "I did have one go missing for a while. Came back yesterday looking like hell—like she hadn't eaten for a week. Thought I might have to put her down."

Mary grimaced. "Sorry. I tried. I fed her as much acacia as I could cut, but she was so huge. She just ate whatever I could give her and wanted more. I don't know how you get this much grass to grow." She waved her hands around. "And no shade for the cows? How do they manage the heat?"

Ian's brow was furrowed. "I really don't understand anything you're saying. If these are your animals, you're welcome to take them. I penned them up, worried they'd pass some disease to my herd. Figured someone might come looking for them. You got a truck to take them home in?"

"No. I…I walked here. Through the paddock." Mary frowned. "It was the strangest thing…like…like walking into a different world."

Ian's eyebrows rose, and Mary knew he thought she was a nutter. She was beginning to think the same, herself.

"Look, I was on my way out to Christchurch. Can I drop you somewhere along the way? You can pick up your truck and bring it back for your animals."

"Christchurch? Where's that?"

Ian's eyes widened. "What rock do you live under, lady? Surely you know where Christchurch is."

"Um…no. I've never heard of it. Is it on Banks Island?"

"Banks *Island?*" Ian took a deep breath. "Okay. How about we just go inside and ring the police. We'll get you to wherever it is you need to go."

Mary let herself be led into the house. It was large and clean, with carpeted floors and strange-looking appliances. "This is amazing!"

Ian scoffed. "Just a house. How about a cuppa while I ring the police?"

"Um…sure. Thanks." Mary looked around the immaculate kitchen. She vaguely recognised items—a kettle, a chiller, a cooktop and oven—but they all looked oddly angular and blocky. Then her eyes landed on a calendar pinned on the wall. She froze.

Her voice came out in a whisper. "Two thousand and seventeen?"

"Huh?" Ian looked up from the kettle he was about to lift.

"Two thousand and seventeen." Mary pointed. "Is that the correct year?"

"Yeeees. What year did you think it was?" Ian filled the kettle from the tap.

Mary swallowed. "Where I came from, it's two thousand four hundred and ten." She turned to Ian. He was staring at her with his mouth open, the kettle forgotten in his hand.

"That's impossible. It's insane."

Mary nodded. "But I'm not. Me, my cows… We live in the year twenty-four ten. I walked from my paddock into yours last night, without crossing a single fence. One step I was at home, the next step I was here."

"You're saying you stepped through time." Ian's eyebrows rose. "Look, I don't know whether you've been smoking something funny, or whether you're a little bit cracked, but you can't just step from one time to another."

"I know that. I haven't been doing drugs, and I swear I'm not insane." She frowned. "At least, I feel like my usual sane self. Except for this." She waved her hands around at the kitchen.

"How could you possibly come from another time? Time travel's not possible."

Mary shook her head. "I know, but… Look, you're a McPherson. I'm a McPherson. My family has been farming the Canterbury Plains—this piece of land—since the 1800s. You and I have never met because we're not neighbours, we're…we're living on the same land. In different times. I don't know how it happened, but I stepped through time from my paddock into yours."

Ian stood frozen for a moment. "This is totally messed up." Then he laughed. "You could be my great-great-great-whatever granddaughter." He set the kettle down with a thud.

Eventually, they both recovered enough to make a cup of tea and sit down at the kitchen table to talk. Mary explained what had happened with the cows over the past two and a half weeks. She described her farm and her crops.

"Why don't you run Holsteins like we do?"

Mary laughed. "I've never seen Holsteins before. If the performance of the one that visited me is any indication, they can't survive in my time. I guess it's too hot and dry."

"And you milk by hand?"

Mary shrugged. "It's the only way I know how. There isn't a lot of dairy on the Canterbury Plains. Small holdings like mine are about it. We supply milk to the towns on Banks Island."

"You mean Banks Peninsula?"

"No. Banks Island."

Ian stood and rummaged in a kitchen drawer, producing a map which he spread out on the table. "We're here." He tapped a spot on the map.

Mary sucked in a breath. "And this is West Melton? So far inland?"

"Yeah, and here's the Banks Peninsula."

Mary looked up from the map and met Ian's eyes. "In my time, West Melton is coastal. The Banks Peninsula is an island. All this—" She looked down and swiped a hand across Christchurch, Lincoln, Prebbleton, and half a dozen other towns. "Is the sea."

"Well, shit."

Running her finger across the map, Mary traced the coastline as it was in her time. "The water at West Melton is shallow. Great beaches, but no port there. We take our milk and grain either down here, to Port Geraldine—"

"Geraldine! That's practically in the mountains," Ian interrupted.

"Or up here, to Port Omihi."

"And it all goes to Banks Pen—Banks *Island*? None of it is exported?"

Mary laughed. "We can barely support New Zealand. There's nothing left over to send elsewhere."

Ian swore.

"You really produce enough to export?" Mary's interest was piqued. "Can I…can I have a look around?"

Ian smiled. "Sure. Come on." They went out to the milking shed, where the cows were still rotating through the milking. He showed her the machinery and the giant milk storage tank. They hopped into his ute, and he drove her around the farm. He showed her the enormous centre-pivot irrigation system, the towering stack of baleage. To Mary's increasing amazement, Ian described his farming system, and how his milk was sent as milk solids all around the world. How New Zealand was a major exporter of dairy products, wool, beef and lamb, fruits and vegetables. She watched, with her jaw in her lap, as the double-trailer milk tanker arrived to carry off the milk to a processing plant in Darfield.

Returning to the house for a late lunch, Mary was astounded at the plentiful food—slivered ham, cheese, beautiful lettuce, soft white bread, crisp apples, and strawberries. She wanted simultaneously to inhale it all in case it vanished, and savour it slowly so it would never end. Ian put the kettle on for more tea.

While they ate, she and Ian continued to compare notes about their respective times.

"So, the economy is largely based on agriculture?" It was hard for Mary to believe that the big AI and space aeronautics companies that dominated New Zealand in her time didn't even exist in Ian's time.

Ian nodded. "Agriculture's the biggest, but tourism is big too. People come to see the natural beauty—mountains, hot pools, glaciers."

Mary cocked her head. "What's a glacier?"

Ian's eyebrows rose. "Snow and ice that never melts. The mountains are covered in them. Franz Josef Glacier, Fox Glacier, Tasman Glacier? You've never heard of them?"

Mary shrugged and shook her head. "I've never seen snow."

They drank their tea in silence for a minute. "Sounds like global climate change turned out worse than predicted." In response to Mary's questioning look, he added, "Climate change? Don't they talk about that in your time?"

Mary shook her head. "No. The climate is just what it is. Oh, we learned in school that it was different hundreds of years ago, but we don't talk about it much."

"Well, I suppose the state of New Zealand in your time is the fault of us in this time." He frowned. "I wonder what we'd do differently if everyone knew what was coming." He rose and refilled the kettle. "There's a lot of talk about reducing our use of fossil fuels, reducing our carbon dioxide emissions. Talk is cheap." He shrugged. "So, we talk, and that's about it." He looked at Mary and his expression changed. "I'm sorry."

Mary looked around at the signs of wealth. The big house, soft carpet, gleaming appliances, plush furniture… This was her family's wealth. Where had it all gone? Her own unending slog to scratch a meagre living out of the hot dust of the Canterbury Plains recalled none of this opulence.

"Yeah. I'm sorry, too." Mary put down her cup, feeling hopelessly out of place. "I should go." She stood. "Thanks for the tour, lunch, tea…"

"Where will you go?"

That was the question, wasn't it? How was she supposed to get home?

"If you don't mind, I'll take my cows and… I guess I'll go back out to your paddock. To the place where I arrived. Maybe I can get back from there?"

Ian nodded. "I guess… It's probably your best chance." He rose suddenly. "But wait a minute. Let me send some things with you."

"Really, you don't need to—"

"Nonsense. You're my great-great-great-whatever granddaughter. I should spoil you like I do my grandkids." He scrutinised Mary. "Now, let's see… What is it you need?"

Mary laughed. "Water. But you can't exactly give me that."

Ian's shoulders slumped. "So, what is it you want?"

Mary thought for a moment. She thought about her life. There were a lot of things she didn't have. A lot of things she'd never be able to afford. Her house threatened to blow away in the fierce nor'west winds. When it did rain, the roof leaked. The floor was rough and softened only by a few battered throw rugs. But she had Les and her cows. She thought about Ian's herd of hundreds. He didn't know each of his cows by name. He didn't talk to them every morning and evening while he milked them. His milking shed of noise and frantic activity wasn't the place of peace and reflection that hers was. She smiled and shrugged.

"There's really nothing I want, except to go home."

In the end, Ian pressed some things on her. She left with a bag full of fruits and vegetables exotic to her—apples, broccoli, silverbeet, blackcurrants. She also carried a nearly-full bottle of drench, because Ian's cow had returned from her place infested with intestinal worms, and Mary admitted she couldn't afford drench.

"Wait," Ian said as they were about to head out the door. "One more thing." He ducked into what looked like an office and emerged a minute later with a handful of coins.

"But these are no good in my—" Mary began.

Ian held up a finger. "They're no good as currency, and if they were, they'd be worth bugger all. But, in your time, these are four-hundred-year-old coins."

Mary smiled as she understood. "Thank you." She held out her hand, and Ian dropped the coins into it.

"Hold out for a good price. Get all you can for them."

Ian helped Mary tie baling twine leads on her cows. They didn't necessarily need them—her cows followed her without leads—but she didn't want to leave any behind when...if...she crossed back to her own time.

Ian accompanied her to the paddock, where his own cows were once again grazing. The sun was already dropping toward the horizon. She'd spent the entire day here, four hundred years in the past.

"So...now what?" Ian asked. "How did you come across before?"

Mary shrugged. "I just walked into your paddock. I…I smelled it. The grass, the moisture."

"Did you see anything?" Ian peered around the paddock, as if looking for a magical doorway.

"Well, it was dark, but no, I don't think there was anything to see. It was just the smell."

"So…do you smell anything?" There was doubt in his eyes.

Mary closed her eyes and breathed in, not entirely sure what home smelled like. She'd never really thought about it. She opened her eyes again.

"Nothing."

"Hm."

Mary began to pace slowly across the paddock, sniffing. Ian and her cows trailed after her. As the minutes ticked by, her thoughts became more and more panicked. What if she couldn't find the way home? What if she was stuck in 2017 forever? What would Les do? What would happen to her cows? Her farm? She struggled to keep her breathing even and to focus on her sense of smell.

"Mary?" Her frightened thoughts were interrupted by Ian's voice. She turned to look at him, and he nodded toward Bonnie.

Bonnie's head was up, her nostrils twitching. She began to lumber away from Mary, tugging on the lead. Mary, Bess, and Lily followed. Ian didn't move. After a few steps, Mary looked back at him. "You sure you don't want to come with me? Just to visit?"

"Nah." Ian swallowed, his throat suddenly dry. "I'll just stay here."

Mary smiled, then hurried up to walk abreast of Bonnie. Five, ten, fifteen steps, and the pair vanished. The only indication they still existed were the two leads trailing from Mary's hand to Bess and Lily. The two cows ambled forward until they, too, disappeared.

Ian stood blinking at the spot for a long minute.

Then he turned to survey his farm. Four hundred years. He tried to imagine his lush paddocks a dry, hot wasteland.

Christchurch gone, nearby West Melton a beach community. He sighed and shook his head. Four hundred years was a long way away.

Hands in his pockets, he slowly made his way back to the house.

About the Author

Robinne Weiss is an author, educator and entomologist writing fantasy, science fiction, poetry and non-fiction for children and adults. Her short stories have most recently appeared in *Andromeda Spaceways Magazine* and the anthologies *Alternative Deathiness*, and *Te Kōrero Ahi* Kā, and have won multiple awards. She's published eleven books, including a series of middle grade fantasy novels infested with dragons, a lighthearted urban fantasy, an epic YA fantasy, a book of poetry, and some rather more serious non-fiction about insects.

Robinne lives in rural New Zealand. Visit her online at

https://robinneweiss.com

or follow her at

https://www.facebook.com/AuthorRobinneWeiss.

Sticky Fingers

by

Aaron Haden

Sticky Fingers

Through a door that had not seen the light in hundred years, there came a girl with dark copper skin and bloody fingers. She was not a small girl, nor was she a tall girl. She was average, with small sticky fingers that caught on the edge of the door when she emerged from it. Her name was Nilam, and she was a curious girl.

Her eyes shone in the darkness of the tower, for she emerged when the light here had not yet broken through the far and few windows. For a time, she wandered around, trying to understand where she was. There were many doors around, one every two meters, and each seemed to lead to somewhere new. Her own door had closed behind her, her bloody handprints the only trace of her passage through it. Not all doors were a proper door, you see, but hers was.

Nilam's door had been made of oak, with a brass handle, and decorations all around the frame. It was something right out of fairytales, with runes written on the side. It was an old door, and it had seen better days, but like all the doors in the tower, we took care of it. It was, and still is, our duty.

The girl, who was of the perfectly reasonable age of eleven and three quarters, had decided that the strange door she had come from had no value for her anymore. She wasn't interested in going back, or at least not yet. She would be later, and when she would try to tug it open, it would simply refuse. But that is for later.

Now, Nilam wandered through the tower, and examined the doors. A few were made of delicate glass that looked like it might shatter at the faintest touch, but when she touched it, she found it stronger than any steel she had ever seen. She liked those doors. She took to calling them the Seeing Doors, as she could see the words that sprawled beyond the doors.

There were doors of gold, doors of silver, and jade. She did not like those doors. It was not her fault; those doors were not meant for little girls with bloody fingers. She took to calling them the Cold Doors. Each time she passed one, it gave her chills, so she grew to resent their very existence.

The doors she liked the most however, were the Animal Doors. Those were shaped in the form of animals, as their name indicated, and they opened for very few people. What happened beyond them could be seen if one peeked through the eyes of the animal, but Nilam was too small to reach most of them. She was able, however, to see through the fox's eyes, and the cat's. There were a few others, but it was those two which interested her the most.

So, Nilam wandered through the tower, her fingers itching to open the doors, to see if they were really doors. Still, she knew she should not, so she waited, careful and tempted. It was not that she had been taught not to open strange doors as much as she had had firsthand experience that doors could lead to somewhere quite nasty. She did not think of her door then, but rather of the door before, the one that had given her the blood on her fingers.

She walked, and walked, and walked. The stairs did not seem to end, although sometimes they would open on a hallway, where more doors were lined. But those doors had no handle, and were all made of the same darkness, so she did not wander there much past the first few doors.

She grew weary of looking through the tower, and for that we do not blame her. Nilam was only a young girl when she came to us first, and she had no such strength as she did when she returned. Wrapping herself in her own arms, she stopped at the entrance of one of those strange hallways, and she slept. It was not a very good sleep, but she had had worse, so she did not feel too grumpy in the morning. She scrubbed her fingers against the bottom of her dress, but some of the dried blood remained anyway. It was frustrating, and she wanted to have it off her immediately, but she could not find water or food anywhere in this tower.

By then, Nilam's mind was well wrapped around the idea that she did not mind this place, although she would not give it any credit, but that it was rather inconvenient. Who could need this many doors, to this many places, and not have any water around?

Surely, walking through the tower as she had done for most of the previous day would exhaust anyone.

She went in search of water, muttering under her breath as she cursed the stairs.

It sounded a bit like this: "Jacin bless me, I hate those stairs, they are so long. Oh no, yet another of those Cold Doors. Why keep those? They are ugly as all Palyssea's eternities, and they don't give any idea of what's behind."

There were many other words she uttered, naturally, but it was those we first heard, when we happened upon her.

Nilam, with all the imperious majesty of a slighted child and all the fright of a hunted animal, shrieked. It was neither a nice shriek or a happy one, and yet it had none of the difficulty an adult's shriek had when they came to us. It was, overall, a rather normal shriek.

"What are you?" she said after a few moments of panting, as we did not move away. She was now our charge, and although we had known she had arrived, we had not hurried. There was never any hurry to be had in us.

The shift had happened when she had first laid eyes upon us. It was not something we really controlled, but such was our nature. We became what she hated most, for she came to us angry and wounded, and we were nothing but her own rage channeled.

You may call us Beholder.

Our voice shook her to her core, and she retreated, placing her fingers over her ears. We did not intend to scare her, and we did not intend to reassure her. We had no intention beyond gathering her and leading her to her door.

"Go away," she shouted, trying to go back on her step, but the stairway had closed behind her.

Come with us. We waved her over, and she did not move. *We will provide food and shelter.*

Humans were fragile creatures, and their children even more so. The tower did not mean to kill, it was simply meant to test. Entering the tower was a choice, and leaving it another.

"What are you," she repeated, and we moved away. She followed. "Are you a ghost?"

No.

"Are you…a zombie?"

No.

"Are you a god?"

No.

That game of hers lasted until we led her to the children's room, where no one resided at this time. It had been empty for as many days as it had been full, although it had grown emptier with the closing of doors. It seemed it would recover from its dry spell with Nilam.

Food throned in the middle of the room, water and tea and juices from fruits we could never taste waiting for her near it. With her eyes of amber, she looked at us, a threat forming on her lips.

Eat to your heart's content. It shall not poison you.

She stepped forward, tentative and afraid, but the food was too tempting to her starved body for her to resist much longer. Still, she held on, and looked at us with her eyes narrowed.

"I don't accept gifts from strangers. My mother says it's not right."

You do not have a mother, Nilam, nor do you have a father.

Nilam froze, her eyes wide, and anger rose within her. Her face did not puff up the way it did with some of the children we had seen before, and she did not cry either. Nilam's anger was a cold thing, and we felt our shape twist according to her, becoming a rag doll for her to clench and break. She was so full of anger for a moment that she forgot she did not know where she was. A tiny little thing like her, fighting against us. We would have felt sorrow, if it had been possible.

"You don't know anything about me!"

We know everything about you, Nilam. We know your past and your future. We know the roads that await you. It is futile to hate us.

"You are just another monster!" Her scream echoed through the room, but we did not flinch. It mattered not whether her voice was a whisper or a shout; we heard her.

We are the Beholder, child. Eat, sleep, gain strength. Your history awaits you.

"No!"

Nilam was a loud child, with no fear to hold her down here. She had known evil before, had seen its like more times than she could count. She could not count very far, but it had never stopped her. She was a child with blood on her hands and a mouth too loud for her peers.

She was a child with a mind so strong that she forced us to change once more. It wasn't the first time that it happened to us, but it was rare that we changed forms more than once for a single person.

Our body shifted, twisting into long shapes that fell against walls and onto her fingers. She did not scream again, and her gaze was not full of fear or fury. We were not her fear, nor her anger. We were her regrets. She had conjured us into this by opposing us.

It was not clear to her then, what our form changing meant. She saw us change and thought we played a trick on her. But tricks were never our way. We let her estimate her own strength, let her think of what she could, or couldn't, do to us. Her regrets wreaked havoc inside us, demanding to be let out to eat at her, but we would not allow it. It was, after all, our purpose.

Calm your heart, child. You cannot change what is awaiting.

"I can and I will," she shouted, and threw a plate towards us. "Get lost!"

The plate hit us, but we did not feel a thing. It had been long ago that we had felt anything. The worlds had been so young then. No, not young. The worlds hadn't been born yet. There had been only us, only the tower and its Keeper.

If you do not calm, child, you will lose your door.

It was not meant to be a threat. We did not know threats, lies, or deceptions. We only knew the doors, and those who passed through them. We knew their hearts, their minds, all that made them who they were. But we did not know their ways.

"I don't care! You are a mean one, and I don't want to see you!"

Our body bent, a slow bow as her regrets surged up once more. Within us, they agitated themselves, demanding to be let out, but we would not allow them to do so. It was our duty to behold, not to free. Only the people passing through could free them. There had not been anyone yet who had managed.

We will leave you to your meal, young one.

We left the room and haunted the corridors. There were so many doors to observe, some demanding to be unlocked in imperious voices, some begging, and some silent. We did not open the doors. Doors were not meant to be opened by our hands. Only humans could pass through the doors, could bring themselves in the tower. The worlds of men did not exist here. It was our world, our tower, *us*. We were its Keeper, until the end of times.

In her room, Nilam raged still. Her anger shook the walls, tore off moss that had grown underneath our windows. She wanted to escape, to leave our tower and the safety it offered her. It was not hard for her to find a way to perch herself on the window.

The emptiness stared back at her. There was nothing for her to jump toward, or to jump on. There was no ground, nothing that existed beyond the tower. In her heart, she knew that she could not escape, that the tower was too perfect of a trap. But Nilam was an angry child, with too many grievances burnt into her bones.

Barely taking the time to close her eyes, she jumped off the tower. She had expected to feel air rushing to her cheeks, had thought that there would be something indicating a fall at the very least. But there was nothing. Everything was perfectly still. There was no indication of a ground to be felt, nothing at all, and she couldn't resist opening her eyes once more.

She was standing a few paces away from the walls of the tower, suspended in the darkness. Her feet were anchored to nothing, her body weightless, and there was nothing. Carefully, she took a step forward, and found herself able to walk. It was an odd sensation, to a girl like her. She had walked on sand, on hard stone, on broken walls and grass. She had walked on sharp glass, and coal, and walked on wood, and metal. This was nothing like those. It was like she was not walking at all. There wasn't any softness, nor any hardness. Her feet moved, but it felt as if nothing happened.

Ignoring the oddness, she walked farther ahead, letting the tower fade from behind her. She regularly threw looks to make sure she was getting away, to comfort herself that she had beaten the tower and its traps. She watched it disappear from view, a pleased grin finding its way to her sullen face. When she turned around, she found herself face to face with the tower again, with the same window she had just left.

She screamed, but no sound echoed. The darkness of the world around her made her feel very small, and Nilam hated feeling small. It was something she despised above all. So, she started to run, away, and away, but still. She always found herself back to the tower.

After too many attempts, she decided that it would be better to try again in the morning. Although, she did not know when morning would be. For a moment, she worried about this. Then, the memory of the food on the table within the room popped into her head, and all thoughts of morning and escape were gone. She was, as was expected from a human child after two days without anything to eat, famished.

Nilam and her hunger climbed back to the room we had set aside for them, and she dined on sweet fruits and candied citrus. Human children were not well known for their ability to know what was best for them and she was no exception. Before eating, she washed her hands, nearly scratching herself bloody as she removed the last specks of blood. Her skin untarnished once more and her belly full, the girl laid down. Amongst pillows and softness, she fell asleep. It was the first time Nilam would sleep so well.

The girl stayed with us for four days and five nights. She was a curious girl, but she was a silent one as well. She wanted naught to do with the tower, but the tower had called to her, and none could ignore our call. Her door had opened, and her door had closed, and until she could find another door that would open for her, Nilam would not be moved. We accepted it.

She did not.

She fought every step as she went up, and up, and *up*. She screamed when we did not answer her questions, never considering that we couldn't. She was a child. She had come to us with blood on her hands, and she was afraid.

On the fifth night, we sat with her as she ate. She did not offer us any food, did not speak to us. Nilam was marble in a living world.

It was the first time we looked at her.

Nilam's door had appeared as she had been running. Her morning had not started easily. The king's son, not the prince, his *bastard*, had insulted her. He had called her a street rat, had said she did not deserve to work in the palace alongside the likes of him.

"Look at you, orphan girl," the boy laughed and kicked her in the knee, sending her sprawling on the floor. "No one wants you. You are just a useless mouth to feed."

In our mind, Nilam snarled and roared, a lioness springing into action. In reality, Nilam bowed her head and did not look up as she stood up once more. She established a safe distance from the king's bastard and spoke in less than a murmur.

"Yes, sir."

It was not allowed to servant to speak to members of the royal family unless given express permission. Nilam was tired of all those rules. Demetrius was not part of the royal family, anyway. He was barely a bastard. Emperor Ellyan had not publicly recognized him as flesh and blood. If he did, Demetrius would become crown prince. He was only a month older than prince Ofelrin, but it was one month too much. The eldest child of the emperor was destined to rule the empire.

"Don't you know better than to speak to your superiors?" Demetrius came closer once more, seizing Nilam's face between two cruel fingers. "You really are a good for nothing, Nilam. I don't see what my sister likes about you."

Princess Deandra was the third daughter of Emperor Ellyan by his wife, Queen Calryn. She had picked Nilam to be her personal servant two years ago, and the two girls had only a few months that separated their ages. They looked somewhat like one another too, and Deandra had once dressed Nilam in one of her dresses. It had been wonderful.

"You aren't a prince, sir," Nilam answered, trying not to let her fear spread. She was already quite courageous then. In fact, she would prove to be only more courageous as she grew. "I don't owe you my silence, sir."

"Watch your tongue, servant," Demetrius growled. He was so much bigger than Nilam had any hope of ever being. The sun had shone four times more on his day of birth than on her own. He grabbed her jaw and squeezed, stopping her from speaking more, but Nilam was a brave girl. Too brave, we would learn.

When she bit his hand, Demetrius howled in pain and let her go. He attempted to kick at her, but Nilam was a small girl. She had slipped away from where he was still nursing his wounded hand, and she was running.

It was not the run that lead her to her door. This run lead her to the closet where Astrid, the head domestic of Princess Deandra's household, hid the cleaning supplies. They were close enough to Deandra's quarters that Nilam could have run there, but she did not think of it. Her thoughts were ours, and we saw the dark closet enclosing on her on dark nights.

She hid there when she was frightened, when the emperor roamed the halls, anger sparking in his voice as he grabbed the nearest available servant to hurt. The emperor's temper was worse than his son's, and Nilam had received enough beatings for a lifetime. She was not keen on receiving another one.

The door of the closet left her in the darkness, and she sighed with relief, crawling to the opposite wall. She enjoyed how cramped the space was. It reminded her of warm arms and the sensation of being loved. Nilam had never known her parents, but she knew they had been servants of Emperor Ellyan. Astrid had raised her, sometimes mentioning that her mother had been a friend, that her father had gardened for the queen.

Nilam didn't need Astrid to tell her in order to know the emperor had killed them both. She could hear the whispers, on nights she accompanied Princess Deandra to banquets and feasts. The low giggles of courtesans, fanning themselves with great fans that hid their faces, did not escape her.

"Isn't it a pity Deandra chose that girl? I heard the emperor wanted to have her executed." One would say, when she passed them by. Nilam was not allowed to talk during those moments. "It would have been more humane to have killed her when she was a babe."

"Oh, don't say that," their partner would answer, guffawing as the imperial procession passed them by. "She is a servant, after all. The emperor might have some use for her, when she grows up some."

She knew what *that* meant, too. The emperor only had one bastard living at court, but his affairs were known to all. Some said a whole city could be filled with only the emperor's bastards. Nilam never wanted to bring more of his children into the world. She never wanted to bring *anyone's* children into the world.

"Open up, you bitch," Demetrius shouted behind her, and the door shook with his fury. Nilam did not move. She made herself smaller and closed her eyes, pushing the palms of her hands against them to create the illusion of protection.

It was a fruitless move. The door fractured under Demetrius' hands, breaking apart easily. She did not cry, did not yell or beg for mercy. She was afraid, yes, but she was a courageous girl. She would prevail. Whatever Demetrius did to her, it would never rival her own anger. The emperor's favorite bastard might think himself Nilam's doom, but the girl knew better.

The door cracked, letting a hand peek through first. It was tinged with red, blood pearling onto the floor as Demetrius reached for the handle. Splinters pierced his soft skin, but he seemed to not care about it. Slowly, he turned the lock, removing his hand from the hole he had created into the wood.

Demetrius, bastard of Emperor Ellyan the third, the golden son of Jacin, god of sorrows, stood in the doorway with a grin Nilam knew too well. It was his smug smile, the smirk that announced pain for those he encountered. Nilam had seen it when he came to visit Deandra, when he would twist the princess' arm in her back as she attempted to make him leave. Nilam would have been afraid, if she hadn't felt the hard edges of a loose nail underneath her uncovered feet.

Nilam was never half as brave as she was clever. When she would grow up, she would sit with us and thank us, but this is not for now.

Now, she let her hands fall to the ground, and dug her nails into the wood until she reached the sharp metal. It scratched at her hand, not enough to draw blood, but she wouldn't have noticed if it had. Demetrius was moving again.

He blocked all the light, and she could only see his sinister grin. Excitement flickered in the bastard's eyes, and suddenly she hated him.

It wasn't a novel sensation for Nilam, hate. She had hated before. She had hated the emperor, and she had hated her parents for abandoning her, and she had hated the whole world too. But she had never truly hated.

It spread through her like wildfire, starting from her heart until it even made her eyes go blurry with furious tears. Opposite her, the smile only grew.

Humans are strange creatures, with instincts and reactions that always seem impossible. They do not understand the bonds of time, or the inevitable ties of destiny. Yet, they draw the strings of life as if they did.

Nilam jumped before Demetrius could reach her. The nail, held tightly in her left fist, found its way into his throat first. The blood that gushed from the wound as she retrieved it, only to plunge it again and again, coated her hands. She howled as she stabbed him, a wolf in a castle full of wild dogs.

Demetrius, despite his age, his height, his royal blood, never had a chance. Nilam's puncturing was too vicious, too precise. He had tried to resist at first, but he quickly found his breath gone. He fell to the floor, but she continued to drive the nail into his skin, again and again. She was angry, more than she had ever been in her life. She half wanted to taste Demetrius' blood.

Everyone in the palace, except maybe Deandra, thrived on the fear they instilled in others. They liked its sour taste in the air, the way it made them bigger. Nilam did not like fear. Even when she would learn to use it, she would never like it the way they all did.

But for a moment, Nilam saw the appeal. She felt the life slipping away between her fingers. Relief, joy, delight… All those emotions ran through her for a terrible moment. This was the high they all sought. It made her skin crawl.

Shouts resonated in the hallway, and Nilam was snapped back to her own reality. The nail fell from between her fingers, and she stood up.

This time, when she ran, it led her to the right door. Her sticky fingers pushed the golden handle of a door she had never seen before, and she joined us.

Nilam sat without a word in front of us, her eyes calculating. The Tower had aged her, and she did not quite feel like she was only eleven and three quarters anymore. That is what she thought, at least, and that is what she would tell us years later, when gold and black silk adorned her face.

For now, she said nothing, and we only watched her further. She kept us in the present this time. We were a shape we did not know, but her eyes were hard on us. Her mouth formed words she would not say, and her fingers gripped the knife tighter. Nilam awaited her doom, even now, but she would not go down without a fight. She was a brave girl.

"I want to leave this place," she said when our silence started becoming too much for her.

Most will say they want to go home.

"I don't have a home," she spat, anger so great that it rippled through us for an instant. "I thought you knew everything about me, aren't you supposed to know that too?"

It was the first time a human had been so fiery with us. Nilam would always be a new one for us. We had seen the eternity of time, had seen empires birthed and destroyed, had seen the first child and the last elder, but the world had never had *Nilam* in it before.

Where would you go, child?

She glared, but it held no heat. Her anger was naught anymore, a soft lull that she kept alive every day, without letting it devour her. She could kindle the flames brighter or smother them in an instant, and if she had wanted, she could have let it consume her, but she did not want that. Or she did not know she could want that. Not yet.

"I don't know, but I can go anywhere through one of the doors, can't I?"

The doors each lead to a single place. You will not be able to use the same door twice.

"I only need to walk through one and I'll never be here anymore?"

You must find your door and open it.

She stood up then, her eyes burning bright with determination. There were no mysteries she could hide, no secrets that would not be ours while she remained here. She was a child of the Tower now, until she found her door.

Without a word, she left the room, walking calmly through the tall wooden doors. The knife she had held previously was tucked in the jacket she had found, forgotten in one of the chests that adorned her room. Many clothes had been left by previous children as they sought out the worlds beyond the doors, and we had never seen the use in throwing them out. We were the Tower's keeper, and the Tower did not mind the clothes.

We did not follow Nilam out of the room. We knew what would happen now. She would walk down the stairs, trying to recall where she had come from, and when she would find the door where her sticky-bloody fingers had left an imprint, she would try to open it.

Nilam had not heeded our warning. Not many did. The appeal of a known space was too strong for them, too bright. Even if no comfort laid beyond that door, they sought to return through it. But it was no longer her door, and she was no longer able to open it. Where before the brass handle had seemed to be fitted to her fingers, molded so it was her touch that made it become a real handle, it was now cold and hard, unbudging no matter how much strength and weight she put on it. She would not cry, for Nilam hadn't cried in years and refused to do so now, but her frustration grew so much that she kicked the door, hurting her foot in the process. She still had no shoes, after all.

After a few more minutes, she stopped her fruitless efforts. It was no good for her to keep going when the door showed no intention of letting her go through. Our words came back to her then, and her rage became so powerful that, as far away as we were, we felt the sharp twists of it, our body turning into the one's she hated the most. It lasted for a few seconds, and then her anger subsided. Cold determination shook her, and she attempted to open all doors, but none would answer her touch.

Seeing Doors, Animal Doors, even Cold Doors, none allowed her passage through. The worlds beyond were outside of Nilam's reach. The Tower would not allow her to choose her door, for it was not how the Tower worked. Doors were created every day, but rarely disappeared. They remained under our care, until the world beyond them was nothing more than a speck of dust, and then they would fade. The door Nilam sought already existed, but she knew not how to find it. Her heart and mind were clouded by the anger within her chest.

We could have gone to her. It would have been easy for us to lead her to her door. We knew where she was meant to go, where she was meant to exist. But it was not our right to guide her there. The Tower was not meant to be a guide. We were meant to be a Keeper of Time.

Nilam's trials did not stop for a few hours, during which she grew more desperate and tired, but she would not stop until all hope had abandoned her. Still, she was young, and exhaustion ran through her more easily than ever before. She sunk to her knees, her back to the Fox Door, and she waited. Still, she did not cry.

For a long moment, she thought she would fall asleep. It was a tempting idea; she wondered if we would bring her back to the beds she had scorned earlier, and idly she wished that we were there with her. The thought had not yet finished formulating when she became disgusted with herself, and she stood up once more. She had never needed anyone to rescue her, and she would never allow herself to become this way.

This time, rather than her mind, she let her heart guide her as she sought out the path to her door. Doors that called not to her, she rejected. Doors that made her skin crawl, she moved past without a look. She did not know which door would be hers, and for now, the knowledge that one would be hers sufficed. She seemed much older than she truly was then. *That* was what the Tower did, to those unsuspecting.

Her door appeared in front of her as she reached one of the alcoves she had seen on her first day. It was large, not quite as large as some of the Cold Doors, but enough that reaching the handle was difficult on its own. This door, she called the Royal Door. It had gold and rubies inlaid in it, surrounding a round mirror. It seemed made for her, even if she could see it had not been created that day. Doors were made for different people and became what was needed for each person. This door would not be used again until much later, when a boy with wild curls and forest green clothing would pass through it, but that is not our story.

Nilam's hand closed around the handle, and she smiled. It was the first time she smiled since she had arrived, and it was the first time she felt something so beautiful in her life. The door opened onto a luxurious garden, where a pond allowed birds and fish to live in harmony.

Through a door that would not see light again for many centuries, there left Nilam, a knife of time hidden within her jacket.

About the Author

Aaron Haden is an academic researcher moving around the world every few years or so, exploring more of the literary field he's devoted to. He is a science fiction and fantasy writer, sometimes getting lost in his own world building. He likes quiet spaces and loud people, which reflects in his writing, and he is always seeking a new adventure to look forward to.

You can find him on Twitter @aaronuniverses.

The Asylum Wall

by

Carol Hightshoe

The Asylum Wall

There is nothing here, I think as I clutch the papers I'm carrying tighter to my chest then force my eyes up from the walkway to look at the building. *Nothing except ghosts and memories.*

It has only been a few years since the place closed, but it looks like it has been abandoned for decades. Almost all of the small windows are broken, giving the building a pockmarked appearance in the light of an early twilight. The doors hang crooked in their frames, and weeds have overrun the once smooth lawn. The place is dead, and only the ghosts and memories remain.

I take a breath and push open the arching main gates; their grinding and squeaking echoes in the silence of the area. "Ghosts can't hurt you," I whisper as the echoes fade.

Broken asphalt shifts and crunches under my feet. Up close, the decay is even more obvious. Deep wrinkles and creases line the front of the building where the paint is cracked and peeling. Moss hangs from the eaves, veiling and shadowing the broken, empty windows. I reach for the partially open door and step through, back into the memories I came here to face.

Dust covers everything in the entry hall, and I swallow the cough scratching at the back of my throat. As I walk through the lobby, the dust swirls around me, creating mists and vapors that bring memories of the people who once worked or lived here back into sharp focus. I am reminded of the doctors and nurses—some of whom were easy to work with and were still fresh enough they hadn't become cynical or callous. There were others who had worked with our patients far too long and had begun to expect the worse behavior from them or had to have it proven which ones weren't BiFFs, or Big Fat Fakers. We did receive a percentage of those as well.

Shadowy forms also became some of the patients I had worked with over the years. There—a young man in his late twenties physically, but maybe four or five mentally and emotionally. He used to follow everyone around like a little puppy. We could never get him to keep his shoes on. I smile as I remember how he used to carry a security blanket with him. Fortunately, one of the other, more stable patients would always seem to adopt him and make sure he stayed out of trouble.

The ghostly figure shifts, and I step back as one of the BiFFs jumps toward me—a young woman who had been ordered here, several times, from one of the county jails, for evaluation. I didn't know her charges, I was never curious about that sort of thing, as I felt it would prejudice my attitude when I dealt with our high security patients. This one though, she was a classic. She wanted to make you think she was crazy, but you could see the calculating going on in her head. Some nights she would create as many disturbances as she could; getting all the other patients on the floor upset and agitated. Then some days she would go into a sweet little girl act, being polite and helpful and other times, she just became as disgusting as she thought she could away with.

We all knew she was a behavior issue, and after a few days, the doctors would release her back to the county jail. But she knew the right buttons to push each time she went to court to make the judge think she honestly had mental health issues, and each time he would order her back here for an evaluation. I always suspected the officers at the jail appreciated the break they got when she was with us. Considering the way we felt after dealing with her, I couldn't blame them.

As I leave the lobby and enter the patient areas, the dust thickens, and I find myself walking in a dense fog that obscures my vision. Still, I know where I am going and only pause to nod a greeting to each of my memories as we pass.

My hand shakes as I reach for the door to this room. A spark arcs from the knob to my hand, flashing bright blue and creating a halo of light in the fog. The bluish glow surrounds the door as I step through and back into my past.

"Deirdre, we just got a call from the sheriff's dispatcher," Marco said as he stepped out of the office. "They picked up some guy wandering around downtown in robes, carrying a staff and talking about dragons chasing him. They'll be bringing him in on an M-1 hold for evaluation." He handed her some papers.

"Did they say how long?" Deirdre looked up and pushed her glasses up on her nose as she glanced at the papers.

Marco looked at his watch. "Should be here in about five minutes. Which room?"

"Let's use room ten."

"I'll get it ready. Let me know when they get here."

"Sure."

Deirdre Ashlyn closed the file she had been working on, pulled up the admittance forms, and started entering the preliminary information from the notes Marco had handed her.

"Where do you want us to put Gandalf here?"

Deirdre looked up from the computer to see two deputies standing at the desk. She shook her head. Tom had never learned to use any of the verbal judo skills she knew his office taught. "Marco should have room ten ready."

She nodded toward the staff the other deputy was holding. "Is that it for his property?" She held her hand out for it.

"We didn't find anything else on the initial pat down," the young man said handing her the staff.

Deirdre took the gnarled wood and gasped as an electric shock went through her arm.

"Are you okay?" Tom grabbed the staff.

"No!" The old man in the robes stepped toward Tom. "That is not for you. You must give it back to the one who has been chosen."

"It's okay," Deirdre said taking the staff back. She smiled at the younger deputy, who had placed a hand on the old man's shoulder but had not thrown him on the floor or into a wall as others would have done.

"Come on old man, let's get you to your room," Marco said.

"I still need a name for the records," Deirdre said.

The old man looked at her, his gray eyes glowing in the dim lighting of the area. "You may call me Brayden."

"Is that your first or last name?" She found herself staring at his eyes.

"Just Brayden." He turned toward Marco. "I believe you said you had a room waiting for me."

"This way." Marco gestured down the hall.

Deirdre watched as they walked away from her desk. *Just a coincidence,* she thought as she went back to filling out the forms.

A sharp pain stabs my hand, the same as I felt the first time I touched Brayden's staff, and I shudder as the electric shock pulses through my body. Even now, I know the name he gave me was only a coincidence, but a part of me wants to believe it wasn't.

As I look around the room, the dust begins to settle on the walls and words start to form on the white paint. I close my eyes for a moment. When I open them, the words are still there—clearer. I stare at the walls and realize that unlike the rest of the building, the walls in this room are still stark white and smooth. The letters seem to shimmer for a moment then swirl and shift. Here and there, I see lines and passages I recognize from some of the stories I had written.

Brayden was a writer also. He would spend hours scribbling on the walls of his room at night. Then, when all of the space was covered, he would clean the walls and start over. I remember asking him what he was writing about once and he turned to me, his gray eyes as dark as storm clouds. "The same thing you are." He smiled then turned back to the wall. "I am looking for a way back to where I belong; while you are looking for the place where you belong. We will both get there one day—through our magic and words."

"Magic?"

"Magic." He smiled as he looked at me. "Stories are a form of magic. Through them you create worlds and people. There are writers who are able to breath true life into their worlds and transport others into them. These worlds really do exist and sometimes they intersect with this one."

I laughed at the image I suddenly had of a unicorn trotting down a street.

"Do not laugh. Bards have always created worlds of wonder for others. Some of these worlds are small and only a handful ever visit, they only linger for a short time, before they are forgotten and fade into mist. But others become a part of the background of this world. They are the repository of the magic your world wants to believe in, but your science refuses to recognize. The more people visit these worlds, either by reading the creative words of the writer or by daydreaming about it, the longer it will last."

He turned back to the wall and placed his hand on it—sliding his fingers under the words he had written before I had come in.

"Sometimes there is enough power in the words that a chosen few can actually cross over and enter the world."

At that point, he started writing again and I decided it was time to leave.

That night when I went home, I found Brayden's staff sitting in the corner of the small room I used as an office. I stared at it for a few minutes then sat at my computer and began typing.

I'd had an idea for a fantasy novel for a number of years, and, while I had sketched out a general outline and knew who my main character was, I hadn't done much work on it in several months. Tonight, though, was different, I read through the notes I had on the story, and on the character I had named Brayden before I ever met the one I now knew as a harmless but delusional old man, and began typing.

I didn't stop typing until I heard the alarm in my bedroom go off, informing me it was time to get up and get ready for work.

I glanced at the staff still sitting in the corner; there seemed to be a soft glow surrounding it. "Good, you have opened the door," I heard Brayden's voice whisper behind me.

My head jerked up, and I found myself sitting in my bed—alarm still buzzing. Had it all been a dream? I thought so at the time. When I checked my computer before leaving for work, I found a new file in the folder where my writing projects were stored. This one though was passworded, and I didn't know the password. I started to delete the file but stopped as I looked up at the place the staff had been—there was nothing there now. *Time for a vacation,* Deidre, I told myself. *You've been working with some of these people so long you're starting to have hallucinations.*

"Hey, you feeling okay?" Marco asked, causing Deidre to jerk her head up.

"Been fighting a headache for the last hour or so," she said.

Marco frowned. "You take anything?"

"Aspirin, but it's not helping."

"Don't go getting sick on me; it's just the two of us tonight, so you can't go home."

"I know. Tonight's my Friday; I should be able to make it till the end of shift."

"That's the spirit. Hang in there."

"Thanks." Deirdre watched Marco walk down the hall to check on the patients.

"He's cleaning his wall again," Marco said when he came back to the desk.

"You might want to make a note on that." Deirdre looked up and frowned. "The walls weren't even a quarter full this morning."

Marco nodded the headed for the small office.

She waited a few minutes then got up and walked down the hallway and paused at Brayden's room. "It's time for the story to be finished," she heard him say. She looked through the small window and saw him sitting on the floor, staring at some papers in his lap. There were several others scattered on the floor around him.

She shook her head and went back to her desk.

A sudden chill causes me to shiver in the room as I remember the scene. Looking down at the floor now, I see a stray piece of paper and reach down to pick it up. There is something written on it, but it has faded to a pale gray that almost blends with the paper. I squint and angle the paper to better catch the little light coming in through the small window. "How?" I gasp as I drop the paper.

I glance at the stack of my papers I had placed on the old mattress. The only words on the top page, *Sylvan Shadows*, stare up at me as I reached for the dropped paper. The words on the page are the same. *Sylvan Shadows.*

"Brayden!" I yell in the silence.

The only reaction I get is dust swirling around me.

The dust begins to settle, and my mind again sees Brayden sitting on the floor with his papers. We had found him in the same position that morning at breakfast. Both Marco and I had thought he had been reading during the night and hadn't disturbed him. However, that morning we discovered he was dead.

There was nothing to indicate how he had died; it was as if his spirit had just left his body. I remembered seeing a slight glow, like a doorway, on the wall, but no one else acted as if they had seen it, so I never mentioned it.

I quit working here about a month after Brayden died, I also stopped writing for a while. There was something about his death that rattled me; it was as if I could feel his spirit watching me, just as I felt he was here with me now. About six months after I quit, his staff reappeared in my apartment, and I found my desire to write had also returned. *Sylvan Shadows* was the result of that return to writing, and it featured a harmless, but slightly delusional old wizard named Brayden.

They closed the hospital about a year later.

Now, something has led me back here. Something that was telling me to bring this copy of the story here, for Brayden. I place the faded page on top of my stack and smile. He once told me he was writing the same thing I was. Perhaps there was some kind of weird psychic connection between us. Maybe there was something to his comments about writers creating worlds with their words. Or perhaps, I had unconsciously plagiarized what he had been writing on the walls when he was here.

"Deirdre."

I jump and turn toward the soft voice. A glowing figure stands in front of a doorway in the wall.

"Brayden?"

"Yes." He holds out his hand. "I was able to open the portal that night and leave your world and return to my own. Stealing your creativity was the only way I could touch any form of magic in this world. Now that you have again found your muse, and your magic, I would invite you to come to my world."

"Would I ever be able to return?"

"Unlikely."

I look past his shoulder and saw the world I had created in my fantasy novel and some other stories. A place that was young and green. A world of magic and wonder. A place I had desired to be for a long time.

I nod and take his hand. There is a sudden spark of electricity, like when I opened the door to the room. It then wraps around my wrist in a glowing band.

"Look," Brayden says nodding toward something behind me.

I turn and see my body sitting on the floor against the bed—just as his had been that night. The copy of my manuscript is still neatly stacked on the mattress.

I smile as I realize *Sylvan Shadows* will probably be a bestseller for my agent, with the added mystique of my mysterious death in the mental hospital I used to work at. I'm sure one of the other former employees will tell someone about the last patient to be housed in room ten as well. And the story of the old man named Brayden who thought he was a wizard from another world will only add to the popularity of the story—keeping it, and this world, alive for a long time.

About the Author

A native Texan, Carol found her way to her current home in Colorado by way of a five-year detour in The Netherlands—courtesy of her husband Tim and the US Air Force.

An avid reader at a young age, her strong desire to write came from her love of (her husband calls it her obsession with) Star Trek. It was this early love of Star Trek that led her to the Science Fiction and Fantasy genres.

In addition to her writing, she has worked as a receptionist/office manager for two veterinary clinics, a deputy sheriff in El Paso County Colorado, Assistant Fan Club Manager for the Professional Bull Riders, and currently as a Rodeo Keyer for the Professional Rodeo Cowboys Association.

She has been published in various anthologies and magazines including "Creature Fantastic," *PanGaia Magazine*, "Stories of Strength", *Baen's Universe*, *Tales of the Talisman* and *Kepler's Dozen.* Her books include: *Call of Chaos*, *Chaos Embraced*, *The Road into Chaos*, and *Chaos Challenged.*

In addition to her own writing, she is the editor and publisher of the online e-zine: *The Lorelei Signal* as well as running her own micro-press—WolfSinger Publications.

The Sea Cave

by
Jodi Rizzotto

The Sea Cave

"For once, I'd like to eat something not burnt to a crisp!"

"If you would unlock your wallet and let me buy some decent pans…"

"All you do is spend my money…"

Even though the day had just begun, Meghan's parents were already arguing. She hoped no one at the campground realized she was *their* twelve-year-old daughter.

"Come on, Noodles," she called to her tiny wire-haired dog, who was busy sniffing every deposit in the dog run. She clipped the leash on him and closed the gate, navigating through kids on bikes and surfers headed for the beach. After looking in the direction of her parents' trailer, she led her dog the opposite way, toward the beach entrance.

A faded sign announced, 'No Dogs Allowed on Beach,' but it was early, and there would be no lifeguards in their towers yet.

Camping was supposed to bring families closer together. Instead, Meghan spent most of her time trying to escape her parents and their endless bickering. She descended the creaking stairs, feeling the tension leave her shoulders. At the bottom, she jumped across the large gap from the cement footing to the sand. Noodles jumped down and sat, looking up at her with worshipful eyes.

"Here ya go," she said as she unhooked his leash.

The black and white dog sped away onto the beach, looped around and headed back to her. He would repeat this pattern during their walk, never leaving her sight. She tied back her shoulder-length ash hair with a ponytail, slipped off her flip-flops, and wallowed through dry sand to the water line. The cool wet sand massaged her feet as she walked.

Crashing waves, hissing foam, and early morning mist blocked out her parents' poisonous words. Sky and sea blended in soothing grey, the horizon a mere smudge in the distance. Dark blobs bobbed on the surface of the water; surfers waiting for the perfect ride. Noodles barked and chased a sea gull on the empty beach.

Meghan smiled for the first time that day.

Noodles continued his chaotic bird hunt until a small ground squirrel poked its head out of a seaweed pile, and the dog changed direction. The squirrel raced for the shelter of the cliffs. With the creature almost in reach of his barking jaws, the dog disappeared into a small opening.

"Noodles, come back!" Meghan cried, fearful her dog would uncover a snake or something worse. She slipped on her flip-flops and followed.

The cave's sudden chill made her shiver, despite her warm hoodie and jeans. Years of pounding waves had carved out a larger space than the entrance indicated. Other than large flat rocks and trails of seaweed, the cave was empty.

"Noodles!" she cried.

"Noodles, Noodles." The cave echoed back to her. She looked everywhere but there was no sign of him.

Plopping down on one of the larger rocks, she pushed tears away, as her parents' endless drama had trained her, took a deep breath, and looked around. That's when she noticed a large gap under the rock facing her. It was large enough for a person to crawl through. She got up and inspected it, discovering familiar paw prints.

Thoughts of rabid squirrels forgotten, she crawled into the hole. The ground below her fell away, and she tumbled downward into soft sand. Pulling herself up, she felt in her jacket pocket for her phone, also still thankfully in one piece, and turned on the flashlight.

The cavern she had landed in was wider than the cave above, like the body of a water pitcher. Next to her on the sand she could see a dog-sized impression and paw prints disappearing into another tunnel.

The sensible course was to follow Noodles' trail, hoping it would also lead to the way out. Fortunately, the passage was tall enough for her to walk standing up. The ground was sandy, but, to her right, a trickle of slimy water flowed, draining from somewhere.

"Noodles!" she called.

"Noodles, Noodles, Noodles," the cave echoed.

No answering bark.

She continued to follow his trail. Her flashlight revealed green, mossy, dripping walls, but thankfully no bugs. Her heart pounded anyway, with the thought that there had to be other creatures down here.

After an eternity of following her puddle of light, she saw daylight as the tunnel curved to the right. When she reached the bend, another large cavern, circular, with natural ledges sticking out like shelves was revealed. The light came from a large hole in the roof, shining down, in a beam, to the ground.

A joyful bark announced the wet dog circling her ankles, and she scooped him up, pressing his matted fur to her face. "Noodles, Noodles," was all she could say.

"Noodles, Noodles, Noodles," the cavern agreed.

Now that she had found her dog unharmed, Meghan turned her thoughts toward getting back topside. She squinted as she looked up to the ceiling. The hole looked large enough, if she could climb up the surrounding ledges. She walked up closer to inspect them.

Suddenly, a loud rumbling, like a train, shook the room. Her feet slipped on the edges of a dull metal plate beneath her. She jumped off it, but the grinding sound got louder. Did she find her dog only to be buried in an earthquake?

With a swirl of dust, the wall split open, revealing a hidden chamber. Maybe it was a smuggler's hideout with an exit. Hopefully, no one was home. Even though her heart was racing, she clutched Noodles and walked in.

Unlike the rest of the cave, this chamber featured walls covered with brightly colored tapestries in patterns of trees, flowers, and fruit. Antique wooden furniture, including chairs, tables, and small sofas, filled the room, all of it lit by a skylight in the center, like the cavern she had just left.

Although she was alone, there was an air of expectancy, like a waiting room or a train depot.

Then she realized she and Noodles were not alone.

"Welcome to Carlsbad Portal, miss," announced a thin, dark-haired man dressed in dark green tunic and pants. He stood near the center of the room, writing on a long rolled out scroll draped over a wooden lectern. "Where might you be traveling today?"

"What?" Meghan asked, her manners compromised by the absurdity of the man and this room hidden inside a cave. Noodles, who usually barked at mail carriers and joggers, was silent.

The man took out tiny spectacles and examined her through them. He narrowed his eyes at her dog and took a cautious step back. "Of course. This is your first time using the Faerie Portal System," he concluded. "From this station, you can visit Summer or Spring Courts. Which would be your destination?"

She stared at the man, suddenly noticing his bright green eyes and slender, pointed ears. "Are you dressed like an elf, like in that hobbit movie?" She looked behind her. "Where are the cameras and the director?"

The man sighed and shook his head. "You're not fae. Not to worry, miss. I have visas here. You can use a day pass." He pulled out a yellowed scrap of paper. "All you have to do is fill in your true name and your family homeland, and you can be on your way. For your first trip, I would recommend the Spring Court. The weather's always lovely, and the flowers are spectacular."

Realizing he was serious, she stood there speechless.

"We're running a special this month. The price for a day pass is a song," the man continued.

"A song?" she said, her curiosity overruling her unbelief.

"Any song will do, miss," the man explained, "but children's songs are preferred. They still contain magic. Come, fill this in, then you can sing, and be on your way." He dipped his long feather quill in a tiny inkwell and offered it to her.

Meghan took the quill and studied the paper. It was a handwritten ticket titled, "Day Pass, Mortal Use Only," and had a rather large paragraph of fine print. At the bottom was a blank line for her name and her hometown. Convinced now that somewhere in the tunnel she had hit her head and blacked out, and this was her dream, she decided to go along with it. She scratched the quill on the paper, trying not to make too many ink blotches.

"You want me to sing now?" she asked. The man nodded, stamped her ticket with the date and handed it back to her.

She tried to remember a song. Maybe her mom sang lullabies to her when she was a baby, but she had a hard time picturing it. Her mom's smile was as hard as a knife and just as sharp.

"Rock-a-bye baby, in the treetop.

When the wind blows, the cradle will rock.

When the bough breaks, the cradle will fall,

And down will fall baby, cradle and all."

Her vision blurred and she stumbled. Her head ached like she'd been up too late. The man helped her to a chair. "Very good, miss, that will do nicely. Now step into the portal. Don't lose your ticket. You'll need it to get back." He gestured toward a metal disk directly below the skylight.

Meghan paused for a moment. Was she really doing this? She never went past the end of her street without letting her mother know where she was going. But lately her parents were too busy fighting to notice her, and this was an adventure she might never find again. If this was all a dream, then it wouldn't matter.

"Thank you, sir." she said, remembering her manners before she stepped onto the disk. The bright light blinded her as the ground below dropped away.

"Hey, watch out!" a tiny voice screamed.

Meghan landed in the middle of a loaded hay wagon. After she regained her breath, she felt movement under her back and then a sharp pain.

"Ouch!" She rolled over, the hay stubble sticking to her jacket. A small creature crawled out from under her. "Did you really bite me?"

"You squash me!" the tiny creature replied, a wide smile showing his tiny, pointed teeth. "Got you off, I did." Although it spoke like a human, it had beady black eyes and large furry ears that stood up like a Chihuahua. It was dressed in a checkered shirt and overalls that almost covered its furry bare feet.

"What are you?" she wondered aloud. The creature frowned. "I didn't mean to be rude," she said. "I've never met anyone like you before. I'm sorry for landing on you. My name is Meghan."

"Apology accepted," the creature said. "Since you have named yourself, I also must. You may call me Malarkey. You are a human tourist, so you not know I am Hob."

"Hob?"

"Hobs are useful persons to have on farm, which is where you are. Mr. Greenleaf's farm," Malarkey continued, as he brushed the straw from his shirt and reshaped his crushed straw hat. "I guide cows to sweet grass. Then lead them home for milking. Sometimes, I grab a few winks on hay wagon. Did not expect to be crushed by visitor." After placing on his wide brimmed hat, he jumped down from the wagon.

Meghan also jumped down, straw falling around her in piles. "It's nice to meet you, Malarkey." She looked around at the lush green pastureland spread out around her on every side. In the distance she could see a grove of trees, perhaps shielding a farmhouse and barn.

Suddenly, she realized she hadn't seen Noodles since the portal. She was no longer holding his leash.

"My dog!" she cried. "Noodles! Noodles! Where are you?"

The field in front of her rustled and waved, and a small black and white dog shot out of the wheat and into her arms. She squeezed her dog close. The clasp for the leash was still attached to his collar, but the length of the leash was missing, roughly chopped off at the clasp.

"Where have you been?" she wondered. Noodles looked no worse for his adventure, jumping down from her arms to bark hysterically at the Hob.

"Be still, beast!" Malarkey commanded, and Noodles plopped down immediately with his head on the ground.

"How did you do that?" she asked. "Noodles usually only listens to me."

"Hobs have ways with creatures," Malarkey answered with a wicked, toothy grin.

A roar in the sky made them look up. Meghan's mouth flew open. She couldn't believe her eyes. Instead of the airplanes she expected, there were large creatures flying toward them.

Dragons soared in staggered formation; long arrowhead tails of the ones in front close to the snouts of those behind them. Their golden bellies faced the ground, shimmering in the sun.

The head dragon roared commands that were repeated down the line, creating an endless stream of sound. It appeared they were going to land in the field.

The leader hit the ground running on all four of its legs, slowing to a stop right in front of Meghan and the Hob. She backed away toward the wagon, holding Noodles close. The rest of the pack landed behind it, creating a trampled down hole in the wheat.

"Won't Mr. Greenleaf get angry about his crops?" she whispered to Malarkey.

"No doubt," Malarkey agreed. "But there's nothing he can do. It's a dragon rider club. Too dangerous to mess with."

"Dragon riders?" she asked, but then she saw the tiny saddles set in between the spiked ridges on top of the giant creatures. Ropes snaked down the sides, and riders slid down to stand beside their mounts, each of which was the size of a one-story house. Each rider spoke words to their mount, and the huge dragons lay down with the rumble of an earthquake.

"Let's get out of here," Malarkey said, pulling on Meghan's leg. "It's never good to have dealings with dragon riders." But Meghan couldn't take her eyes from the young man walking toward her.

A tall, slender man, appearing to be in his early twenties, wearing a black leather jacket, leather pants, and boots stopped in front of them. He quickly shed his heavy gloves and leather helmet, extending his hand toward her.

"Good morning to you, miss," the faery said. "Visiting on a day pass?"

"Yes, I am," she said, shaking his hand. He had long fingers with pointed nails. Almost like claws. "Good morning to you also. I'm here on an adventure."

"Well, no better place than Spring for adventures," he said, motioning for his companions to join them. "The DOGS welcome you to the Spring Court."

"Dogs? She looked behind them. "You have dogs, too?"

The faeries behind the leader chuckled at her joke. "No, miss. We're the DOGS—Dragon Owners Group. We're a dragon club. See?" He turned around to show her the green and gold embroidery on the back of his leather jacket. It showed a dragon twisted around in a circle, clutching a knife in his mouth and a very human-looking skull in its front claws.

"I see," Meghan said. The faeries surrounded her, watching her curiously. Malarkey folded his arms and stood as tall as he could. She compared them to movies she had seen about faeries. Unlike the on-screen versions, these beings were at least six feet tall, with no visible wings. They stood in military readiness behind their leader, coiled like rattlesnakes. Apart from their pointed ears and piercing eyes, they looked human. The kind of humans you wouldn't want to meet on the street at night.

"We were headed to the farmhouse for tea," Malarkey said firmly. He started leading Meghan down the dirt road between fields. "Good day, riders."

The leader called after them. "Hold up there, Hob. The young lady wants to ride a dragon. Don't you, miss?"

Meghan turned back and met his piercing green eyes with her own. "I'm not sure that would be a good idea. Is it safe?"

The riders roared with laughter. "Of course not!" the leader said. "You don't ride a dragon to be safe! But think of it! The wind rushing through your hair, the land below you a patchwork quilt of colors!"

"I'm not sure about this," she said, but she allowed the dragon rider to lead her over to his creature, who turned his long neck to watch her. With its tail wrapped around it like a cat, it was larger than any of the elephants she had seen at the zoo. Noodles, realizing he was in the presence of larger dogs than he could ever imagine, hid his head under her arm. The dragon paid no attention to him.

"It's amazing," she said, wanting to reach out and touch its shiny green scales, but its bright red eyes made her pause.

"You can touch her," the faery said. "She's tame enough, especially with me by your side." He took her hand and placed it on the side of the creature's neck. It felt cool and slick, like a lizard. The dragon regarded her with intelligent eyes.

The other riders came up to their leader. "Should we go, Hardly? We should reach the forest before nightfall," one of them said.

The faery gave a quick nod, and they sprang into action. They replaced their helmets, buttoned up their jackets, put on their gloves, and climbed back up onto their dragons. The leader took another leather helmet out of his saddle bag and offered it to her.

"Come with us," he said. "My name is Hardly, and I'll make sure you have a great adventure."

She looked back at Malarkey, who was shaking his head vigorously. Was she really going to do this? It was only a dream after all.

"My name is Meghan. I'll come with you." She took the helmet from the faery as Noodles licked her chin. "What about Noodles? Can he ride, too?"

The faery laid his hand on Noodles' trembling head, and the dog was still. He pulled out a leather harness from his bag and slipped it over her head. After fastening it securely around the dog, he smiled. "He should be fine. Let's go."

Meghan slipped on the helmet, pushing her bangs out of the way. She fastened the leather buckle under her chin. Hardly climbed up on the dragon and secured an extra saddle behind his saddle. Then he called down to her.

"Climb up the rope and sit behind me."

With an apologetic look back at Malarkey, she took hold of the rope and found herself seated on a dragon, taking off into the blue sky of Faerie.

Two weeks later, Meghan chewed on a roasted turkey leg, listening to riders swapping stories over the fire. A faery called Never, who had curly black hair, was spinning a tale about the time he and his dragon had landed on Mount Tabletop, the highest mountain in Spring. The others listened with skepticism. They had accepted her easily into their company. Even though they were hundreds of years old, they seemed like friends her age.

She inspected her bone for any last strips of meat, but it was picked clean, so she threw it behind her into the woods. Noodles sat gnawing his bone at her feet. She wiped her greasy hands on the back of her jeans and took out a folded paper she kept in her jacket pocket.

Meghan opened it up and looked at it again. It was her day pass, her permission to enter Faerie. In vain she tried to read the text at the bottom above her signature, but the print was so small there was no way she could see what it meant without a magnifying glass.

Although she had enjoyed the past weeks riding with the Dragon Owners Group, she was a little worried about her visa. What would happen to her if someone asked her for her pass and saw that she had been here past its expiration? She usually was not a rule breaker, preferring the security of boundaries. Except when taking Noodles down on the beach. Her whole adventure wouldn't have been possible without breaking rules. Carefully she folded it back up and put it away.

"Meghan, sing us a song." A ginger haired rider, named Sometimes, pulled her out of her thoughts. "You know, the one about the kids who climb the hill and break their noggins!"

"But it's only a nursery rhyme!" she protested, knowing that she would be forced to give in. They constantly begged songs from her.

"There's a price for traveling with us," Hardly reminded her with a smile. "Come on, now. Your voice is so lovely."

There was a time when she would have been too embarrassed to sing in front of people, but much had changed in her time with the riders. She made them wait as she took a pull of water from her waterskin, swallowed, and looked around at her attentive audience.

"Jack and Jill ran up the hill to fetch a pail of water,

Jack fell down and broke his crown, and Jill came tumbling after."

The riders cheered and toasted each other with the strong dark ale they drank. Stories resumed. She wrapped up in a blanket close enough to the fire to enjoy its warmth, Noodles curled up beside her. There was a simple peace in this nomad life.

That next morning began as any other. Steamy porridge with strong tea, then everything packed up and loaded onto the dragons. During the night, the dragons had hunted and slept, so they were ready to go. Hardly's dragon, the largest with the longest spikes, was named Petal. Petal had warmed up to her early in their travels, purring in a low growl, and thrusting his head in her chest for petting. Even Noodles adjusted to being around the dragons, although he always kept close to her.

Hardly called out, "Time to fly!" and the riders mounted the dragons. Watching the magnificent dragons bob their heads and let out clouds of steam made Meghan feel like an ant crawling on the ground. Yet she also felt bold perched on the back of one. If her parents saw her now, they would not see their daughter, but a strange adventurer, clad in black leather clothes and helmet.

She supposed she should feel guilty for not missing them, but it was such a relief to be away from their drama she pushed them out of her mind. There would come a time when she would have to think about her old life, but not now.

Hardly nodded to Never, who waited while the rest of the dragons rose into the air. Never was their sweep, so he would ride last to make sure everyone stayed together. The riders rode west, away from the still pink morning sun.

Last night, Meghan heard Hardly say they were headed toward the Great Grove, a birch forest a day's flying distance away. Noodles slept peacefully in the pack, by this time accustomed to this strange form of transportation. Below her the farmland formed a green patterned quilt, broken up by brown dirt roads and dots of trees. Then the dragons pierced the canopy of puffy clouds, and all she could see was a landscape of white.

Hours passed without the dragons tiring, and she pulled her scarf tighter around her neck. It was cold up here, cold enough to keep her awake even with the monotony of white. Up ahead, she could see a black speck. As she watched, it grew larger until it became the shape of another dragon.

"King's boils!" Hardly cried, and he held up his left fist, signaling the others for a landing. The riders followed him down as he shot suddenly through the clouds, dropping like a duck shot in a hunt. She held Noodles close with one hand, and with the other clasped her saddle horn desperately.

The quilt of farms below her had been replaced by woods and hills. The ground came up quickly as Petal put them down in a tiny valley. Her stomach flipped as she braced for the jolt when they hit the ground. The dragon's strong legs slowed them to a stop.

"Hurry, Meghan, get down!" Hardly shouted to her as he slid down the mounting rope.

"What's going on?" she asked. All around her riders were rushing their dragons under an opening in the rocks. She kept Noodles in her pack as she picked her way through the piles of jumbled stones.

"The queen's sky patrol," Hardly said as he caught up to her, carrying a folded green cloth. Sometimes and Never helped him open it. She watched in amazement as they kept unfolding until it took six faeries to hold it out. It was some sort of magic blanket. They attached it to the top of the rocks to make a shelter.

Never lit a small lamp, and everyone sat down, seeming to hold their breath. They heard a dragon roar somewhere out in the valley. No one spoke a word. The whoosh of flapping wings came close and then faded away. Minutes stretched into at least an hour before anyone moved.

"Come on," Hardly said. "He's gone."

"Why did we hide from the queen's patrol?" Meghan asked as they prepared to continue their journey.

Never paused and looked at Hardly, who nodded slightly. "Once there were many dragon rider clubs. We used to have parties and races. But one night in Littleton, things got out of hand. No one was watching the dragons, and the next thing you know the whole village was burnt down. Now the queen hunts us like animals."

"How terrible!" she said. She had forgotten the Hob's warning back in the field. The dragons were dragons after all, fire-breathing beasts that could be destructive.

Just then a large group of soldiers holding swords stood up from the rocks surrounding them. A tall faerie in chain mail shouted something, and a large net flew and trapped the dragon riders. Hardly and the others took out their knives and tried to cut free, but they couldn't break a strand of the enchanted trap.

Never looked at Hardly and said, "I told you something bad would happen if the dragons got into the ale."

Meghan and the dragon riders, cocooned by a regiment of faerie soldiers, walked directly to the queen's audience chamber. Meghan's stomach still felt queasy from their portal jump. Besides the stationary portals, the faeries had field portals that could be transported easily wherever they traveled. So here they were, moments after they had been caught in a net like witless rabbits.

Meghan wondered what had happened to Noodles. Her terrier had been ripped from her arms when they were captured. Her heart ached with his absence. She glanced behind her at Hardly, Never, and the rest of the Dragon Owners Group. The riding club walked with their heads down, their hands bound behind them, and their mouths gagged. Their captors took no chances that one of them would cast a spell. Their dragons were back in the woods, still held in nets.

Since the soldiers knew she was human, Meghan walked in front, unbound. She looked around at the overarching trees forming the hall they walked. Behind the trees, tall hedges formed walls on both sides of them. Tiny lamps hung in strings from the trees, glowing with an unseen power.

At the end of the hall stood a large oak tree with an enormous knot that formed a door. A soldier knocked, and it was opened by a guard. They exchanged words in that strange murmuring language that soldiers had heard Hardly speak with the other riders. Then the door opened wide, and they were escorted inside.

The chamber inside was vast, impossible to be contained within the oak tree. She squinted at the tiny bright lights that filled the ceiling like stars. On both sides were faery courtiers, in silk gowns every color of the rainbow. Their male companions wore embroidered tunics over bloomers and stockings. Their beautiful faces frowned at the procession.

Meghan and the DOGs approached the base of steep stairs leading up to a dais. Upon the dais sat a throne made of two living birches, twisted together to form a chair. The soldiers stopped in unison and dropped to one knee. When Meghan saw the dragon riders fall on their knees and bow their heads, she copied their pose. Out of the corner of her eye, she saw the soldiers look up, so she followed their gaze but remained on her knees.

On the tree chair sat the most beautiful woman Meghan had ever seen. Her flawless face was ageless, yet old and wise. The faery queen's arms were bare and covered in sparkling bracelets of gold and jewels. Her hair was twisted on top of her head where rested a crown covered in glowing opals. Her pale grey eyes pierced Meghan's mind, rummaging through her thoughts and memories like thrift store owners at a garage sale. One moment, Meghan was playing catch with Noodles in her back yard, and the next she was back in the cave, looking for her lost dog.

Noodles! Meghan gasped when she realized her tiny dog was sitting on the queen's lap, her hand on his head. Why didn't Noodles run to her? Perhaps he was under a spell, but at least he looked unharmed, nestled into the dark green silk of the queen's ruffled gown.

"A human child, in the company of dragon riders?" the Queen wondered in a voice like a babbling stream. She frowned, and it seemed that everyone in the room frowned with her. Then her face brightened. "The DOGS are brought to judgment, and yet they bring us a gift." She stroked Noodles' head. "Human, show me your pass."

With trembling fingers, Meghan took out the folded paper and handed it to the guard. Dread gripped her as the queen read it.

"Let me explain," Meghan said, rising to her feet.

"Do not address the queen without permission," a guard growled, pushing her to the ground.

"Just keep quiet." She could hear Hardly's whispered advice.

The Queen's voice was amused. "Someone broke the rules. We will deal with this later. Guards, take this child to get cleaned up. She smells of dragon."

As she was going through the door, Meghan turned when she heard the Queen say, "Guards, unbind him."

Hardly was dragged to his feet and the ropes undone. Then she commanded, "Heatherope Hallowhill McDreary, explain yourself."

And Hardly answered, "Uggh! Come on, Sis. You know I hate it when you call me by my true name!"

Washed up and dressed in a green gown, Meghan was escorted to a large dining room lit by giant pinecone chandeliers. All the chairs were filled except one, and the human servant gestured toward it. She tried to speak with her, but hand signs revealed the servant was incapable of speech.

As she sat down to her meal, Meghan noticed Hardly was the only dragon rider present, seated next to the Queen, his sister. He looked stiff, and his eyes never turned her way. He was too far away for conversation, so she turned her attention toward the servant waiting to give her some meat. It looked and smelled like beef, seasoned with herbs and roasted to perfection. Another servant brought her potatoes and tiny carrots. All the food tasted delicious after being out in the wild for weeks.

But Meghan's eyes kept wandering back toward the Queen and Hardly. Why hadn't he told her he was the Queen's brother? Seated on either side of Meghan were faery ladies, one in a shimmering dove grey gown, and the other wearing yellow satin. Maybe Meghan could find out more from them.

"Pardon me," she asked the one in yellow. "I love your dress. It's beautiful!"

"Oh my," the faery said, wrinkling her tiny nose like she just had a whiff of something foul. "I shouldn't have insulted the queen's baker. This is how she repays me. Seat me next to a human." She turned her shoulders to face the faery on her other side.

That didn't go well. She waited until after a few more bites of potato. "Excuse me," she said to the faery on her right. "The feast tonight is unbelievable! Is the food always this good?"

But the faery ignored her.

After everyone had finished, the servants whisked away all the plates, and all eyes looked expectantly toward the Queen at the far end of the table. She blotted her mouth with a linen cloth and then addressed her guests.

"We thank you for joining us at this feast. We celebrate the return of my brother, Heatherope." The assembled faeries hesitated before clapping politely. It seemed Hardly wasn't popular with his sister's court.

"Today we have captured the DOGS. They await judgment for their crimes. Their foul creatures will be destroyed at once." Hardly looked like he might throw up.

Destroy the dragons! What fate awaited the dragon riders? It appeared that Hardly's relation to the Queen had saved him, and possibly Meghan, but had not extended to his friends.

"What do to with the human child," the Queen said. "Her day pass has expired. One month ago. According to our laws, we could keep her. Enchant her tongue and make her one of our silent servants." Meghan panicked. That was why the servants couldn't talk to her. Then she felt the pressure of the Queen's mind prying into her memories again. Images of her parents fighting flashed through her mind.

"Or perhaps it would be punishment enough to send her back," the Queen said. "Her memories of our fair land will poison her short human life. But she'll have to buy another ticket."

Meghan stood and fought her legs as they, against her will, brought her over to stand beside the Queen, who smiled at her like a cat does at a mouse. "What can she do for the price? Can she weave gold or bring down shaved ice from the mountains for our drinks?

"I don't think I can do anything like that," Meghan said quietly. Hardly was right at her side, and, while she did not look at him, she could feel his nervous energy.

"She can sing human songs," Hardly said, standing up and moving her to the side.

Murmurs rose around the table as the faeries looked at each other in pleased surprise.

"We care nothing for silly human songs!" the Queen scoffed. But the faeries murmured amongst themselves, their faces excited. Seeing them, the Queen relented. "A song then. Make it a good one."

Meghan knew this was her chance. All the beautiful yet cruel faces turned toward her, some truly noticing her for the first time. In the front of the Spring Court, she began to sing a familiar song:

"Ring around the rosy, pockets full of posies,

Ashes to ashes, we all fall down."

She sang it three times, each time more confident than the previous. The faeries were captivated by a song that mocked the Black Plague. A children's song about death.

When she finished, the guests erupted with applause. The Queen didn't rise, but she gave a slight nod of her head. Hardly relaxed slightly.

The Queen took one tiny silver band off her finger and handed it to her brother. "Hardly, take her to the portal. This ring is her ticket home."

To Meghan, she added, "Few have charmed a faery court. Farewell, human child."

On the way to the portal, Meghan and Hardly were lost in their own thoughts. The faery's boots pounded on the polished wood floors. Meghan's sneakers made no sound. She had changed back into her own clothes and held Noodles firmly in her arms. One of the silent servants had brought him back to her, which earned the girl a huge hug of thanks.

When they reached a door at the end, Hardly opened it with the ease of someone who knew the palace well. He spoke a word and torches burst into life down the stone staircase. As he led Meghan down the smooth steps, she could stand it no longer.

"What about your friends?" she said. "You're just going to leave them in prison?"

The faery turned toward her, his eyes full of pain. "Of course not! I'll find a way to break them out." His eyes gripped hers with determination. "I'll free the dragons, too. The Queen shows me no favor on account of the dragons. She hates them with her entire being."

"But why does your sister, the Queen, allow you to remain free, and me to return to my world? It seems like favor to me."

Hardly sighed and turned to continue down the steps. "She knows keeping me at court and sending you away is the perfect punishment."

That caused her heart to jump. She'd always wanted an older brother.

"Can your sister read minds?" she asked. "I felt like she was rummaging around in my memories."

The faery stopped at the bottom of the steps and faced her. "You are more aware of her talents than most. My sister has a rare magic that allows her free access to anyone's mind, faery or human. She uses what she discovers against you. Even I can't keep her out. That's why I can't remain in her palace."

They walked down a tunnel, his steps echoing off the earthen walls until they reached a large cavern with a wood shack at one end. A porter emerged and waited for instructions. A familiar beam of light streamed down from the ceiling and a disk sat below it. Although she had been eager to escape the attentions of the Queen, Meghan was reluctant to approach the portal. Riding with the Dragon Riders Group had been an exciting adventure and going home only meant locking herself away in her room to avoid the war between her parents.

"Welcome, Prince Heatherope," the porter greeted his ruler with a deep bow.

"Come on, Greyleaf," Hardly protested. "It's just me."

"Of course, Your Highness," the porter replied as he raised his eyes. "Where are you going today with this pretty human child and her creature?"

"I'm not leaving, but they are," Hardly answered. "And she's my friend. Her name is Meghan. The creature is a dog, and he's named Noodles."

"Welcome to the Queen's portal, Meghan and Noodles," the porter said. "Friendship with Hardly is not easily won. You must have some magic of your own." He bowed to her with a knowing grin. "Your ticket and destination, please." He held out his hand.

She had the overwhelming desire to turn and run back down the tunnel toward the palace. Maybe she could help Hardly rescue the other riders and dragons. She turned toward him. He stood there with an unreadable expression. If only she had the Queen's mind reading gift for five minutes!

"I want to stay and help you," is what blurted out of her mouth. Tears trickled down her cheeks.

Hardly smiled. "I know you do, but it's too dangerous for you here." He handed her an embroidered handkerchief from his pocket. "Come now, Meghan. You've had your magical adventure. Now it's time to go home."

She gratefully took the tiny linen cloth trimmed with blue flowers and dabbed her face. Noodles sniffed at the handkerchief curiously. It felt awkward to allow herself to feel loss. It was too embarrassing to let people into your life when your parents might erupt like a volcano at any time. For a long time, it had been Noodles and her only. But the dragon riders had changed her, and now perhaps she could be allowed to cry.

"Thank you for being my friend," she said, trying to smile. She reached over and hugged Hardly, clutched Noodles in her arms, and handed the silver ring to the porter. Then she stepped onto the portal disk. "Back to my world. Carlsbad campground, please."

The faery prince acknowledged her with a bob of his head right before the light whited out everything around her. She felt like she was flying, riding on Petal again, but she could see nothing.

Then she landed firmly on wet sand and realized she was back at the mouth of the sea cave once more. Noodles barked and wriggled out of her arms to chase a sea gull. The surf crashed close to her feet. She got up and brushed off sand and headed off after her dog.

Meghan checked her cell phone and was amazed to see that, while she had been in Faerie for a month, only a few hours had passed here. At least her parents wouldn't have reported her disappearance to the police. She called Noodles to her and attached his new silver leash the Queen had given him.

As she ascended the creaky stairs back up to the campground, her breathing remained slow and even. Her stomach wasn't churning like it usually was when she had to return to her parents.

In her heart, she kept the memory of Hardly's face at the portal. She reached into her pocket and took out the crumpled handkerchief the dragon rider had given her. A token to take into battle. At the top of the stairs, she turned to look back at the endless crashing waves.

The Queen wasn't wrong. Meghan would never forget Faerie. She had crossed the skies with dragon riders, been captured by soldiers, and even sang for the Faery Queen and the Spring Court.

She could handle the problems in this world as well.

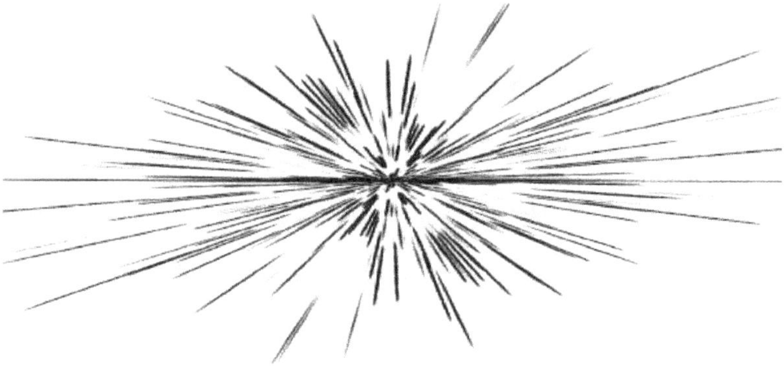

About the Author

Jodi Rizzotto is a full-time writer and former elementary school teacher living in Southern California. She holds a Master of Teaching degree from California Baptist University, Riverside. After growing up on Tolkien and C.S. Lewis, she prefers to write fantasy for adults and children. When she's not writing, she and her husband love exploring back roads in their Jeep and camping at the beach. She belongs to the Society of Children's Book Writers and Illustrators and the California Writers Club.

Her nonfiction Harley travels have appeared in *2019 Anthology Inland Empire California Writers Club*, *Courtship of Winds*, *Blacktop Passages*, and *Cold Noon Travel Diaries*. Her magical realism short story "Angry Man" appeared in *Altered Reality Magazine*.

Connect with Jodi at:

https://www.facebook.com/authorJodiRizzotto

https://twitter.com/rizzotto_jodi

https://www.instagram.com/jrizzotto/

https://jrizzotto.com/

Samhain Night

by

Brenda Carre

Samhain Night

The streetlights were out for some dumb reason, and I was hurrying the few chill blocks down to my best friend Elsie's costume party using the flashlight app on my smart phone to guide my way. I was creeped out by being alone, by being in the unusual, almost complete dark. There were noises—shushing ones right beside me—and far away screams and bangs, the smoky smells of exploded fireworks, and the rotty smells of dead leaves.

I shone my thin beam from side to side as I clicked down the sidewalk. A lot of kids didn't come down to our end of the block even when the lights are on, because we live so close to the forest.

My neck itched like spiders were crawling down my coat collar. What if something was sliding through one of those 'thin spaces' between the natural and the supernatural world my writer mom liked to talk about?

Wasn't Samhain famous for that?

What if a coyote came out of Pacific Spirit Park and attacked me? I glanced behind me at the darker shadow of the forest, the hundred-acre green belt right in the middle of our Point Grey neighborhood. People got dragged in there by murderers sometimes, didn't they?

Was that a murderer attacking somebody a block away? The screeches were blood curdling.

What if three coyotes were working together, and the only warning I got was something grabbing my ankle with teeth that wouldn't let go? Coyotes were smart. I'd found the back leg of a cat on our sidewalk a week ago. Even then, I'd wondered what it must feel like to get eaten alive.

I hurried faster.

I wobbled a little on Mom's stiletto heels. I should have worn flats, but dammit, Mom's shoes were perfect for my outfit—medieval-looking cross-ties all the way up to my shins. I should have asked for permission before she went out for the night, but I hadn't.

Mom was going to kill me if I ruined them.

A few blocks. It's only a few blocks.

I clutched Mom's trench coat closer around me and the fairy-tale gown I was wearing, crinolines swishing and tangling around my legs. Rats! Why didn't I go with something more fitted?

Yeah, and there were rats in our neighborhood too, and raccoons with claws that could rake open a dog in seconds.

Why hadn't I brought Mom's camping lantern? My phone only seemed to illuminate the ghostly swirls of stinky, sulfurous air in front of me.

Should I go back? No way! It was even darker in that direction.

My heart sped up. I heard a strange noise like a grunt. A pig? What would a pig be doing on our street? Did rabid raccoons sound like pigs? What was that big reddish hump across the street? Did I remember a mailbox on that corner…?

"Auuuhh!" I screamed, pitching into something that jerked its pointy head up from the curb way too late for me to stop.

"Aaahh!" yelped the thing.

Still screaming, I grabbed what felt like a warm head, neck and shoulders and tumbled onto the huddled body.

It happened fast. One of mom's shoes broke. I felt the laces give. My phone flew out of my hand and clattered somewhere. The light went out. No!

I fell onto the boy—it was a boy, I realized even as I went flying—he twisted and grabbed me so we both turned into a heap of arms and legs in the gutter.

Me on top.

My crinolines hadda be in his face—and other bits of me too. I was semi-relieved, insulted and embarrassed. Never mind the hideous bruise on my elbow that just everyone was going to ask about tomorrow,

I squirmed out of his grip, feeling like an idiot. My heart was hammering.

"What the heck!" I gasped.

"Žao mi je. Izvinite," he cried at the same time, cutting my rant at him off in mid word.

What in holy hello was some Russian-sounding boy doing lurking, literally lurking, on the corner of my block, unless he was up to no good? Was he pouring poison down the drain hole? Getting ready to egg cars?

"So sorry," he answered and hissed.

That was pain I heard coming out of him. He was hurt! Now I imagined he'd gotten one of my stilettos in his eye or something… I needed my phone.

What if a car came along and ran over it? What if a malicious car without lights came along and ran over me? My entire contact list was in my phone, never mind every class assignment I'd been given by my teachers and my journal, and…

I groped across the road still dazed, limping around on one stiletto and one stocking. Now I really felt like an idiot. It hadn't rained in Vancouver for a couple of days. The heaps of moldering leaves were slimy and cold and ukky, and the road was gritty and hard, but miracles of miracles, there was my phone.

And it was working!

Letting out a whimper of relief, I limped back and shone the white beam into the boy's face. He ducked and winced, but not before I caught the shine of his eyes. Animal.

I yelped, but the shine had been a trick of the light. Now his eyes blinked back at me like a normal human being's.

I recognized him!

"Luc?" I said surprised.

This was the new exchange boy. Not in any of my classes, but I'd noticed him right away, keeping to himself, except for a couple of stoner guys I never talked to. Now his hair glowed flaxen in the white beam of my phone, pale startled features, cute. Cross between Chris Hemsworth and Peter Pan.

He was all in black, wearing the tackiest Prince of Darkness costume imaginable. Black pants, black hoodie with "girl power" written on the front in pink letters, plastic horns, and what looked like a dirty tea towel hanging half-stitched off one shoulder. Totally rumpled even before he'd got in my way.

No wonder I'd tripped on him.

He held out Mom's shoe. "This is yours, yes?" he said tightly, in that way of someone choosing his English with care.

Now worry took over again. "My mom's. She's gonna kill me." I grabbed the shoe. The laces were broken, but I could fix them enough to tie the shoe back on.

"What were you doing here?" I said. *Sitting huddled like a ghoul on the dark corner,* I wanted to add. Something was still making me uneasy, but I couldn't say what.

Luc tried to struggle to his feet, but he didn't make it.

"I fell," he said at last, as if that explained it all.

"Show me," I ordered him.

"Is ok," he said.

"No, it's not ok, you could have broken something. Let me look, you hold my phone," I demanded, handing it to him. "I'm a first responder at school."

I sat down on the cold curb, skirts pooling around me, and grabbed his hand to point the beam on his ankle.

'I am knowing this," he replied. "I see you at help in school office."

"Then you know I mean business—show me."

He sighed and rolled up his pant cuff.

There was a new cut on his ankle from where he'd tripped on the curb, but below that was an ugly sore, almost right to the bone. It looked at least a week old. By the direction of the gouge, it appeared somebody had hung him up by his ankle and he'd managed to struggle himself free. There was a livid blue-black bruise as well.

"Oh No," I gasped in upper case font. "You didn't get that just now?"

"Yes, I am getting it now," Luc said defensively. I touched it and he winced at the pressure of my fingers. The skin was really warm, too warm, but the ankle moved. There was nothing I could do at this point but let him heal on his own.

"Is ok. I can deal. I am kind of first responder in my own country."

"Oh, like I believe you," I said taking my phone back, "And who is it gets your first response?"

Luc shrugged, and again his eyes picked up the light as I shone it into his face, clear but impenetrable. I felt like I was looking down into a deep pool of clear water, beneath which the rocks moved. Sly rocks, in a world of their own, that moved by other powers than our own world could bring on them.

I shuddered. Touching Luc hadn't felt like touching anybody else. Not evil exactly, but something. My fingers still tingled. Luc was telling me the truth about his being a first responder, but this was first responding on a scale that was way bigger than anything I could ever imagine. All my frights on this Samhain night were nothing compared to this boy sitting next to me. If that's what he really was.

"Is your other ankle as bad?" I whispered.

He nodded. "Is healing. I fell," he said again.

"From how high up," I said.

"Please to not asking. I am here only little while, for one reason, then am going."

"Where and why? Or, would you have to kill me if you told me?" I blurted. Something terrifyingly evil swirled around Luc though it wasn't of him. Yet I could help him tonight, I felt it in my bones. I think he felt it too.

"It's going to happen tonight, isn't it? It's Samhain. You were on your way somewhere around here to do whatever you need to do. Are you after the ones who did—that?" I didn't need to explain what I meant.

He winced again. "No. The ones who hurt me are no more. You are in none danger, from me nor from them, Kelly Greene. You are first responder. It is for those like you the world is made safed by those like me. You should put on your spike shoe now, and go where you are to go. I am sorry again, if I am tripping you."

But I didn't want to go. If I left it at this, I'd be wondering for the rest of my life. It would kill me. He'd just told me people had hurt him, and in the next breath, he'd told me they 'were no more.'

He'd killed them somehow. I was fascinated and terrified too. But I couldn't let it alone. Now I knew, for the first time, what it was that made those brainless slasher movie chicks look behind the forbidden door.

"Who—what are you?"

"Better not to asking." Luc stood with care. He unfolded upwards like a spire of deadly nightshade. A dark figure in a dark world. "You should be wary," he said in that precise accent of his.

I shook my head. That accent was fake. He was putting it on to distract me from the truth. It scared me now to know this, but I did. I had to know more now. There was no turning back.

"Who were those people, and why did you kill them? I'm afraid but dammit, it'll be worse if you lie to me. I over-think things. It drives my mom crazy, but if I know what's going on, I can deal with it. Together, we'll think of some way to deal with this."

He took my phone out of my hand and turned it off. He looked at me for a long time in the darkness as if every part of me was visible to him.

"You would knowing whom I am?"

"Yes," I said. "Now give me back my phone."

"No. Is better to talk in darkness."

He sighed as if coming to a decision. When he spoke again there was no accent. None at all. Neither Russian, English, French, Germanic, American, Canadian. Nothing. And his voice? It was soft like grass whispering in the wind, the grind of wood against stone, or like the whisker of a mountain lion tickling your neck.

"I fell a long, long time ago, because somebody had to. There was too much evil in the world, and there had to be someone to find it. Someone who had to go into the camp of the enemy, and someone who had to find others like him."

My spirits rose. "So, you're like an avenger?"

He laughed bitterly. "My name is Lucifer," he said.

My mouth fell open. If you'd asked me to breathe right then you'd have needed a respirator.

Nothing he could have said, or done, could have prepared me for the ice of horror that rolled through me. This boy in his black hoodie and that stupid tea-towel cape? No. He had to be insane, or…

"I'm not crazy," he said. "I tell you the truth because your own truth isn't hidden from me, Kelly Greene. Your thoughts are as bright as the sun. You saw me clearly in your school when I was looking for the one I've come to take tonight. Call it Hell. Call it a testing ground. I search out the bitter, the broken, the angry and the mad. I enlist them into my army of the damned. Or, I kill them before they go the way of the Lost. At least by doing that I take away most of their power over the living."

"The Lost?"

"Those who have no hope of redemption. You never want to meet them, Kelly, though there is that in you that is foolish and wants to. They look as human as you do, but they aren't. Not anymore. They are lost and rotten through and through. I lead them to me. They try hard to kill me, but I take them apart and they are gone."

He said this so calmly. I imagined him hanging by his feet in some cellar. I imagined brutal hands on him.

"Don't," he said. "The more you imagine them, the easier it will be for them to find you. I don't want them to find you. The fires of Hell are real, Kelly. It is the good like you I hope to save."

His voice continued to come out of the night, more real to me than the ground I stood on. More real than the screech-a-roos a few blocks down and the occasional cracks of sparklers.

"So many over the ages have glimpsed me," he continued, "but all they've seen is illusion. A thing with goat horns and cloven hooves. But you didn't…"

"You look like a boy," I interrupted him.

"This is how I look. My appearance will never change. I was created in this form. You have eyes to see past illusion, and if you were taught, you could walk through illusion too. But you would fail, Kelly. You aren't dark enough. You tripped over me; you want to heal me. I will not be healed."

"What…?"

"What am I?" he said, and I felt him smile sadly. "I am the great balancer. One day I may go home to my brothers, but not yet. Maybe never."

I couldn't stand the ache in his voice. It hurt me. No amount of imagination could have prepared me for the depth of pain and loneliness I was facing. It was as if he'd created a void around us into which nothing could penetrate. No wonder the streetlights were out. No wonder there were no cars. My mouth was so dry, I could hardly talk.

"Who—who're you meeting?"

"Perry Wills."

That made sense. I'd seen him with Perry at school. Perry Wills was in Hell if anybody was. He was a murder scene looking for a place to happen. Bad home. Abuse, drugs. The worst. Rumor was it had been Perry set fire to an elementary school nearby, though it hadn't been proved. Perry had beaten his terrible dad to a pulp then run off and gotten himself stoned. He'd stolen a car, gotten into a high-speed police chase, slammed into a house and killed three people.

"He's going to turn up at a party close to here," said Luc.

I gasped. "Elsie's party. That's where I'm going—Oh No—Perry's going to crash Elsie's party, isn't he?"

"So, I heard, earlier today. I need to turn up before he does and give him a choice."

"What kind of choice!"

"To choose to be lost no longer. I've come to help him. One way or the other, tonight he's going to vanish. If you hadn't tripped over me..."

"But I did and now I'm in this too. Let's go," I said. "Can I have my phone back? I have to see to put this blasted stiletto back on. I'm not going to limp all the way to Elsie's like a doofus."

I was trying for humor and not doing well. Maybe, if I gave him a nick name. They called the devil 'old scritch' or something didn't they? I guess you could call that humor of a kind, and here was this guy in horns and a towel, wasn't he?

Why wasn't this funny anymore?

Quit babbling at yourself like you just had about five energy drinks in a row.

Luc handed me my phone. "Leave it off. I'll carry you."

"Carry me, Tolstoy? On those ankles? Are you nuts?"

You're right; at least the nick name is helping me some.

"No," he said, picking me up before I could yelp.

It was after him picking me up that I yelped. I'd got too close to lightning. Being carried by him was like being torn in two by delight and extreme terror. Like hang gliding off of Mt. Everest.

"At least let me give you some light," I gasped and turned on my phone.

He growled. "Turn that off while I'm carrying you. You'll look like you're floating. I don't want anyone freaking out."

"Oh," I said trying to process the idea of people seeing me floating. I didn't want that kind of notice. I was already stirred up. It was taking us no time at all to get to the party now. He was really strong. I weighed a buck-twenty, and he was carrying me like I was a kid.

"So, why Perry? Isn't he kind of a smallish fish to be one of the Lost?"

"Not too small to be used by them," he said. It was simply said, but I felt how big his battle was against the Lost.

"You feel like an exile," I said. I didn't know why I said it, except that there's a spark in me that knows when it's the perfect word.

"I am an exile," he said. "It will always be so until the end of the world and perhaps beyond that. My brothers sit in the light, but for people like you to know light there must be dark, Kelly."

"But, you're not the monster, Tolstoy. You're an avenger."

He set me on the ground. Oz couldn't have done better with Dorothy. We were at the end of the block from Elsie's.

"I am what children fear. I am the thing in the dark, the monster lurking beneath their bed. I am your nightmares. The unknown. I am the barrier between what is real and what is not. It is very right to fear me, because, to draw the Lost to me, I must be like them."

"But you know good too, don't you?" I breathed.

He laughed but there wasn't anything funny, and we both looked down the block at the Jack o' lanterns twinkling all over Elsie's lawn. The power was out on this block too, but I could already see there was some kind of commotion down there, a big crowd spilling onto the street. Shouting.

Luc took off at a sprint like a hunting panther. He left me standing there, and now I felt really cold. Having him leave me like that—no, this was Samhain. The doors were open, but if I didn't do something quick…

I tore off Mom's other shoe and ran, stocking feet and all, toward impending disaster.

People milled around on the lawn like lawn flamingos dressed like nightmares. I heard sirens in the distance. The police were coming. It smelled like weed and raw burgers.

Perry Wills stood on the sidewalk screeching his filthy head off and waving a broken bottle at everybody like a club. He was dressed like the Prince of Darkness too; only *his* costume was perfect, right down to the goat legs, the goat horns, the fangs and the pointy tail.

"You don't f…ing tell me to get out, *Daddie*," Perry roared, swaying on his feet. Even in the dark I could see spit flying from his mouth.

As I got closer, I saw a big splash of something red on Elsie's front door, and a ripped bag on the doormat that spilled something gross looking. Elsie and her twelve-year-old sister had stepped over that and were cowering behind her dad. Muffy was Totoro and Elsie was in jammies and mouse ears, being a lab rat. Eric wore his perennial Halloween lab coat disguise.

"Hey you reprobate. I called the police on you raising hell like this."

"So, what!" Perry roared back. "You and your f…ing party of rich guys don't know how it really is in Hell!"

I'd caught up to Luc who stood now between me and Perry.

"But you do, don't you, Perry," said Luc, grabbing Perry by the shoulder.

Perry wheeled around like he'd seen a ghost. His eyes bugged out and the bottle dropped with a *thunk* onto the grass. "Wher'd you come fr'm, man?" he slurred.

"You know where, don't you, Perry?" said Luc.

"No, I don't, man. Oh, please man." Perry tried to back away. He stumbled and started to weep. He was seeing what I saw. Luc grabbed him and hauled him back up by his scruff with no effort, but nobody else could see that.

"You're pitiful, Perry, but you'll learn," said Luc.

Everybody must be thinking Perry was high. He sure looked it. "I ain't ready yet, man. Busy here. Go 'way!" he slurred as the screech of police sirens grew louder.

Luc's shadow was huge. I saw it dwarfing everyone else's. Heck, it dwarfed the entire house.

Luc snarled at Perry, shaking him like a hound. "I'm not here to damn you, Perry. At least not yet. You have a choice. You can see me. You have always been able to. Tonight, on Samhain, you can also choose between Good and Evil. You have the luck to be given the chance to redeem yourself. I can train you, or I can kill you. Either way you will vanish from this world. Do you understand?"

Perry nodded miserably and Luc growled. "Good. Then we're agreed. Come with me."

Perry Wills went limp like a piece of flaccid celery, and now it was Luc supporting him, and it was Luc who dragged him away down the sidewalk.

Luc turned to me as they passed me. "Do not follow. Please Kelly Greene. The police will come. Say nothing. They will not find us. Remember me kindly and do what you do in the light. If ever you see my brothers tell them…"

"What, Tolstoy? Tell them what?"

He shook his head. "Never mind. They do their work as I do. Just don't follow," he told me.

With an audible *humm*, the streetlights winked on. The nightmare flamingos gasped, and there was no sign at all of Luc or of Perry. Later they'd all say different stuff, that a wind had come up or some fog, or the lights blinded them. It had been really dark, and now it wasn't.

By that time, Elsie and her dad were out on the lawn with everyone else. There was hugging and carrying on. But behind it all there was a kind of hallowed silence, as if something eventful had happened, but nobody quite knew what. Elsie's dad ran up by me and shouted. "Don't think you're getting away!"

Never mind they were gone. It was still dark down the way Luc and I had come.

"Dad!" cried Elsie grabbing his arm. "Don't make him mad, or he'll come back…"

"I don't think he will, Else," I said, standing there in my socks. Luc was gone.

"Tolstoy," I whispered and burst into tears.

"Yeah, War and Peace for sure," said Elsie, grabbing me into a hug. "Oh man, Kelly. I'm sorry. Did you see? Are you hurt? Did he punch you? Perry brushed you, I saw…"

"Man, I never seen a kid walk like that. Like he's got no bones! Yuk! How'd he do that ghoul walk, huh?" said Muffy.

"I don't know," I said, pulling away from Elsie's fluffy warmth. I felt like an idiot, but then I *was* standing there in my socks like a doofus.

"Who was that other guy helping Perry?" said Muffy

"What other guy, Muff?" said Elsie.

"The one in the black hoodie. You saw him too, didn't you, Kelly?"

I stared at her, my whole spine curling up with horror. What could I say? I needed to lie, but I liked Muff, and she'd know I was lying…

I just stared at her like I didn't believe her.

Muff's eyes narrowed. "Hmm. I guess not," she said thoughtfully.

I knew this wasn't over.

When Perry's mother reported him missing a couple of days later, nobody really wondered. Nobody figured he'd run away. We were the last to see him alive, staggering and stoned on his way to the forest. Everyone knew there were coyotes in there, and maybe worse—if people let their fears get hold of them.

Perry's body never turned up. Surprising how many of us turned out to his memorial, despite the noise he'd caused and the lives he'd wrecked.

Y'know, since that day, I decided to read the Bible and the Qur'an and the Baghavad Gita. I've read Rumi and a bunch of other good books too. It's a start at least, for a first responder needing to brush against either Heaven or Hell.

I'm the kind that needs to know. I still don't know what I'm going to do about Muff, but I'll figure that out. But I sure know what I'm going to do about Tolstoy.

I was given the chance to see him for a reason, to help him, if only for a bit, and to know who he really is. There'll be other Samhain Nights and doors to open. I can do it. I won't pull Muffy in, but if Perry can go fight the Lost, so can I.

About the Author

Brenda Carre lives on Vancouver Island, British Columbia, in a place steeped in lore where myth arises from the waves of the Salish Sea on the backs of Killer Whales. A love of lore and myth and emotion creeps into everything she writes. Her short fiction crosses borders into the realm of weird fiction, ghostly visitation and the terrifying unknown: A paranormal sleuth and her side-kick genie solve X-file-style crimes in Victorian England. In small 1960's town in the Pacific Northwest school girls resurrect road kill to deal with bullies and killers.

Brenda writes long epic fantasy with voice and a kiss of grimdark.

In her upcoming portal trilogy, an intrepid young witch comes of age in a world where ghost dragons fight a cosmic war against demons of anti-matter. A taste of Brenda's prose can be found in "The Clunkety" (*Superpowers/Fiction River Anthology* #26 2017. Edited by Rebecca Moesta) and "Birdie" (cover story in *Pulp Literature* summer issue 31/2021). Talk to her about ghostly encounters, the strange and unseen and weird fiction.

Sign up for her newsletter and get a free publication at:

https://mailchi.mp/627eb341fe91/gret

Find her at https://brendacarre.com/

and on Twitter @brenda_carre

The Wild Hunt

by

Carolyn Kay

The Wild Hunt

Jace pushed her skis through the deep powder, fighting against the wind, which hurled snowflakes like tiny daggers at her face. Cross-country skiing into the depths of Norway to photograph the Aurora Borealis at the winter solstice seemed like a grand adventure yesterday in the warmth of the hotel.

A late start and a surprise storm turned a difficult trek into an impossible one. She wanted to turn around and go back to their cabin base camp, but they were closer to their shooting location now. And she couldn't wuss out on her first big trip with her photography mentor, Mads.

Jace had idolized his work for years on Instagram. She still couldn't believe she'd won the contest for this trip. The winning photo was one of her favorites—Blarney Castle shrouded in fog with a rainbow arching over the ruins. Part of her wished she was back in Ireland right now.

She pulled her hood tighter and pushed on. As bad as the wind was blowing, she hoped it meant clear skies later.

Mads and his assistant, Sven, got the tents pitched with practiced ease. The wind had died down as they'd entered the broad river valley, the name of which was unpronounceable by Jace's American tongue. The sun had set an hour before, taking the scarce winter light with it. Camp lanterns now created little puddles of light in the snow, helping drive back the gloom.

The three of them talked around a small space heater in Mads's tent while they ate a small meal. Mads instructed Jace on the best settings to capture the aurora. She asked about the pros and cons of various lenses, taking detailed notes of everything the National Geographic photographer said.

With the meal done, and her head full of ideas, she excused herself, heading to her tent for a nap before the night's shooting began.

The howl of a wolf startled Jace awake. She lay in her sleeping bag, heart pounding. Another howl answered, closer. She rose, brushing curly brown hair from her face, and checked her watch; eight p.m. They weren't supposed to head out until nine, assuming the clouds had cleared.

The wolf howled again. The eerie sound echoed across the valley, followed by the sound of horses running. Was that a horn? Mads and Sven must be watching something saved on a phone or tablet—there was zero service out here.

Jace toyed with trying to go back to sleep, but she knew it'd be pointless. She was too amped from the wolf howl. She'd never heard one in the wild. Her curiosity was piqued.

She bundled up and grabbed her smaller Nikon. Might as well play around a bit. If she was lucky, she might get a shot of the wolves.

The cold air shocked the lingering fatigue from Jace's head and almost made her retreat back into the tent. Chicago's winters could be brutal, but they didn't hold a frigid candle to winters in Norway. Steeling herself, she crawled out of the tent and closed it tightly behind her. She might never get another opportunity like this. If she could get some good shots of wolves or the aurora, or both together, it would be incredible. She'd only ever seen wolves in a sanctuary, and those were mostly hybrids.

Jace scanned the valley before her. They'd camped near the tree line for some protection from the wind. A wide braided river ran from her right to left. A small cliff edged the valley on the far side. Mads said it made a good backdrop for the aurora, giving the scene some depth of field.

The valley was quiet, the only sound was the river gurgling over rocks. The stillness was as unnerving as the complete lack of ambient light. There wasn't a man-made light within a hundred miles. Even Mads's tent was dark.

A wolf howled again. Jace jumped, fumbling her camera in her hands. "Get a hold of yourself, girl," she chided herself under her breath. In the dark and quiet, it felt disrespectful to raise her voice. She also didn't want to wake Mads, relishing the time alone to experience this place.

An answering howl came from her right.

Jace scanned the valley again. Faint moonlight shining through the clouds cast long shadows over the landscape. Movement near the river caught her eye. Fumbling with gloved fingers to remove her lens cap, she finally succeeded. Aiming her camera at the river, she turned it on and looked at the LCD screen, zooming in about midway.

After several minutes she found what she was looking for. About halfway between her and the river, she caught the misty breath of a howling wolf and followed it to its source. A large white wolf with a gray mantle sat near a small rock outcropping. Whispering a prayer it would stay put, she marked the spot visually, hooked the camera to the harness across her chest, and pulled out her tripod. She didn't try to set it up with her gloves on. Her tripod was set and her camera mounted before her fingers started hurting from the cold. Using the rock outcrop as a guide, she sighted back in after setting her camera to compensate for the lack of light.

The wolf was right where she'd left it. Its head was turned, looking right at her. Jace took a step back from the camera, surprised only for a moment before realizing the wolf would have heard her fumbling around.

She stepped to the camera and looked at the LCD. The wolf was still there. She took her time to frame the shot and took several photos, then changed the angle, and took a couple more before the wolf stood. Without a backward glance, it trotted off behind the rocks and disappeared.

"Thank you for sticking around for a little while," Jace whispered.

Excited, she toggled the camera's screen to see what she'd captured. There were a few shots not quite dialed in, but the rest were pretty good. The wolf's pale blue eyes bored into her from the photos. She shivered with more than cold.

As she clicked through the images, something in the last one caused her to look closer. A pale purple-blue glow hovered in the background by the river. She manipulated the controls to zoom in to the spot.

She stood there in the cold, her breath fogging the LCD, not sure what she was looking at, until the sound of running horses caused her to look up.

A line of horses and riders made of mist ran along the river toward where the glow was in the photos. Only, to her naked eye, there was no glow.

One by one, the riders disappeared with a faint flash as they rode through that spot. The sound of laughter and the jingle of bells and tackle reached her ears a short time later, as if the sound was lagged on a slow computer video.

As she watched, the last rider looked in her direction and raised a horn to its mouth. It sounded a long and mournful note as the rider disappeared. The sound hit Jace in the chest, filling her head with images of bright, warm homesteads filled with laughter and tables full of sweets and barrels of mead.

It was both familiar and strange to Jace. As the descendent of enslaved Africans, mead halls were not something in her heritage, yet it felt like home.

Jace blinked, finding herself at the river's edge, not far from where the last horse and rider disappeared. There was still nothing for her to see, no doorway, no glinting portal. Still, she walked toward the space where it'd been, curiosity overriding caution.

Pacing around where she knew it to be, she felt nothing, saw nothing, heard nothing but the wind in the trees and the gurgling of the river.

She walked back toward the camp, maybe thirty yards, before turning and taking several pictures in the direction of the enigmatic glow. She checked the images. Nothing. She sighed, her frustration rising.

A sudden gust of wind tried to push her over, driving snow with it. Resigned, she trudged back to her tent.

Several days of near-constant darkness must be messing with my mind.

She crawled into her sleeping bag. Drifting off to sleep, she heard laughter and the jingle of belled bridles.

"Miss Thompson, are you awake?" Mads's baritone voice pulled Jace from an uneasy sleep.

"Uh, yeah." She opened her eyes expecting it to be light, but it was still dark. "What time is it?"

"Eight o'clock. The storm raged through the night, so we didn't wake you. We've got coffee on. The light will be good for landscape shots in about half an hour, if you're interested."

"Sure, yeah. I'll join you in a few." Jace stretched. She instantly regretted pulling her arms out of her sleeping bag. It was frigid! How could people live this far north and still be happy?

The soft swoosh of snow being shoveled from the front of her tent made Jace shiver more as she hurried into her snow gear and grabbed her camera backpack. Before stashing her Nikon, she turned it on. The wolf photos were still there, but none of them had a shining gate in the background. Had she imagined it all? Should she ask Mads and Sven if they'd heard anything? She didn't want to sound crazy. Maybe she'd just mention the wolf and see where it went. At least she had proof of the wolf.

She was careful to push the thick canvas tent door out as she unzipped it to keep any remaining snow from falling in. Her breath immediately condensed into a cloud of ice, but the biting wind was gone. There was easily another foot and a half of snow on the ground. It squeaked as her boots stepped through it.

The white landscape shone with an ethereal glow. Stars blanketed the sky, and a crescent moon hung above the treetops. The Milky Way paved a bright path through the stars. Jace had never seen so many. Places without light pollution were few and far between in the States. It was only after traveling from her home in Chicago she actually got to see the constellations she'd learned about in school.

"You think it's impressive now, wait until tonight." Mads handed her an insulated coffee mug.

She nodded her thanks and inhaled the fragrant steam, feeling more awake as she continued to stare at the sky.

Sitting around the fire with Mads and Sven, Jace pushed thoughts of the previous night away as they talked shop and discussed the best settings to use with the approaching dawn.

Sven suggested hiking up a nearby hill to capture the valley with the river's mist. She agreed without hesitation.

Jace's muscles protested snowshoeing up the low hill, and she had to remind herself this was a trip of a lifetime. The pictures she took over the next couple of days would round out her portfolio and hopefully get her a chance to work for National Geographic, or at least get space in a gallery.

At the top of the hill, the trees cleared about twenty feet from a short cliff overlooking the river valley. Sven set up his own gear and Mads's, while Mads gave Jace a lesson on composing landscape photos. Jace lost herself in the instruction, committing it all to memory. The strangeness of the night before lingered in the back of her mind, but she didn't let it distract her. Her mother's voice whispered in her ear, "Keep your focus, sunshine. Bright and shiny might be fun to look at, but they don't get you closer to your goal."

Jace's heart constricted with the memory of her mother. Rosaline Thompson was a fiercely determined woman who'd raised a daughter single-handedly while also earning a degree. She was one of the first people to learn to use the precursor to a personal computer at a well-known aerospace engineering firm. Her mother worked on several top-secret projects there. Only one, the SR-71 Blackbird, had been declassified before she died.

Jace couldn't fathom the strength it had taken to do all of that, not only as a woman back then, but as a Black woman. Her mother was a constant source of inspiration for her, and the reason why she had quit her corporate slog of a job to pursue her dream of being a world-renowned photographer.

Turning her attention back to the brightening landscape, Jace composed her shot, waiting for the right light. The sun didn't rise far above the horizon here. This far north, it skimmed the treetops for about five hours before setting, casting everything in a perpetual pinkish/orange twilight. Jace followed Mads's lead and waited until the winter sun warmed the river enough to create a low mist hugging the valley's lower elevations before taking any shots. The mist thickened, creating islands of some of the larger rock outcroppings, while the snow-covered hills across from them sparkled in the early light. Sven was right, this was a great spot to shoot from.

The vista before her looked surreal. A stag walked into view at the top of a hill across from them. They all repositioned their cameras to capture it, rapid click-click-clicks filled the quiet morning air. The stag paused to look in their direction for a moment, its ears flicking back and forth, before leading his herd down to the river to drink. As the mist shrouded their forms, Jace pondered what she'd experienced the night before. She debated if, or how, to bring the subject up without sounding insane, and then an idea struck her.

Jace waited until they were shoeing back to camp before broaching the subject. "Hey Sven, do the Norwegians have any legends similar to the Irish Wild Hunt? Seeing the stag reminded me of stories my grandmother used to tell."

Sven glanced at her, but not with the look she usually got when she mentioned her Irish heritage. The lack of concern over her race she'd experienced in Norway was refreshing.

Her father's grandmother had been a house slave to some Irish landholders in Tennessee and passed down the folk tales she'd heard to her own mixed children. Each generation since had done the same. Her grandmother told stories of fairies riding through the countryside hunting stags and any unlucky children who happened to be up past their bedtime. Jace's belief in the veracity of the stories faded as she grew older, but now, she wondered.

"We do have a Wild Hunt here too, though slightly different," Sven said. "Odin rides his steed, Sleipnir, leading a troupe of elves and fallen warriors on a hunt around Yule time." Sven glanced back at her, his eyes glinting through the gap in his balaclava. "If you see the Hunt, be careful not to be spotted, or you risk being caught by them and whisked away." He laughed. "But if you are caught, be sure to tell of your deeds. If you're lucky, and Odin finds you worthy, he'll grant you a boon, and they may let you go."

Jace looked back on her life. There wasn't much there a god would find interesting. A degree in business administration, a divorce, no children. Her few photography trips to the western US were the only exciting events she could talk about.

"I'll do my best to not get caught then. No one wants to hear about life in south-side Chicago."

Jace couldn't help but grin under her scarf as Mads and Sven chuckled. They were good guys, genuinely kind.

What would she say if she were caught by the Wild Hunt? It was something she'd have to think about.

They napped again that afternoon, after doing some post-processing on Mads's laptop. He joked his gear was equally split between cameras and batteries. He wasn't wrong. They had a pretty solid photo studio in the front half of the ten-person tent Mads shared with Sven. All they were missing was an internet connection.

Jace dreamed the dreams of someone obsessed. Random bits of taking photos, processing them, nonsensical computer commands, and the image of the stag coming to life and running at her through the laptop screen, laughing.

She woke with a start, her heart pounding, the bizarre image of a laughing stag stuck in her mind's eye. Reaching around inside her sleeping bag for her water bottle, she took a long drink. The cold water helped clear her mind and settle her heart. "Well, that was fun," she muttered to herself. She clicked on the electric lantern and checked her watch. 11:59 pm.

Panicked, she scrambled through her tent, looking for her extra thermal top. Mads said he'd wake her at ten. The aurora was supposed to peak around midnight. Had his alarm not gone off, or worse, did they leave her behind? Jace couldn't hear anything outside but the faint gurgle of the river. Taking a deep breath, she forced herself to calm down. Sound carried easily in the valley. If the guys were awake, she'd be able to hear them. They must still be asleep.

Still, she hurried to gather what she'd need for the night's shoot.

The horn sounded as she was unzipping her tent, sending her heart racing again. Jace hurriedly slipped into her boots, hoping to catch a glimpse of the ghostly riders. A glance at Mads and Sven's dark tent told her they were still asleep. The horn sounded again, this time louder. She decided not to wake them, instead making her way toward the river as quietly as she could.

She made it to the rock outcropping from night before just as the host of spectral riders appeared, racing along the edge of the river. Some of the horses ran in the water, kicking up a sparkling mist. The aurora overhead cast everything in green hues. Riders and their mounts raced by her as she hid. Wolves howled from the hills across the river, and black spectral hounds with glowing red eyes brayed in response.

Jace tensed, holding her breath when one hound stopped and looked back at her. She curled in as small as she could make herself behind the rocks and waited. A terse command, in a language she couldn't understand, forced the hound to move on. She waited a moment more before breathing again and peeking over the rock.

The last of the Wild Hunt was disappearing through a glowing archway about ten meters down the riverbank. Within the archway, Jace could see warm firelight flickering in a wooden hall, and beings of all sorts drinking and dancing.

Without thinking, she stood, then froze, hearing the clatter of horse hooves on the rocky riverbank.

"Who are thee mortal, who braves the Wild Hunt?" a heavily accented voice said behind her. She turned. A black horse with a cloaked rider stood right behind her.

"Oh, crap—" Her mind raced, going through all of her grandmother's stories, searching for the right response. She knew not to give her full name, and her nickname sounded more badass anyway. "J-Jace." She responded, embarrassed by her fearful stutter.

"You carry strange weapons for the Hunt, Jace," the hooded figure nodded to her chest. It took her a second to realize the apparition referred to her long lens camera strapped to the harness on her camera vest.

She responded spontaneously, "I didn't come to hunt, but I did come to shoot."

The black horse snorted and stamped a plate-sized hoof. Jace stepped back, surprised at the warm breath coming from the beast. Its rider laughed and pulled back the hood to reveal a tan, ageless and androgynous face framed by white hair gathered into a multitude of braids. Long, pointed ears pierced the curtain of hair.

Jace had to be dreaming. None of this was real, was it?

The horse snorted again, enveloping Jace in pungent breath.

"Well, Jace, I'm afraid you're too late for any shooting, but you are just in time for the revelry." The elf held out a hand to her. "Come, Woden is waiting."

She was pulled forward, and in a blink, found herself on the horse behind the elf.

The elf looked over their shoulder at her and grinned, revealing pointed teeth. "Welcome to the Wild Hunt."

Jace grabbed the elf's waist as the great black horse reared and galloped toward the gate.

One moment Jace was holding on for dear life. The next, she was standing in a warm, fire lit hall, surrounded by fae. Hanging sconces lit the large wooden hall, and a central fire in a rectangular pit provided warmth. Long tables filled the space, piled with every imaginable food. Roast duck, pigs on spits, piles of exotic fruits, tables of sweets and cakes, and pitchers of amber-colored liquid filled the room with mouth-watering scents. The folk here were as diverse as the food. Elves, fairies with butterfly wings, humanoid creatures with stag's heads, and many more sat at the tables and gathered in small groups along the fringes, talking and laughing. A troupe of musicians played in a far corner near a dais set with a large wooden chair. Upon the chair sat an imposing man with long gray hair and a braided beard set with thick silver beads. A patch covered one eye.

A light touch on her arm brought her attention back to the elf who'd brought her. Bowing, the elf said, "Forgive me for not introducing myself sooner, I am Airdan. Please, be at ease. Nothing will harm you within Woden's hall."

Jace's stomach rumbled, awakened by the savory scent of roasted meat coming from a nearby table. She resisted the desire to sit and eat. There were too many tales of mortals being trapped in the fae lands because they partook of fairy food and drink.

"Thank you, but I really should go. I'm going to miss my chance to photograph the aurora."

Airdan looked at her for a moment before a look of understanding crossed their face. "Ah, you are referring to the device I mistook for a weapon. Fear not, Jace of the mortal realm. All you wish can be yours for the price of a tale."

Airdan's choice of words made Jace look down. Her vest was gone, along with her camera. In fact, everything she'd been wearing was gone, replaced with a long dress made of some thick woolen fabric died a pretty grey-blue, and edged with elaborate embroidered Nordic knot work.

Panic seized her voice for a second. "Where-where is my camera? My gear? My clothes?"

Airdan bowed again, motioning toward the tables. "Your belongings are safe, do not fear. I simply thought you'd be more comfortable in the attire of the evening. Please, eat, drink. Enjoy yourself. It's not often we get the company of mortals."

There was nothing in Airdan's voice to indicate anything but sincerity, but she didn't trust the elf. She had no memory of actually getting on their horse which didn't help feeling she was, while not necessarily a prisoner, definitely not free to leave. She decided to test that theory.

"Please, Airdan, I am honored by your hospitality, truly, but I do need to go. My friends will worry if I don't return."

Airdan smiled, their pointed teeth making the gesture less than friendly. "Your friends are still asleep, dreaming of their next adventures. Please, you are our guest. We would be offended if you did not join us in our feast."

A purple-skinned fairy, about three feet tall, fluttered before her, taking her hand. "Come, dance with us," she said in a high soprano voice. She pulled Jace through the tables to a space where others were dancing a reel.

The room tilted sideways for a split second, and Jace found herself hand to hand with a large, black-furred Minotaur. The bull-headed being nodded to her and turned, passing her off to a fair, dark-haired elf in a blue doublet. The elf spun her around, and Jace found herself paired off with a green woman clad in leaves and tree bark.

Jace passed from fae to fae, the steps of the reel coming to her as if she'd practiced them her entire life. Was something or someone, controlling her movements? She didn't feel like a marionette, yet she didn't feel entirely in control either. Maybe it was the fragrant, purple haze from herbs set on the fire. No doubt something here was clouding her mind.

The music changed, flowing seamlessly into a more African beat. The drums took over with an earthy, deep, heart-pounding rhythm. The dancers moved into a circle and started stamping their feet and hooves in time with the music. As the musicians threaded Celtic rhythms into African ones, this too felt familiar to Jace. She lost herself in the pounding of the drums, stomping her feet and tossing her head side to side.

After what was both forever and no time at all, the music rose to a crescendo, and ended with several heavy drumbeats. The entire hall erupted in cheers and applause as the dancers clapped and tried to catch their breath. Next to her, a tawny satyr with autumn leaf-colored dreads and ebony horns bowed and kissed her hand before leaving the dance floor arm-in-arm with the purple fairy who'd brought Jace to the dance floor.

Winded, Jace found an empty bench off to the side and sat. She breathed deeply, trying to clear her head. It didn't help. The room wavered, silver sparks dancing at the edges of her vision. She gripped the bench, trying to regain a semblance of balance.

Airdan slipped onto the bench next to her, a pewter goblet in their hand. The elf offered it to her. "Here, drink this. It will clear your head and revive you."

Jace eyed the goblet, thirsty after all the dancing. She sat on her hands to keep them from reaching for the cup. The darkness of the metal hid the nature of its contents. "Thank you, no," she made herself say. "I've heard too many tales of mortals trapped in fairy because they ate or drank something offered by the fae."

Airdan laughed. "Ah, yes. I cannot say those tales are false, but this is only water, and on this Solstice night, in Woden's hall, you are safe. When the tales are told, and boons given, you may stay or leave. The choice will be yours. Eat, drink. Nothing of that nature will trap you here. You have my word." The elf bowed from the shoulders, one hand coming to their ribs, the other offering the goblet.

Jace swallowed, her throat dry. Her grandmother's admonishing voice was silent in her head. Her thirst got the better of her. She accepted the goblet and drank deeply. It was, in fact, only water, but it was the crispest, most refreshing drink she'd ever had. She emptied the goblet in one pull. When she set it on the table behind her, it refilled. Airdan snapped their fingers and a plate piled high with roast duck, herbed potatoes, fresh bread, and a chickpea curry appeared in front of her. With a flourish, they produced a set of silverware, presenting it to her on an aubergine linen napkin.

"Enjoy," the elf said, their eyes twinkling. "I'm afraid I have duties to attend to, but the telling of tales will begin shortly. Think about what life tale you will tell the Yule Lord." Airdan winked. "I'm sure you will come up with something enthralling."

Jace paused, a curry-dipped piece of bread halfway to her mouth. A life tale? What exactly did that mean? She turned to ask Airdan, but the elf was gone. In their place stood the purple fairy.

Her confusion must have shown on her face, for the diminutive fae said, "Don't worry about your tale. Simply tell us something meaningful which happened to you this year." The fairy giggled and flew away, leaving a trail of lavender sparkles in her wake.

I have to be dreaming. Maybe I have hypothermia, and this is just my neurons firing frantically to stay warm.

Hypothermia did seem like the more sane possibility. Jace pinched herself, trying to wake up, but her surroundings didn't change. The hall was warm and comforting, and the aromas from her dinner plate made her stomach growl.

"You should try the duck," a bass voice said next to her. "The Brownies outdid themselves this year. I think they added coriander to the glaze."

The Minotaur took a seat next to her, facing outward, a large leg of roasted meat in his grip. "The tales are about to start. This is my favorite part of the evening." He took a bite out of the leg, exposing a row of sharp, non-bovine teeth.

The hall hushed. Jace grabbed her plate and turned around in time to see two ravens fly across the room and land on the shoulders of the man sitting on the dais. The ravens cemented her suspicion he was, in fact, Woden, the Yule Lord.

Woden clapped his hands and the hall fell silent. "Friends, it is good to see you all gathered here on this Solstice night. Come forth, share your tales, and ask of me a boon." He looked directly at Jace before he sat back in his chair, taking a goblet in one hand, and stroking the head of one of the two wolves at his side with the other.

Jace's heart skipped a beat. She focused on her plate, selecting a duck wing and taking a bite, hoping if she looked like she was busy eating, they wouldn't pick her to go first.

No one else looked at her as excited chatter filled the hall. After a moment the tawny satyr stepped forth. He'd acquired golden ribbons around his horns. He bowed to Woden, then stepped to the side to face the entire hall. "Brothers, sisters, and guests," he said, looking at Jace at the last, "let me tell you a tale of sun-swept meadows, jealous gods, and a fierce goddess of battle…"

What followed was an X-rated tale of a bet between two Celtic gods, and the satyr's exploits with the Morrigan, the Celtic battle goddess. The crowd jeered and yelled suggestive comments throughout and cheered loudly when the satyr's tale concluded.

Turning to face Woden, the satyr took a knee.

"Ah, Pan, your tales become grander with each passing Yule. If you truly satisfied the Morrigan, then you are a blessed fae indeed." Woden laughed, his entire form shaking and causing his ravens to ruffle their feathers before settling down again. "What boon would you ask of me?"

"Great Yule Lord, I ask only for continued virility and stamina, so I might continue to please my Goddess and the dryads within my grove."

There were whistles and shouts of approval. An onyx-haired woman in a gown of black and blood-red stood near the front of the assembled fae. A ruddy dwarf elbowed her in the thigh, saying something Jace couldn't catch. The woman glared at him, her eyes flashing red. With haste, he bowed, backing away into the crowd. She watched him retreat, smiling like a cat watching a mouse.

Jace shivered and looked away.

One by one, the fae in the hall stepped forward and told a tale. Some were fairly mundane—stories about creating a work of art or discovering a new recipe—while others were more fantastical, though none as X-rated as the satyr's. All asked for and were granted a boon when they were done.

Throughout, the minotaur, whose name was Druzus, gave Jace a running commentary, telling her whether or not he thought the tales were true or false, or somewhere in between. His own tale was a combination of the mundane and fantastical. He'd spent the entire year creating a warhammer for Hadúr. Jace pieced together through the tale that Hadúr was a war god, but she didn't know exactly from where. Druzus described the hammer in intricate detail, and as he did, it appeared before them, as if it were being 3D printed with magic. For his boon, he asked for enough star metal to complete his next commission—a set of daggers for Coyote.

Woden didn't immediately grant the minotaur's boon. Instead, he thought for a moment, his hand stroking his beard. "Star-born metal is a powerful thing to give to a trickster, and were it not Yule, I would not grant such a boon."

The hall fell silent once again. Many fae looked at each other with expressions of surprise. Woden hadn't yet denied a boon.

"However, I cannot deny you on this night, Druzus. You shall have it."

Everyone cheered. Several beings clapped Druzus on the back as he returned to his seat next to Jace.

All eyes turned and focused on Jace. Her stomach turned to butterflies, and her face flushed.

"I believe it is your turn, my mortal friend." Druzus clapped her on the back, pushing her forward.

Jace rose slowly. She wiped her sweating palms on her thighs as she walked to take her place before the crowd. She looked to Woden and took a deep breath to try to calm her nerves. This was just a hypothermic dream. She had nothing to worry about, right? This wasn't a board meeting where she might get fired if she didn't have an optimistic enough financial projection.

Woden's gentle smile reminded her of a kindly mall Santa—if the Santa had been a bit metal. He nodded his head as if to urge her to begin.

She'd tried to think of something exciting to tell while the others told their tales, but compared to everything she'd heard, her life was too mundane. But maybe mundane was fantastical to these beings.

"I'm afraid mine is just a mortal tale," she began. When no one jeered or booed, she continued. "I've spent my life doing what was expected of me. I went to school, I got a degree. I got married and had a decent job. But I wasn't happy. I needed to do more, to be more. I owed that much to my ancestors who'd been enslaved, who'd had their dreams taken away and shattered."

A few beings in the crowd hissed, but Jace got the feeling it wasn't at her, but at the injustice dealt to her ancestors. She kept going, feeling more confident.

"A few years ago, my mother was diagnosed with stage four cancer and given six months to live. She made it a year before she died." Jace had to stop and breathe to keep the tears at bay. "On her deathbed, she didn't tell me life was short. We both knew that already. Instead, she told me to quit my job and do something which would bring me joy, something which would light a flame in me and could be a beacon for others to follow." She wiped the tears from her eyes and looked at the fae before her. A few surreptitiously wiped away tears, while others smiled kindly at her.

"After Mom passed, I took her advice. I quit my corporate job and divorced my narcissistic husband. With the little bit of money Mom left me, I bought a camera and took some classes. About six months ago, one of my photographs won me the opportunity to learn from a master in my craft, and that's how I ended up here." She chuckled. "Although how exactly I got here, in this hall, will be a tale none of my friends will believe." Shrugging, she turned to face Woden. "That's the end of my tale."

Polite clapping came from behind her. There was an air of expectation, of unanswered questions. She waited.

Woden leaned forward, resting his forearms on his knees. "I sense there is more hardship and strife in your tale, Jacqueline, daughter of Anesa."

So much had happened during the evening, Jace wasn't surprised Woden knew her full name or her mother's.

"You carry the weight of your ancestors on your shoulders and bury the pain of living in a hostile society beneath a skin thick as armor. I hear that pain and would lessen it if I could. What boon do you ask of me?"

Jace had thought more of what boon she'd ask than what story she'd tell. There was a lot she could ask for which would make her life easier, but her grandmother's stories of the fae were still forefront in her mind.

"My lord, you are kind and have been generous beyond measure tonight. My mind has spun around what I could ask of you. I could ask for instant fame and recognition of my art. I could ask that people of color and those who are different from the majority not be looked down upon and prosecuted. But I also know those would come with a price."

There were sharp inhales of breath, and Jace knew she was treading on thin ice, but she pushed forward.

"I know your boons are given freely, but there's always a cost to pay for instant gratification, even if the price isn't paid by me. I want to be a photographer for National Geographic. I want my photos, and my accomplishments to be an example for other young women of color to follow. To show them they too can pursue their own dreams—that they don't have to be shackled by what society expects of them. But if it's given to me, if I wake up tomorrow with a contract and fame and a pile of emails offering me gallery space, then how much is it really worth? I want to do these things, to accomplish these things, on my own. I need to prove to those who follow in the years to come, that they too can do these things—that they are just as worthy as anyone else, no matter what society says."

Woden sat back, steepling his fingers beneath his chin. "You are a rare mortal, Jace of Chicago. It surprises me not you found your way here to my hall. Since you wish no boon, I will simply wish you good luck in your endeavors."

The Yule Lord stood and clapped his hands twice. The hall fell silent once again. Raising his goblet, he said, "I thank you friends, for warming my hall and my heart this night with your revelry and tales. Go now, with my blessing, and return a year hence. I expect great things of you all. Sköll!"

The entire hall responded in kind, lifting their goblets and drinking.

Jace returned to her table only to be engulfed in a crushing hug from Druzus.

"Your tale was not exciting, but it was heroic, nonetheless." He set her back on her feet. "I hope you succeed, my mortal friend, and return here to tell us of your triumphs." He bowed and disappeared into the milling crowd of fae before she could respond.

"I'm afraid minotaurs are a bit light on manners," Airdan said from beside her.

Startled, she turned to the elf. "I thought he was quite pleasant."

Airdan sniffed. They clearly had other opinions. Airdan put a hand on her back, steering her through the crowd. "I hope you had a pleasant evening. If you'll follow me, I'll guide you back to the mortal realm."

The crowd in the hall began to dissipate, the fae literally disappearing. Some stopped Jace briefly to wish her well with "whatever 'photography'" was, and others wished her a long and happy life.

Airdan walked her to the large oaken doors of the hall, which were open to the winter air and snowy river valley beyond. "Here is where we part ways, Jace of Chicago. I hope you have found me true to my word?"

"I have, Airdan. Thank you for a...fantastical evening. Maybe one day we will meet again?"

Airdan smiled, keeping their teeth concealed. "Mayhaps, one day, little mortal. Blessed Solstice."

With a firm hand, Airdan pushed Jace across the threshold. Bright light flashed into Jace's eyes before darkness engulfed her.

Jace adjusted the photo canvas on the gallery wall and smiled. The Aurora Borealis photo was one of her favorites from her Norway trip two years ago. The neon greens and nearly ultraviolet purples swirling in the sky popped against the dark cliffs and icy river. A wolf howled in the foreground.

The trip had been transformative in many ways. She'd learned a great deal from Mads, not only about the technicalities of photography, but how to refine her portfolio and reach out to galleries. They talked weekly and were set to travel to Iceland together in May. It'd been a lean, hard two years, but things were coming together.

Her dream of Woden and the hall of fae still occupied her thoughts from time to time. There was an older gentleman, with a short grey beard and an eye patch, who'd become a recent patron. He reminded her of Woden, until he spoke, his Texas accent shattering the semblance. Occasionally, she'd catch a glimpse of the gallery owner's diaphanous purple shawl from the corner of her eye. She usually did a double-take, thinking it was the wings of a fairy. It was nothing but happy coincidences, but they made her smile.

Jace smoothed her dress and pulled a section of dreads over her shoulder. Taking a deep breath, she nodded at the gallery owner to open the doors. Smiling, she stepped forward to greet her patrons.

About the Author

From an early age, Carolyn Kay's been steeped in the worlds of fantasy and science fiction. She watched *Star Wars* at the drive-in and viewed *Star Trek* (the original series and Next Gen) religiously with her parents (yes, she's that old). Legos and Star Wars figures were her favorite toys, and Madeline L'Engle and Tolkien graced her bookshelves at a young age. So it's no surprise that she writes stories in a variety of genres, or that her first novel was an Avengers-Star Wars crossover fanfic.

Carolyn melded two of her favorite genres, steampunk and fantasy, together into a series titled, *Galessel's Tale,* set in a world co-created with her husband and award-winning illustrator, Chaz Kemp. She's also authored several short stories and a sci-fi novelette.

A government drone, she carves out time to write in between the day job, belly dancing, gardening, photography, and herding two very independent felines.

You can find her at carolynkayauthor.com and on most social media platforms under the username, Bewitchinghips.

The Open Road

by

Claire Davon

The Open Road

The lemon-yellow Datsun 240Z let out a rattling sound, and died.

"Darn it." Nicole blew out a breath. She'd followed all the instructions to rebuild the engine, but so far nothing had worked. Greasy fingerprints marred her open laptop.

The car had sat in her parents' garage for years, decaying with each passing day. Nicole had asked to fix it up for years, so when Dad finally gave his okay, she wasted no time. Now, six weeks in, she wondered if she'd been too optimistic. She couldn't figure out what she was doing wrong.

"You still trying to get Grandma's old hunk of junk running?"

Her brother Teddy stood in the driveway, peering into the open garage door.

"Almost there. I think I've got it." She wouldn't admit defeat.

"Better you than me," Teddy said, glancing around at the strewn parts. "Mom said to tell you dinner is in a half hour. You'll have to clean up first. You get oil on her chairs, and she'll have your head."

"Noted. Just a few more minutes. I think this baby is ready to come to life."

"Whatever you say, sis. See you inside."

Grandma's old car would not best her. If Grandma could do it, so could Nicole. Her ancestor had a touch with cars. No matter what model she touched, there wasn't a piece of machinery that didn't purr under her hands. She had kept the Datsun running for far longer than anyone thought possible.

"Everything is tight. Nothing is dripping." She glanced at the laptop where a refurbished engine stared back at her. "I'll give it one more try. Maybe third time is the charm."

Nicole shut the hood and got behind the wheel. She turned the key, sending up a prayer to various gods. A clicking sound made her hopes soar, and then the engine caught. She fed gas to it a bit at a time. It wheezed and backfired but continued to run.

A broad smile crossed her face, and she patted the dashboard. "Good car. Stay on. Please."

She held her breath as it shuddered and coughed, but didn't stall.

Dinner could wait. The only way to be sure she'd succeeded was to try the car out. Nicole eased out of the garage, nerves skittering through her belly.

The half mile to the old access road felt like a hundred. It once led to the highway, but a bigger one had replaced it. Now it was cut off from its original use and was growing more decrepit every day. She had fond memories of this place. Her first kiss had happened here. She didn't run into Joe Tonning around anymore, now that he had graduated high school.

Nicole pulled onto the abandoned lane and set the hand brake. She waited, listening to the pulse of the engine. When it showed no signs of stalling, she shifted into gear, and continued on.

The forest lay in dappled strips around her. Weeds poking through myriad cracks in the asphalt. It had to be a dozen years since anyone had used the road. Nicole checked for anything moving before stepping on the gas. The car lurched forward. She whooped and raised a fist. It bumped along the hard ground, the shocks groaning with the punishment. Satisfaction burst through her with each foot they moved. She had done it.

White light filled the cabin, blinding her. Nicole shrieked at the unexpected illumination. This was an old growth forest, and light didn't penetrate to the bottom of the trees.

Nicole braked, not wanting to risk hitting something in her sunblind state. She knew where she was from her childhood adventures with her brother, back when she and Teddy were good friends. Up ahead, a gap in the trees gave way to open fields.

Nicole gasped in surprise.

The tableau in front of her didn't fit her mental image of her location. She was on a street, with houses on the hills, and pasture in between. It took her a moment to register that this was a different part of the town. She recognized the house—but that was impossible. She couldn't be at the Tonning's place. They were ten miles away, on the other side of town. Yet there was their red barn with its collapsing roof, a structure that somehow was still upright. There were their cows—she recognized the one with the distinct patch on its side that resembled a giant handprint.

Nicole shifted into reverse, turning to ensure the way was clear before backing up. The cow mooed, its sonorous bellow echoing.

Light filled the interior. She put her hand on her forehead to shield her eyes, wishing she'd brought sunglasses.

Then she was back on the path, about a half mile from her original spot. Nicole slammed into park. Sweat beaded her upper lip, and she licked it away. Perhaps she'd been hallucinating, or had some sort of waking dream. Otherwise, she had no explanation for how she'd wound up at the Tonning's place.

When her pulse had slowed, and her nerves stopped jangling, Nicole shifted into drive again, and continued down the road.

As she re-entered the wooded area, the sun again filled the cabin with light. She took a wary glance around.

Smooth dirt, unblemished by weeds or cracked black tar, ground under her wheels. A meadow with waving grasses and a low wood fence paralleled the route. The scene was so pastoral that the dread left her. Nicole rolled the window down and breathed the fresh scent of newly cut grass and beyond that, cow patties. The pungent odor made her wrinkle her nose.

To the side of the path was a farmhouse with clapboard siding and an open door. A saddled horse, with a cart attached, stood in front of the door with an air of patient waiting.

A cow mooed, startling her. She shifted her gaze from the white house to the bovine who was staring at her. It nosed the fence, and she was reminded that a rampaging cow could trample small cars. Dad's warning about the Datsun being unable to protect her echoed in her mind. Nicole glanced back the way she had come and saw fields and a dirt path. She couldn't make out any sign of the road she'd been on.

The interior filled with blinding light, erasing all other images.

When her vision cleared, darkness loomed, the kind of blackness that pressed like a living thing. The headlights didn't penetrate more than a few feet. She couldn't glimpse very far ahead.

Nicole revved the engine, listening to the idle. To her relief, it stayed steady.

Fear curled through her. She had no reference points, nothing to tell her where she was or where she was going. If she lost her way, she might not make it back.

Nicole gripped the wheel and started driving. Light filled the cabin again. She prayed it would take her back to her original spot.

Cracked asphalt under the tires and the forest behind her showed a relieved Nicole she was indeed on the access road. Nicole let out a grateful sigh and turned for home.

Nicole checked the oil and fiddled with the spark plugs, aware of someone's focus on her. When she glanced up from the engine, her dad was sitting on a sawhorse, watching her. He had that intense air that he got when he had something he needed to say.

"Hiya, Dad." She kept her attention on the engine, dismay filling her at the sight of him. She'd been about to head out. The knowledge of her adventure draped around her like a cloak. Maybe she should be scared, but she was more exhilarated. Nothing that exciting had happened to her in her entire seventeen years. She'd gone *somewhere else* and come back home safely.

"You've done a fine job with this car," he said, rising and patting the front fender.

"Thanks." She tugged on one of the hoses.

"Your grandmother appreciated this car, but one car alone captured her heart. Did I ever tell you about it?" He ran his hand over the side mirror and met her gaze.

This she could be interested in. "I don't think so. What kind of car was it?"

"A turquoise 1958 Packard."

"Nice! Those are sweet with their fins and side detailing. Too bad she didn't keep it. That would have been fun to drive."

Her father was staring into space. It seemed he'd lost the thread of their conversation. Then he shook his head and continued.

"It resembled a rocket ship with whitewall tires and big fins. It had this leather interior with a bench seat and state of the art dials. I loved riding in it. It got stolen when I was a kid, and we never found it. She tried for months but could never find it. Grandma was always fussing with that car. I bet you could have kept it running, considering what you've accomplished with this bucket of bolts here. She loved taking the Packard out on solo rides."

The grandmother Nicole had known was an old woman who was too frail for car repairs. Not the free-spirited adventurer Dad was describing.

"This is my bucket of bolts. The Datsun is never going to be as cool as a Packard, but it doesn't have to have fins and chrome to get me places."

"That is true." He ran his hand along the panel. "Often when she came back from her solo rides the Packard it would be muddy, with vegetation and bugs in the grill. Her hair would be tangled, and she had a glow about her that told of great adventure. She hadn't been gone long enough to accumulate that much debris. Your Aunt Sally sometimes pestered her to go along, and your grandmother refused. Said she was going into an alternate dimension, and it wouldn't be safe. Sally didn't believe her, of course, but Mom held firm. She was a unique woman. In all my life, I never met anyone like her."

"I wish I'd known that person instead of old Gran."

Sadness moved over his face. "She would love the woman you're becoming. Nicole…I am past being able to tell you what to do. Nonetheless, I'm your father and I'm always going to worry. You're safe where you're going?"

Nicole opened her mouth to tell her father the things she witnessed. Then she shut it. This was her secret—hers and grandma's. She picked up a wrench, waiting until her voice was steady before speaking.

"I'm not going anywhere special, Dad, just along that old access road that got replaced by the highway. That's all."

Her father stood to his full height. If disappointment lined his face, she refused to acknowledge it.

"You be careful. Don't go too far. There isn't enough car to protect you if something happened."

Nicole flashed him a bright grin, remembering the light that presaged her entrance into the new places.

"I won't, Dad. Just the road."

"As you say." He went to leave, and then turned around again, piercing Nicole with an intent stare. "You take after her. Watch yourself, okay?"

Nicole swiped her rag across the radiator, and then eased the hood down. She checked all the hoses, refilled fluids, and tightened the frame bolts. Some of those tracks were bumpy, and she intended to ensure everything was in top shape before she dared another trip.

"You taking that car out again?"

Nicole whirled. She hadn't detected her brother's approach. She groaned at the additional interruption.

"Yes, I am."

"I'll go with you."

She shook her head. "No." *Your grandmother said that she was going into an alternate dimension.* "Mom would have my head if I stranded us both."

He lowered his head and glared at her in much the same way her mother did when she got angry.

"I want to come."

He yanked on the passenger side door so hard she feared he might break it. Climbing in, Teddy sat there with a mulish expression on his face.

"I'm coming."

"No. This is my car, and I am going alone."

He glared at her from his lower position. "Don't be a b-word. I want to ride along."

She considered letting him come, just for a second. Then she remembered the places she had gone. She couldn't take him on too, just herself.

"No." Nicole tucked the keys into her back pocket. "I'm going nowhere with you in the car."

She wondered if he suspected about her unconventional trips. If so, all the more reason she couldn't allow him on her rides.

He huffed out a breath and glared at her. "You suck," he said, jerking open the door and stomping toward the house. He called, "Mom!" as he went inside.

She had to go before her mother stopped her.

Nicole tried to suppress her irritation as she went to the access road. She had worked for weeks on the car—her and nobody else.

Teddy had no business horning in on her adventure. He hadn't spent hours on the Internet figuring out how to remove the rings. He hadn't sourced parts from local junkyards. She had done all the work, and she deserved this.

She cursed her brother as she went down the lane. This wasn't about him. All their petty grievances surfaced in her mind, and Nicole sifted through that exasperation as she drove. Younger brothers were a pain.

Then the sun was blinding her, and Nicole held her breath to determine what world she emerged into.

Fog lay heavy on the ground, and she couldn't see more than ten feet beyond the windshield. Nicole crept down the clearing, her heart in her mouth. The landscape outside her window reminded her of a primeval forest, filled with vines and vegetation, and she wondered if the area were crawling with hostile reptiles. Everything was coated in fungus. The trees were heavy with moss, and water dripped from them in an intermittent ping on the Datsun. Creatures stirred below the water of a nearby lake, disturbing its murky surface.

The susurration of crickets, and the low sounds of animals, reminded her the window was open. The air was thick with humidity, and the pungent odor of decay.

She saw nothing but forest in any direction, unless you counted the alligators—or crocodiles, or something worse—living in the water.

She heard a noise like a cross between a pterodactyl and a tiger. The sound came again, closer. The trees bent toward her, their branches closing in like hands. She had a vision of a tree reaching down to pick up the Datsun and pouring her out so it could eat her.

Her hands were shaking on the wheel. Terror filled her. Nicole was convinced that something bad was up ahead. Or the thing was in the trees—and coming for her. Fear danced along her nerve endings, and her breath was shallow as everything in her urged her to run, run, RUN!

Nicole slammed the gear into reverse, fearing she was lost forever in this terrible place. Light filled the cabin, and she prayed that it would take her back to safety.

The familiar access road jostled them. She threw the emergency brake with a shaking hand. Nicole took several deep, shuddering breaths, her mind racing.

She had never gone to such a horrible location. Then again, this was the first time she'd been in a bad mood when she went out. Maybe her spat with Teddy had blackened her spirit and affected her ride. It had fed on her darkness and took her to a place that matched what she was feeling.

Nicole pondered this revelation even as her heart slammed in her chest from the near miss. She didn't breathe until she was off the access road and heading for home.

Several days passed. The moss coated trees, with their malevolent branches, danced in her mind. Nicole considered not going out again. The memory of what lurked beneath the surface made her shudder. Indecision filled her every time she thought about getting behind the wheel. Part of her yearned to get back out there, but she was paralyzed by doubt.

"Check this out."

Nicole studied the thing Teddy had tossed before her. She recognized it as one of those old photo albums that boomers loved, with plastic to protect the developed photos. She glanced at Teddy, and then to the scrapbook. If he wasn't going to say anything about their earlier spat, neither was she.

"Whatcha got, bro?"

"What's it look like?"

She licked her thumb and paged through the yellowed album. The cover was embossed, and someone had taken great care with the photos, aligning them to the page and each other. The early ones were in sepia tone, and pictured people she was unfamiliar with. Judging from the clothes, they were last century, or perhaps the century before. Back when cameras were giant things and you had to stand still for several moments as they took the shot.

Nicole flipped through the stiff pages until she reached a page Teddy had put a sticky note on.

"This is the one I wanted to show you."

This was not the grandmother Nicole had grown up with. This was a woman in her thirties, with a kerchief around her hair, bent over a car. She had a wrench in her hand, and her culottes were grease stained, but she was beaming, pleasure radiating from her expression.

The turquoise color told Nicole this was the beloved Packard. Her grandmother's affection for her vehicle was there in the way her hand rested on it, her fingers splayed. The paint gleamed everywhere except the front, where grandma had been working. Nicole had little doubt that the hood would be scrubbed clean of any grease once her grandmother was done.

"She was beautiful."

"Yeah, she was all right." Teddy tried to turn the page, but Nicole stilled his hand.

She studied the lines of the car, from the fins to the hardtop roof to the grill. Then she leaped up, startling Teddy.

"I have to go."

Nicole raced to the garage and slid behind the wheel of the 240Z, mouthing silent apologies for neglecting it this past week. It sputtered in what appeared to be recrimination.

She wished she'd understood about this person and asked about her before the old woman passed away. Nicole bet there were a million different things the woman could have taught her, if she had understood the value of her insight.

Nicole pulled onto the access road, Grandma's image floating through her mind. Within a few minutes, the now-familiar bright sunlight filled the cabin. Nicole breathed a sigh of relief that the gift had not abandoned her.

The deserted highway must have been somewhere in the middle of the country. The hills in their small Massachusetts town made seeing into the distance impossible, unless you were on top of one of them. Here the countryside was flat all the way to the horizon. The highway stretched in both directions with level land on either side. She didn't know her U.S. geography well—but something told her this was Kansas.

Nicole stepped on the gas. She could open the engine up in this deserted plain in who-knew-where. The car responded, gathering speed as they cruised. It bucked a little but smoothed out as they flew down the road. She went for miles, and the terrain never changed. Wind whipped her hair around her face. She grinned with satisfaction at being able to tear through the scenery without running into other cars.

After what seemed like hours, Nicole heard a car approaching, and glanced in the rear-view mirror. The other vehicle was gleaming turquoise with protruding headlights, and a grill that resembled teeth. She slowed down a bit, watching in her rear-view mirror as it got closer. She hadn't dared hope until she got close enough to identify it as a 1950s Packard.

The 1958 Packard.

It wouldn't be long before it caught up to her. Nicole shifted and floored it. As she raced away the person waved out the window. The other car shot ahead, its wheels gripping the asphalt, the hubcaps spinning. Nicole barreled ahead, part of her attention on the road, and part on the auto gaining on her.

As they came alongside each other, Nicole darted a glance into the driver's side.

Her grandmother looked as she had in the picture Teddy showed her—early thirties, with brown hair that was tied back with a kerchief. Strands were flying around her face, and she had a broad grin on her face. She nodded toward the 240Z. "Nice car," she mouthed. Then she darted in front of Nicole and dashed ahead.

They raced for several miles. First one pulled ahead, and then the other, their cars moving through the countryside.

Nicole wasn't sure how long they drove. After an indeterminate time, the other woman slowed, and Nicole decelerated with her until they were side by side.

A hint of sadness showed on the other woman's face before she made a V for Victory sign, and then turned that into a wave. She blew Nicole a kiss.

"Thank you for the car," Nicole yelled. "It takes me to incredible places."

"It's not the Datsun. It's you. The power lies within us. Use it wisely, Granddaughter."

Then she revved the engine and gestured to the road. They began racing again. A hill showed in the distance where there had been none until now. Her grandmother crested the slope and vanished out of sight.

When she cleared the rise, Nicole was not surprised that she was alone. Once again, she was blinded by light, and then the Kansas landscape was lost to her.

Nicole was breathing hard as she bounced along the once-again familiar path. She stroked the black dashboard of the 240Z. The events of the past hours crowded her mind. A smile curved her lips. She had little doubt she would see her ancestor again.

All she needed to do was find the right road.

The house was quiet when she parked in the driveway. The car idled hard before sputtering off. She would need to check into that. She couldn't have her ride die when she was out exploring.

"Your grandmother always had that appearance when she came back from her journeys."

Nicole met her father's eyes.

"Did she?"

His expression was bittersweet, regret moving across his face. "She tried to tell me about her adventures once, but I was too young. 'Mom is weird,' I said to Dad. I heard them arguing later. She never brought it up again, even when I asked. My father was a good man, but he didn't understand her at all." Her father put his hand on the door across the open window. "I have to know if it is safe where you are going."

The concern on his face made an easy affirmation die on her lips. "I can't promise you that, not for sure. Many places are scary, but I figured out how to avoid them. I…" She paused, trying to frame the words the right way. "I saw Grandma just now."

Her father gave her a sad nod and opened the door. "I hoped you would. Be careful, that's all I ask. You're almost an adult, but you're still my little girl. Please watch yourself. For me?" He held out his hand to her. "If you encounter your grandmother again, tell her hello—and that I miss her."

Tears misted her vision, and she couldn't speak for a few seconds. Then she nodded and dabbed at her cheeks.

"Oh, and don't be too hard on your brother. He's got—what is it you kids call it? FOMO?"

She grinned at her father's attempt to be cool. "I'll try, Dad. For you. I can't take him with me, though."

"I get it. Come inside. Dinner is almost ready. Afterward we'll watch some YouTube videos and figure out how to fix that hard idle."

Nicole accepted his hand and got out. Her father took her into a loose embrace and held her. Startled, Nicole returned the hug. She felt his sense of loss, of time passing, in his tense body. Soon she would be heading out for new frontiers. She was not his little girl anymore.

He released her and pushed back her tangled hair. “I love you, Nicole. Always remember that.”

“I will. Love you too, Dad.” She hugged her father again.

She had many open roads ahead of her, but she had a life here too. She would travel into strange places, but in the end, only one spot called her every time—the same place her grandmother always returned to.

Home.

About the Author

Claire Davon can't remember a time when writing wasn't part of her life. Growing up, she used to write stories with her friends. As a teenager she started out reading fantasy and science fiction, but her diet quickly changed to romance and happily-ever-after's. A native of Massachusetts and cold weather, she left all that behind to move to the sun and fun of California but has always lived no more than twenty miles from the ocean.

www.clairedavon.com

Witness for the Prosecution?

by

Lucinda Gunnin

Witness for the Prosecution?

Ellen Elizabeth Booth looked across the courtroom to her attorney, a tall, thick, redheaded woman in an ill-fitting suit. The woman, public defender Margaret—call me Peggy—Black, remained adamant that Ellie should not testify. The forensics experts testified that Ellie had no gun powder residue on her hands or clothing. When the coroner testified that the shot which killed Alex came from about three feet high, the prosecutor had scrambled, trying to cast Ellie as some sort of Annie Oakley with a killing shot made from the hip.

"All those things instill reasonable doubt in the jury, Ellie. If you testify, you may undo all that we've accomplished," Peggy said over coffee.

Ellie handed her a napkin to wipe the lipstick off her teeth. "I appreciate your advice, Peggy. I understand what you are telling me, and I even realize that if I testify, there's a better than average chance the jury will decide I killed Alex. But if I testify, what I say will make the papers and then maybe someone will be prepared when the invasion happens."

Peggy shook her head and started to protest, but Ellie lifted her hand to cut her off.

"No one is going to blame you for losing this case, Peggy. I sound like a lunatic when I tell people what really happened to Alex. My own father thinks I did it."

"If you know that, why won't you consider a mental illness plea?"

"Because I'm not mentally ill. I'm going to take the stand, swear to tell the truth and then testify that dwarves are planning to invade."

"I can't prevent you from taking the stand, but I am going to object to it," her attorney said.

Ellie replayed her attorney's advice in her mind even as she raised her right hand and swore her oath. Knowing she was going to have to fight her own attorney to get the word out was daunting. Ellie took a deep breath and waited as Peggy spoke.

"Your honor, if it pleases the court, I'd like to note that my client refuses to consider a plea of diminished capacity, and is testifying against my advice."

The judge was a Hispanic man, graying at the temples, and on loan from a nearby county because all the local judges had to recuse themselves due to their relationship with either Ellie's father or her husband.

The prosecutor was Alex's best friend, formerly his assistant, a man Ellie had served dinner in her home the night before Alex died.

"Your objection is noted, counselor. Please proceed with your witness."

Peggy's hand trembled as she poured herself a glass of water and then took a sip. She walked around the table to stand between Ellie and the jury box.

"Ellie, can you tell me about your hunting trip with Alex?"

Peggy hadn't wanted her to talk about the marriage counseling, but Ted, the prosecutor, had been well-aware of it. He mentioned it in his opening statement as a reason why Ellie would kill Alex. Ellie disregarded her attorney's advice. Her face flushed with embarrassment and her voice trembled as she spoke.

"Alex and I had been having some trouble. He'd had an affair and, at first, I just wanted a divorce. I couldn't imagine staying together after that, but, mostly to make our families happy, and for his career, we decided to see a marriage counselor, to see if we could work things out. Our marriage counselor suggested we try spending more time together, to remember why we got married. Alex said he would join my book club if I would go elk hunting with him."

Ted scribbled something on the legal pad on the desk in front of him, and Ellie stared at the man she had once called a friend, as her mind drifted back over the conversations with the pastor who provided marriage advice.

"...before?"

Her inattention caused her to miss Peggy's question, so Ellie asked her to repeat it.

"I asked if you had ever been hunting before."

"No. Guns made me nervous. In fact, when we first got married, I asked Alex to keep his guns away from the house. He insisted we needed them for protection, so I relented as long as they were kept locked up." Ellie shook her head to clear her mind before she continued. "We started seeing the marriage counselor last summer, so I took a hunter's safety class in September, and Alex took me out to the range to learn to shoot."

While the prosecution was making its case, Ted had asked the range owner how often Ellie had been there. Ted looked triumphant when the records showed she had been there every weekend from August to November, but on cross-examination, the range owner confided she had never been there without Alex. Alex had been unimpressed with her skills, he said, deriding her the last time they were there.

"Were you any good?" Peggy followed the notes with the questions Ellie told her to ask.

"Objection, calls for speculation." Ted's objection wasn't unexpected, but Ellie wanted to make sure the jury understood her skill level.

"Counselor, can you rephrase the question?" the judge asked.

Peggy obliged. "Ellie, did you think you were a good shot?"

"No, I wasn't. I hit the target five times in 14 weeks at the range. Not the bullseye, the target. Alex almost called off the hunting trip, but instead he decided I could go along as long as I kept the safety on."

"And did you?"

"Yes. I never touched the safety on my gun." Ellie tried to keep her answers short and direct, hoping that would help stave off the tears that threatened every time she thought about Alex and that day.

"So how did Alex come to be shot with your gun if you kept the safety on?"

Ellie had written the question, verbatim, for Peggy to ask her, and still, she reeled from the emotional impact.

"Early that morning, before dawn, we got to the canyon where we were going to hunt. I was finishing up my bagel and sat my coffee on the seat next to Alex. He leaned over to kiss me and the coffee spilled on his jeans. He got angry, yelled at me for leaving it there and then dug through the glove box to find some tissues or napkins to wipe it up. I got out of the truck while he was yelling at me, so I didn't notice that after he slammed the glove box shut, it bounced back open."

Ellie scanned the faces of the jurors, wondering if any of them believed her.

"From there, the day went downhill. He was mad at me because his leg was wet and cold and I...," Ellie sniffled and wiped the tears from her eyes. "I told him that I hated hunting and maybe if he had brought his mistress, she'd be willing to keep him warm."

"How did he respond?"

"He told me I was right, that we should get a divorce because he hated being married to someone as frigid as me. After that, we didn't speak for hours, except for Alex occasionally telling me I was being too loud."

"Why didn't you leave?"

"We only took the truck. I tried to call my mom to have her come pick me up, but I couldn't get a cell signal in the canyon. And, to be honest, by that point I wanted to be able to tell my parents and the marriage counselor that it was his fault we were getting a divorce."

"Did you get your elk?"

"No. Alex said I scared them off being so loud, so just before dusk we started heading back to the truck. When we got there, the battery was dead."

"From the glove box being left open?"

"We thought so. Alex kicked the tires and yelled a bit, and then I laughed. He was furious at me for a minute, but then he started laughing too. He said, 'I guess this is what the reverend meant about facing adversary together.'

"That Alex was the one I fell in love with, the one I will always love," Ellie said, twisting the tissue in her hands.

Peggy's voice was soft, almost kind when she asked, "So, what happened next?"

"We decided to walk out of the canyon, at least as far as Sawmill Road, hoping we could call a tow truck from there. We walked for an hour, talking the whole way. He apologized for the affair, swore it was a one-time thing when he was drunk and angry. He told me he felt like I wasn't supportive of his career. I told him he should have told me."

Ellie looked defiantly at the prosecutor and then at her father. "We decided we were going to save our marriage come hell or high water." She barely whispered as she added, "That's what made it so much worse when I lost him—and it was my fault."

Ted looked triumphant and Peggy paled. She went back to the defense table and finished the glass of water before turning back to Ellie.

Ellie's head was bowed, and her weeping bordered on sobs.

"Do you need a minute, Ellie?" Peggy asked.

Ellie shook her head.

"Why do you think it was your fault Alex died?"

"Because I called him over to look. I had stepped off the road to go to the bathroom and I saw a shimmering spot in the snow. My dad always said I was too curious for my own good. He was right. I asked Alex to come look at it with me. I didn't know it was a doorway."

"A doorway?" Peggy tried to mask the disbelief in her voice, but Ellie heard it. She was certain the jurors did as well.

"A doorway or a gate, whatever you want to call it. We walked through it and suddenly we were somewhere else."

The looks on the jurors' faces made it clear she had lost them.

"I know it sounds insane. My own family doesn't believe me. If someone else told me this story, I wouldn't believe them. But walking through the shimmering spot felt like dipping your hand in warm wax. Not unpleasant, just a bit of resistance. On the other side, we were still in the forest, but it was warmer, and the sun was brighter, more like afternoon in mid-spring. We hadn't gone far when we started hearing the drums. I was frightened, but Alex reminded me that we had our guns."

Her voice trembled as she continued. "Alex left me hiding behind a rock outcropping and went to see what was going on. When he came back, he grabbed me by the hand and said we needed to get out of there before they found us. I asked him who and he described them: tall, muscular humanoids with pronounced jaws, tusks and green skin. He was practically dragging me back toward the shimmering."

Ellie looked directly at Ted as she continued her story, willing the man she once called friend to believe her.

"We could see the shimmering ahead when another creature right out of Tolkien's imagination stepped into out path. He was maybe four feet tall, with long red hair and a beard half-way down his chest. The dwarf surprised us by speaking to us in English. He asked why we were running, and Alex told him about the orks. The dwarf nodded and introduced himself as Baxton. He said his raiding party was hunting the orks but were outnumbered and overpowered."

"Alex told him that wouldn't matter if they had guns. Baxton asked what guns were. Alex told him all about the rifle and how it worked. Baxton asked to see my gun, and we thought that with the safety on, it would be fine. Baxton looked it over, checked the sight and then flipped the safety off as though he'd been doing it his entire life. Alex told him that was a bad idea and went to get my gun from him, so Baxton shot him. Twice."

The tears broke through again and Ellie's body shook with her deep sobs. Peggy asked for a short recess to "allow her client to regain her composure," and the reporters who filled the courtroom jumped at the chance to call their editors and say that federal prosecutor Alex Booth's wife had just testified that dwarves had killed her husband.

In the conference room, Peggy handed Ellie more tissues and wrung her hands. "Those reporters are going to write stories that say you believe dwarves killed Alex."

"Good. They did. And maybe, someone will believe me."

"Only the crackpots."

"Then the crackpots will be the only ones we have to defend us when the invasion begins."

Peggy's sarcasm was obvious when she asked, "The invasion of dwarves?"

"Yes. The orks had been stopping them."

"But if they don't have guns, we can easily send them back where they came from."

"They lied to Alex. While I was trying to stop the bleeding, someone told Baxton that he needed to kill me too, and he just laughed, calling our rifles antiques. He said once they wiped out the orks and their portal-blocking magic, they would invade. He taunted me and said no one was going to believe a woman who just killed her husband. Then, he threw Alex, me, and our guns back through the portal."

"Baxton sounds like a supervillain revealing his plot just in time for the hero to rush in and save the day."

"I would like to think so, Peggy, but I've been telling people this for months and no one is listening." Ellie couldn't keep the censure from her voice as she added, "Not even you."

Peggy blanched and tried to apologize, but Ellie just waved it off. She dried her tears and returned to the courtroom. Once there, she recounted Alex's final moments and Baxton's threat to invade Earth. She held back the tears as she finished her testimony. Then she held her breath waiting for Ted's cross-examination. Alex had commented many times how brutal Ted could be to witnesses. She had tried to prepare for it but knew she would likely fall apart again.

"Ms. Booth, can you tell me how your clothes came to be covered in Al—the victim's blood?"

Ellie noted that Ted could not look her in the face. His Adam's apple bobbed as though he was swallowing hard when he asked the question.

"After Baxton threw us through the portal, I applied pressure to the chest wound and held Alex's hand. Someone had heard the shots and found us about 10 minutes later, but it was too late to save Alex."

"No further questions, Your Honor."

The judge excused Ellie, and she made her way back to the table next to her attorney. She sat numbly through the closing arguments and instructions to the jury. Whatever else happened, she had gotten her story out to the world.

The jury was still deliberating when they broke for the night, and, from her jail cell, Ellie watched as her testimony led the evening newscast in Denver. The following morning, the headline asked, "Prosecutor's Death: Warning Shot in Dwarf Invasion?" The story mostly focused on mental health experts saying that she was clearly delusional and needed treatment more than she needed prison. Most predicted a quick guilty verdict.

Peggy was cautiously optimistic when deliberations stretched into a third day. They were eating lunch when the announcement came that the jury had reached a verdict. Ellie's heart pounded as she walked back into the courtroom. She'd done her duty, warned the people she loved. That was the best she could do.

The world seemed unnaturally quiet as the bailiff said, "All rise," and the judge entered the courtroom. Ellie shook, clasping her hands together and trying to remain calm. The concept of fighting the charges all the way, of making sure her story got out, had seemed noble and the right thing to do until this point. Now, visions of cold gray walls and orange jumpsuits swam before her eyes. Her knees threatened to buckle as she stood and waited for the jury foreman to read their verdict.

A woman who looked like someone's mother began, "We, the jury, find the defendant…"

"Stop!" Ted shouted, looking down at his phone. "Your Honor, may I approach the bench?"

"This is highly irregular, counselor."

"Yes, sir, but the news..."

"Approach. Now."

Ted and Peggy walked up to the judge's podium. Ted was whispering and waving his arms, then handed his phone to the judge. Peggy's forehead glistened with sweat and her knuckles turned white as she held on to the edge of the judge's bench.

Her question, "Is this real?" echoed through the courtroom.

Ellie turned to watch her father, a decorated veteran of the state police and a firm believer that she should face the death penalty for killing her husband, take the phone out of his pocket and turn it on. He looked at the phone and then up at his daughter, his eyes filled with tears. The courtroom noise grew louder as more observers brought out their phones and found the news.

A seven-foot-tall, green-skinned man had walked into the state capitol during the lunch hour. Though he could not seem to speak English, his mere presence was seen as confirmation of Ellie's story.

The judge pounded his gavel and demanded order in his courtroom.

"It would appear that there is perhaps another witness for the defense, though they will need some time to secure a translator. The prosecution informs me that, to avoid the expense of another trial, they are dismissing all charges against Ms. Booth. Case dismissed."

About the Author

Lucinda Gunnin is a reformed journalist turned author and commercial property manager in the suburbs of Philadelphia. She moved to the end of the Main Line long before she knew what that meant and now finds herself surrounded by old money, the country's biggest shopping mall, and historic sites. When she's not at her computer, chances are she's at the gaming table. She's a fan of old school TTRPGs, war gaming and cooperative board games. She'll probably get around to having an author website again someday. For now, send sushi and find her at:

Twitter: https://twitter.com/LucindaGunnin

Facebook: https://www.facebook.com/lucinda.gunnin

Lucinda Gunnin

Hold The Mayo

by

Diane Arrelle

Hold The Mayo

Edgar stood by the food concession counter at the rest stop. "I remember when this place had real live servers," Edgar snapped and watched the frown lines around Gregory's mouth deepen.

"I know Dad," Gregory said, "you've told me enough times."

Edgar noticed his son's gaze never flickered from the red, white, and blue trimmed menu board above them. "I also remember when you used to give a rat's ass about the things I said."

Gregory's shoulders tightened, but he didn't turn around. Edgar watched the movement under his son's lightweight jacket. He knew Greg always scrunched up when he was upset and trying to hide it.

"Hey, look son," Edgar shouted. "Your mother wants to take your order. See her behind the glass partition working the computer. Look, she's waving at us."

Greg spun around. "What did you say?"

"I said stop acting like an old fart and lighten up. I just want to reminisce a little, and all you can do is think, 'Uh oh—definitely time for the home!' " Edgar looked his son in the eyes and, in a totally uncharacteristic move, spat on the floor.

Greg flinched, opened his mouth, but only sputtered. Both men stared at the glistening glob on the spotless floor. An alarm went off behind the glass partition, and a spider-like thing scurried out from a slot under the counter. It squatted down on jointed metal appendages and sucked up the wet spot.

Edgar snorted. "I can remember when they used to have people to clean up. Hey, I even remember when it was considered disgusting to spit on the floor in public. Why, I even remember when in public meant other people around and music playing over the loudspeakers. Even if it was only crap elevator muzak."

He glanced around the room, noted the three 4th of July cardboard cutouts taped on the walls, and saw only two plastic booths occupied by other travelers. "Hell, those alarms didn't even faze sleeping beauty back there manning these mechanical nightmares." He pointed to the only employee at the rest stop, the one sleeping behind the food dispensing machines. "I—"

"Dad, please!" Gregory whispered. "Come on, Dad. Please order. After all, this trip was your idea. You wanted to take a drive to the cemetery."

"Yep, Greg, it's so good of you to humor the old man like this, kind of eases the guilt before you send me to the home. Hey, I understand, boy. Peg didn't grow up around old people. She just doesn't understand an old geezer around her house. She thinks I'll be happy stuck in a disguised prison filled with senile fools, drooling mental black holes, and all those nice shiny nurses and cameras to watch over me."

"DAD," Greg shouted, finally red in the face. "Please!"

"So, son, you can do more than just get embarrassed. What are you feeling, shame or anger?"

"Anger, Dad. Anger!" Greg said lowering his voice as the other people in the room turned to stare at them. "I'm sick of you trying to make me feel guilty. Well, I'm not feeling bad! I'm not in the least. You are always putting me down, always comparing me to some absurd standard from your pathetic excuse of a past. Peg isn't just uncomfortable with you around, she hates you! You are making our lives a terrible strain."

Edgar laughed. "So, Greg, you do have a little spine, don't you? You actually came out and said hate, and in public too. Good thing the Polite Police didn't hear you, huh. And gee, I'm a terrible strain, mighty harsh words, mighty tough talk for now-a-days."

Greg sighed, his shoulders slumped, and he turned back to the menu. He touched the pictures of what he wanted to order, then touched them again for Edgar, who refused to communicate with machines.

"Ah, Greg. I just want you to see that you and the rest of the sheep are condemning yourselves to an existence of empty, polite crap. Everybody's nice to each other, nobody has to ever get their hands dirty, but nobody's happy either." Edgar watched his son walk away from him with the tray of food following on wheels. He sighed with frustration. The world was never meant to be like this, he thought. Nobody allowed to complain, nobody allowed to get angry, everyone so considerate of everyone at the cost of everything.

When did we stray so far from reality, he wondered. He struggled to let go of the anger he seemed to feel all the time and followed his son to a booth. "I think I miss the music the most. All there is today is silence, nothing piping through to upset anyone. I can't stand the idea of having a speaker embedded in your head or else you gotta live with this infuriating silence."

Greg sat and began to silently eat.

Edger shook his head. He was sorry that Greg thought him a foolish, wasted, old man, but he wasn't. He wasn't! He was just tired of living in a society based on lies. "Look son, I'm sorry I've embarrassed you. I just miss the old days."

Greg picked up his sandwich and took another bite. He chewed, swallowed, and said, "I think I understand, Dad. But anger is so counterproductive. We live in the best of all worlds. Just look around, everything is clean, sanitary, peaceful. There is no need for anger and lies and bigotry anymore."

He took another bite and added. "I just wish you could learn to enjoy life. The village you are moving to is so perfect. You're not going into a home like your dad had to. This is just the way it should be, everyone living with their proper group, the elders together in the villages, and the family units together in their complexes. No more of that forced intermingling of cultures, no more ethnic or socioeconomic slurs, no more fighting, no more anger! A good world."

"You really believe that?" Edgar asked, then started to eat his bland sandwich. He wasn't even sure what it was, pseudomeat or processed non-dairy cheese. "I'd like a hamburger, dripping grease and covered with mayo, pickles, and fresh, outdoor-grown onions."

Greg shuddered, "Ugh...sounds kind of disgusting. Dead flesh, muscles and fatty tissues ground together, fried in its own carcinogenic excretions, then covered with a vegetable grown in insecticide polluted soil. Thanks, I'll stick to today's food."

Edgar caught a movement off to the side. He turned his head, but whatever he thought he saw disappeared. "Guess I'm just stuck with my yesterdays, or at least wishing for them," he said to Greg and began to hum a song from his past.

The movement caught his attention again. This time he didn't turn his head. Instead, he waited, and it moved into focus a little, just inside the line of his peripheral vision. It was a waitress, dyed red hair tousled and falling out of a ponytail, short-skirted uniform bouncing over long tan legs. He could have sworn he'd seen her a thousand times in a thousand places when he'd been young.

But her type was gone, just like the restaurants, the hangouts, and the life he had known. And yet, she persisted in playing on his vision.

Maybe the boy and that bitch wife are right, maybe I am ready for the old folk's home. Edgar chuckled softly. They may have cleaned those old age centers up, taken away the stench of piss and shit, and made the residents look presentable and functional—it was amazing what they could do with implants and chips—but when the mind gives up the fight, the only thing left is a senile old fool, too dumb to know when to die.

He closed his eyes, then opened them. The waitress was gone, but he could sense more than see shadows moving all over the room. He squinted and the shadows deepened into misty people milling around an old-fashioned turnpike rest stop complete with food stands, canopied shops, vending machines, video games, and huge smelly rest rooms. Edgar sighed and closed his eyes again. He ate that way, eyes closed shutting out his silent, sullen son and a vague world he longed to see again.

Finally, he heard, "Ready Dad?"

He nodded and got up, opening his eyes. The shadows were still there, and he could swear he could hear noises, people talking, shouting, laughing, sneezing, coughing, and even the crying of a baby.

He rushed to the glass automatic doors that went out into the almost empty parking lot. He was going to leave as quickly as possible.

Then he heard her.

"Come back now, real soon."

He jerked to a stop. Greg crashing into him. Edgar turned back and there she was, the waitress, waving good-bye. "Real soon, Honey. We'll be waiting."

"Dad, what's the matter?" Greg asked, stepping back from his father. "Dad, are you all right?"

Edgar went out the door, then asked, "See anything interesting in there?"

Greg's expression turned to concern, "No... Did you? Dad?"

"Of course not, what do you think I am, crazy?" Edgar snapped and walked toward the car.

Greg drove the solar powered car on the almost deserted superhighway. "It's funny, what with public transportation so good, you'd think they'd close those rest stops and tear up the roads."

"Some of us still like to drive, and, as for the rest stop, well, as clean as they've made us humans, they still haven't figured out how to make us give up food and voiding."

Greg sighed and fell silent.

Edgar looked out the window at the bleak landscape covered with landfills, high-rise cites and cemeteries. He sighed and thought about how the future had become the present, how man didn't need the land anymore, what with submersible living and superstructures reaching to heaven like successful towers of Babel. The earth was only good for storing the trash and the dead. Edgar thought about ending up in one of the endless graveyards tended by machines, never visited except by fools like himself. He wondered if Greg would ever visit him after he died. Would Greg visit Peg the way he visited Janet?

He'd had hopes for that boy. He remembered how like himself Greg had once been, before Peg, success, and children turned him into a modern-day automaton.

"Greg?"

"Yes Dad?"

"You ever think about your mother?"

Greg turned from the road, "Of course!"

"Ever miss her?"

Greg smiled a little, "Not like you do."

"Are you going to miss me?"

"Hey Dad, I'm sorry I blew up back there. You'll only be a few minutes away from us by metrotube."

"No, son, I mean when I'm really gone. Will you ever come out here to visit?"

"Of course, Dad," Greg's cheek twitched, and Edgar knew he was lying, just like when he was a kid.

"Perhaps you will," Edgar said and returned to studying the road and the occasional tree with yellow and dying brown leaves.

They stopped at the cemetery for just a few minutes before Greg said he wanted to return to the rented car.

"Wait son," Edgar said reaching into his jacket pocket. "I've been saving this for you ever since I found it in a container last year."

Greg's eyes lit up. "Why it's my old smartphone!"

He grabbed the small portable unit from his dad's outstretched hand. He opened a compartment and took out the cordless buds and slipped them in his ears. "Hey, do I look as cool as I did when I was eight?"

Edgar nodded. "You sure do, son. Cool."

"Shame batteries are outlawed. I wonder if I can find an energy source to make it work? I had tons of music and movies stored on it." Greg smiled "Boy, I sure would like to hear those songs."

Edgar fished out a holographic photo and handed it over. "You find all sorts of stuff when you clean out a lifetime."

Greg's expression softened even more, and he got a faraway look. "Wow, me and my first car. The old shitmobile."

Edgar laughed. "Yeah, those manure driven babies weren't around all that long, thank the Lord. But they were efficient little stinkbombs."

Greg put the picture in his pocket. "You know, Dad, sometimes the past does look good, probably better than it really was. But this world is a good place."

Edgar nodded and rested against Janet's gravestone. "That's because it is your world. My world is in that picture and all around us right now. When you don't fit in anymore, you have to move on."

Greg looked sad. "I wish you could see that you are wrong. This planet is big enough to be everybody's world."

They walked back to the car, neither one breaking the silence that had formed. On the drive back, Edgar found himself thinking very little of his late wife and a lot about the rest stop.

"I'd like a coffee," he announced.

Greg sighed. "Dad, we have to get back."

"Come on, son. Humor an old man with a weak bladder."

He watched Greg grind his teeth.

They turned off the road and back into the rest stop parking lot. Except for the two cars which had obviously left, the same few cars were still there. Edgar wondered, if he walked up to them, would they be covered in dust?

They went inside and the shadows were gone. Edgar fought off the feeling of disappointment. What had he expected anyway, a welcome wagon?

Greg walked up to the counter to punch in two coffees. "Want any dessert, Dad?"

Edgar thought for a moment then said, "I'd like an apple pie a la mode."

He sat at a booth and waited, not sure for what, when he suddenly saw her, plain as day.

"Hi ya, Honey," she said. "Glad you could make it back. So few do any more, but it's a slow time. In a couple of more decades we'll be swamped, just you wait and see."

Edgar sat there mesmerized. As he stared at her, he realized he was hearing music, music decades old, from the turn of the century when he was young, it was Boulevard Of Broken Dreams. It all started to sink in.

The waitress was standing in front of him, pad and pen in hand. "Well doll," she said. "What will it be, processed pie with sonny-boy over there, or the real thing forever."

"Am I dead?" Edgar asked.

She laughed. "Hell no, Sweetcheeks."

"Then, am I dying, is that why I have a choice?"

She shook her head and few strands of her rich, red curls tumbled from the scrunchie.

"Well then, what's going on?"

She shrugged. "Hey, I'm just a waitress, came here about thirty-five years ago and took the job. All I know is, if you can see the past, you can get there."

"This is the past?"

"Well, it's a rest stop on the way to the future."

Edgar looked over at Greg, who was still at the counter. He smiled. His dour, middle-aged son, who was always in such a rush, could never make up his mind when it came to desserts. He'd be there another ten minutes without Peg nagging him to hurry.

"How do I join you?"

She smiled, a sweet, crooked grin. "Just order what your heart desires."

Edgar thought for a moment then said, "A stop from reality, with a juicy, rare burger smothered in pickles and fresh onions."

She wrote furiously and asked, "Mayo?"

"Nah," he said. "Hold the mayo...this time."

The room suddenly filled with a crowd of people, souls just like himself, who had tired of humanity's schizoid race to assimilate as well as segregate. The music tempo changed. The Beatles sang Twist and Shout as several of the people around him got up and began to dance.

Edgar ignored the dancers and watched Greg turn and look for him. He felt a pang at leaving the only living soul who mattered to him.

The waitress put her arm around him and said in a soft voice, "Don't you worry, his kind always comes back when they're ready. After all, he's a chip off the old block."

Edgar nodded and walked up to his son. "Greg, I know the most you can see is a shadow that you won't accept as real, but I'll be here waiting when you finally decide to return someday. And, Greg, I'll make sure the desserts are fresh for you."

He wiped at his eyes and turned away from his son, who was obviously searching the huge empty room for him.

Then Edgar walked back to his table and ate the first real burger he'd had in fifty years.

About the Author

Diane Arrelle has sold more than 350 short stories and has three published books including the rerelease of her updated and expanded short story collection, *Just A Drop In The Cup*, and, *Seasons On The Dark Side*, her collection of horror stories. She is the editor of the anthology *Crypt Gnats: Horror You've Been Itching to Read* and the mystery anthology, *WhoDunit.*

Retired from being director of a municipal senior citizen center, she is now co-owner of Jersey Pines Ink LLC. She resides with her sane husband and her insane cat on the edge of the New Jersey Pine Barrens (home of the Jersey Devil).

www.arrellewrites.com

Facebook: Diane Arrelle

www.jerseypinesink.com

Find What's Lost

by

Dana Bell

Find What's Lost

But Your Majesty," Cameron objected, "you ask the impossible!"

"Of course I do." The king yawned, barely covering his mouth with his pudgy hand. "That's why I hired you and not that insipid wimp who runs errands for me." A glare nailed the poor skinny man who kneeled at the monarch's feet, shackled in arm and leg irons.

"I tried," the captive wailed.

"Oh, shut up," the king ordered. He narrowed his red eyes and looked at Cameron. "That witch took my son and hid him. Your job is to find him." He waved his hand, indicating the audience was over.

Cameron bowed out of the room, and two guards clad in loincloths, with crossed leather over their muscular torsos, closed the door behind him. He gazed uneasily at their scimitars, each held at the ready, and fled down the darkened hall. Once outside, he dared to take a deep breath.

How in the solar system was he supposed to find the lost royal heir when his mother, a renowned healer—not a witch as the king had called her—could be anywhere from one of the colonies, like Mars, to the farthest mining colony on Titan?

"I should have never accepted the commission," Cameron mumbled, knowing precisely why he'd been hired. He had a knack for finding the unfindable. No thanks to his heritage. His father had been a sorcerer, from a long line going back generations, and his mother a distant cousin to the missing queen.

One problem. His mother had no idea where the queen had gone. He'd asked her when he'd gotten both the payment and summons to appear at the royal court. No doubt the king knew Cameron wouldn't turn down the assignment.

"She's always been a tricky one," his mother had told him. "Take care or you might vanish, as have all the others who have sought her."

Not real encouraging. Still, he needed the silver, and a referral from the king would bolster his reputation. Not that he really needed it. Everyone came to him to find what had been lost.

Opening his office door, Cameron scratched his beard, glad he'd trimmed it before the royal audience. One should always look their best, and he prided himself on always wearing the appropriate attire.

Tessa, his black cat, blinked yellow-brown eyes at him from where she sprawled on his wooden desk.

"Hello to you, too," he grumbled. "You know you're not supposed to be there."

The feline ignored him and used her tongue to give her gleaming fur a bath.

He shook his head and walked to his window where he could see the alley. A few beggars huddled in blankets as the rapidly chilling wind picked up. Several children laughed, chasing each other until their mother's called them home. The night ladies hadn't come out yet.

Of course, they weren't the only creatures who roamed the streets. Making certain the window was secure, Cameron pulled the drapes. Time for a hot dinner of stew, hard bread and a brisk tea. Afterward, he'd have a word with the gatekeepers. Maybe one of them had escorted the royal lady and her son to their new home.

Eliza knew the king would eventually try to find her. Her tired eyes rested on her twelve-year-old son Fredrick, who sat at his computer listening to his teacher, who lived at the Rhea colony and taught history to students all over the solar system. Since a shortage existed in the profession, they often shared an instructor.

Turning back to fixing lunch, Eliza mixed dried meat with cabbage she grew herself. Gardening had been her specialty, and, here at their new home, her talent was appreciated. She taught others the skill of growing plants, and, over the past seven years, no one had starved.

"Cabbage again," Fredrick griped as he sat down at the counter. He wore what the other kids did: gray pants with a white top and flat shoes.

"How was your history lesson?" she asked her son, putting his plate in front of him.

He sniffed and forked a mouthful before answering. "Boring."

"History is important." He wouldn't have any idea how important until he took his father's place on the throne, if that is what he wanted.

"It's boring." He frowned, his face a younger version of his father, with high forehead and cheeks, a full mouth and coppery skin. Though he had her blue eyes, height, and toned body.

"Why do I need to know the history of witches, vampires, shifters, and an assortment of other creatures. They don't have much in common with humans." He speared more cabbage. "And they can't travel in space."

"No, but they can come through the portals." *Like we did*, she silently added.

"Not for long." His fork twirled his food. "Don't they die?"

"Some," she agreed. Pouring a glass of oat milk and taking a swallow.

"Wish you didn't have to work in the mine, Mom."

"We need the coin." They had the same conversation every day before she went to work.

"You don't eat enough."

She knew she was thin, but muscular from working the drill. "I eat enough." One silver lining—she didn't miss the fancy gowns, preferring the simplicity of her brown trousers and matching tunic.

Fredrick narrowed his eyes. "No, you don't."

"Be good boy while I'm gone and do your homework." She missed the days she could hug him and kiss his cheek. He'd outgrown that when he'd turned six.

"Be safe," he returned, taking another bit of his lunch.

"Dinner is in the cooker. When you're hungry just serve yourself."

" 'Kay," he answered, watching as she left.

Outside the doors Eliza took a deep breath before heading for the pit. Her shift lasted ten hours in a heavy suit. For her son's sake and safety, she endured it.

Since magic had replaced things like cars, buses, and public transportation—not because they didn't work, but because using a gatekeeper was easier and quicker—Cameron went to one he knew just down the block.

"Hey, Sim," he greeted the green being clad in shimmering colors. Cameron had changed to black pants and an open necked shirt with silver braiding.

"Hey, Cam," Sim answered. "Where to today?"

"No destination."

"Ah. Information."

"You ever escort the queen and her son?"

The other bit and chewed its lips together, considering the answer. "Not me. Might want to ask Sham."

"Who's Sham?" He shrugged on his brown cloak, which wiggled like it wanted to get away. How had his father ever worn the temperamental thing? Luckily, Cameron was tall and lean. Despite the twin scars on his cheeks, his looks didn't matter to him. Women could look elsewhere for a mate.

"Old keeper who retired about a year ago." Sim rubbed his hairy neck. "Think he settled in the Bahamas. Want me to transport you there?"

"Thank you, Sim. Your usual fee?"

"Always."

Cameron gave him a small silver piece and stepped through the rainbow portal and onto a sandy white beach. Deep green water spread out as far as he could see, and above, a cloudless blue sky greeted him. Not far away, an old mottled green creature sat in a hammock strung between two palm trees.

"I'm retired," it groused when Cameron approached. "Sat is keeper here."

"You Sham?"

The keeper's eyes were clouded over with black, and it squinted. No doubt it would be blind in a few more years. "Who wants to know?"

"My name's Cameron. I find things."

"Sorcerer who finds things. Fancy that." The other laughed, its naked body very different from a human. Keepers were neither male nor female.

Forcing his eyes away from the odd anatomy, Cameron asked again, "You Sham?"

"What'cha want?"

"You escort the queen and her son somewhere else?"

Sham scratched its chest with chipped nails, slinging the damp off and hitting the sizzling sand. "What's in it for me?"

"What do you want?" Cameron waited. Negotiating with the keepers took patience.

"To be left alone."

A damp breeze slid over the waves and embraced Cameron. He recognized the feeling. A siren lived closed by.

"Circe will take you be if I tell her to," Sham threatened.

"Sorcerers aren't good prey."

With narrowed eyes, Sham pointed to Cameron's face. "Tell me how you got those, and I'll tell you where I took them."

With a sigh, Cameron relived the incident, and Sham happily gave him the information asked for.

Her shift over, Eliza returned to her quarters, smiling at her son, whose draped body covered the couch. A blanket covered him from the waist down, and one arm was slung over his eyes, while the other hung over the side.

Taking care not to wake him, she pulled the blanket up over his chest and resisted the urge to kiss his forehead. His skin had the same sensitivity as his father. One of the reasons she was happy they lived where it was dark all the time.

Entering the scrubber, she washed off the sour sweat and tossed on her soft nightie. Snuggling under the covers, Eliza grabbed her small portable computer and pulled up the book she'd been reading. She'd found a number of paranormal romances in the shared library and found them quite amusing. Not one of them came even close to an accurate portrayal of being with the undead.

Keeper Sat did not want to transport Cameron off world. "Makes me toes curl and me sides turn." Instead he'd been taken to the main hub. "Ask for Shiek," Sat instructed before vanishing.

Shiek lived on the outskirts of town, in an old military bunker. Climbing down the ladder into a deep dark narrow tunnel unnerved Cameron, even more so when his shoes encountered water reaching his ankle. His cloak jerked, and he yanked back. "Stop that."

"Stop what?" a croaky voice echoed out of the dark.

"I seek Shiek," he replied instead of answering the question.

"I'm Shiek."

Cameron started, surprised the keeper was beside him. He frowned, surprised the keeper proved to be short and small. Whirling greens, mixed with yellow, covered its body.

"I'm Cameron," he introduced himself.

"You're a sorcerer."

"I am." His cloak pulled at him, and he hissed at it. The fabric gave him an insolent slap and then behaved. "I need to go to Io."

"You do, do you?" Shiek cackled.

"I'm seeking a lost person." No need to lie, even if it were not the full truth.

"Io bad place. Worst colony." A grin split the green face. "Take you to Mars. Much better there."

"I don't have time to catch a ship." He put one foot on the ladder. "Take me to Io or I find another keeper."

Shiek laughed. "Won't find another keeper, or else you wouldn't have come to me."

Those words froze him. Was that true? Would another keeper refuse to take him off world? "Why?"

"Farther from Earth, weaker the magic." Shiek narrowed slanted eyes at him. "You should know sorcerer."

No, he didn't know.

"That's why they go. The humans. No magic out there." Shiek scratched its arm. "You on one way mission. No come home."

Stunned, Cameron stood there absorbing what the keeper had told him. He'd never heard of anyone from the various colonies returning to Earth. Did the king know, and was that why he'd wanted to send Cameron?

"Who send?" Shiek demanded.

"The king."

"King bad." The colors around Shiek twirled faster. "Hungry soon. No more prey."

The red eyes! How could Cameron have missed the obvious clue?

"More and more humans leave every day." Shiek poked a nail on Cameron's chest. "I take them. Gonna leave us creatures here. Be free. Live longer." The keeper peered up at him. "Sure you want to go?"

"There's no way back?" He wanted the point clarified.

"Not unless they build ship." A brief silence followed. "I not know."

Nor did Cameron, and he could be risking his life for a one-way trip. "I have to think."

"No take long. King know humans leave. And he's hungry."

Eliza sensed the stir of magic and woke from her fuzzy dreams. She sat up and looked around her room. The feeling had been close, but not inside her quarters. Tossing on a robe she quietly checked on her son, who still slept and stepped out into the hall.

A figured lurched down the hall, and she sensed he was a sorcerer. "How did you get here?"

"Same way you did." He stopped and stared at her. "Your Highness." He bowed.

"Not anymore."

"The king sent me to find you."

"The king sent you to leave a trail so he could track his precious food source." She glared at him. "He doesn't care if I'm found or not."

The man looked puzzled. "He told me you stole his son."

"He's lying." Her eyes searched his. "Were his eyes red?"

"Yes."

"Means he's starving." She found satisfaction in that. "Come." Eliza pulled the man inside and touched her finger to her lips. He nodded his understanding, and she led him into her room. "We're almost ready to leave."

"Leave?"

"Io and all the other colonies." She smiled. "The ships are almost ready."

"Ships?" He sat on her bed.

"Ships," she confirmed. "We're leaving the solar system."

"Going where?"

"We found a habitable world." She glanced at the door. "I'll no longer be the king's enticed."

"Enticed?" The man sounded angry. "I had no idea, cousin."

"Cousin?"

He nodded and rose to his feet. "My name is Cameron. Our mothers are distant cousins."

Explained a great deal. "You'll stay with me until we leave."

"Thank you."

Everyday Cameron watched to make certain the king did not come through and try to stop the mass exodus in the final stage of preparation. He'd seen the ship, nestled in a canyon, attached to the base by a long vacuum tunnel. Eliza had trained him how to get into a protector suit, but assured him when the time came, there would oxygen pumped inside so they could all escape.

He felt the tingle of magic and raced to the spot. Shiek stood there, shackled to the king. The keeper moaned, keeping its eyes on the metal floor.

Without regard for his own welfare, Cameron pulled the alarm and sealed the section.

The king grinned. "I can get out."

With a smug look, Cameron retorted. "Not in time."

From her seat on the ship, Eliza looked back as Io retreated into the darkness. Eight hundred souls had escaped. Ten had stayed behind to fight the king's guard, who tried to enter the tunnel as they boarded the ship. She knew the plan. Let them enter and then empty the space to vacuum.

"You'll be missed cousin," she whispered. "And thank you for your sacrifice."

A puff of magic, and a body dropped on her floor. The cloak crossed its ends, and she could feel its smugness.

"Annoying cloak," Cameron groaned rising to his feet.

"The king?" she asked.

"As close to dead as he can be. No way back to Earth. No air. No food."

"And with any luck, he'll never be found." Magical creatures never left Earth. They'd been left behind to either survive or perish. The choice was theirs. Humans had made their decision and embraced their future.

"To the future," Eliza breathed.

With a grin her cousin agreed," To the future."

Fredrick stood in the shadows and listened to the adults. What his mother didn't know was he had begun to drink blood. With a grin, he realized he would have as much food as he needed in order to survive.

The humans were all his.

And he would be king.

About the Author

Owned by two cats Taj and Esther, Dana Bell often uses felines in her various tales. She is notorious for mixing genres and tying her various universes together. These include her Winter Trilogy, Five Systems/Borders and vampire cats. Currently she has three books released *Bast's Chosen Ones*, *Winter Awakening* and *God's Gift*. She is an editor as well with seven anthologies compiled and published. Belle Blukat is the pen name she uses for Paranormal Romances. Her first novel *Blood Bride* will be released soon. Hobbies include, flower arranging, making candle holders, soap, and building/decorating dollhouses.

The Cartomancer

by

Tim Newton Anderson

The Cartomancer

I am a map maker, but my master was a Cartomancer.

I take old charts, scribbled drawings, journal descriptions, and the ramblings of sailors and explorers, and try to draw maps which detail the world as it is.

My master can take a pen and ink, both blessed in arcane rituals, and produce a map of places that have never been, but through his artifice, become. Old voyagers, when they reached the limit of their knowledge, used to write "here be monsters" on their maps to indicate this terra incognita. If my master writes "here be monsters," then monsters there will be.

In the seven years since I became his apprentice, I have asked him several times how he does it. At first he would just say that it was none of my business. My job was to do whatever he directed, and not to ask questions. After a couple of years, he would simply say "magic" and leave it at that. In the past two years he had started to prepare me to follow in his footsteps, having taught me the basic art of ordinary mapmaking, and he had begun to explain that there are more worlds than one. The art and magic he wrought (as one of a small number of Cartomancers) built bridges between the worlds, and, rather than creating the landscapes and creatures he drew, he was allowing them access to our world.

We did not advertise my master's true vocation. As far as most of the world was concerned, we were simple mapmakers, producing charts for sailors and those planning new construction or new military campaigns. Only a few cognoscenti were aware of the full range of my master's abilities, and they came cloaked and disguised to ask him to produce a map of a country where they could find rare treasures or other things they could exploit for their own advancement.

As a rule, these transactions were ones that benefitted both sides, although the rule of caveat emptor was never as true as with my master. He had an impish sense of humour, and, if he did not take to his client, he would ensure any loopholes in the customer's specification were exploited to their disadvantage. The benefit of being one of a very elite group of craftsmen was that there was little choice but to accept whatever he provided.

He also had a strict rule that any lands he created could only exist for a short, fixed period of time. Long enough for the client to visit and retrieve whatever they were searching for, but not so long that they would damage the stability of the rest of the world. A temporary alteration to geography could be accommodated, but leave it in place for too long and the new features would move mountains, bend rivers, and displace seas. At the end of the agreed period, the markings on the map would be erased with another magical fluid, and the new land would cease to exist. However anything brought out of it would be permanently in our world.

I loved working for him and would sit at my drawing table in the window of our shop, charts spread in front of me, copying and refining them to create the most accurate representation of the world I could. Eager though I was to learn the full extent of my master's trade, I still revelled in the more basic tasks assigned to me. I especially loved interviewing our more mundane clients and hearing tales of faraway lands and their explorations. Sometimes my master would sit in on these consultations and bring his immense knowledge to bear on improving my work, but, as often as not, he would be cloistered in his back room, carrying out his secret commissions or conducting the ceremonies needed to create the tools for that work.

At night, we would retire to our quarters above the shop, and I would cook our evening meal while he smoked a relaxing pipe and drank one of the rare wines our clients provided as part of their fees. He especially relished wines not of this world and insisted clients bring some for him from the lands he created for them to visit. If I am honest, many of those wines seemed not designed for human palates and I found them undrinkable, but my master relished them all the more for their bizarre tastes.

As I was clearing the table one night, there was a loud knocking at the front door. Our business hours were clearly stated on the shop sign, and even the most demanding clients had never attempted to access us outside of those. We were also left alone by the civil authorities, as my master's reputation was valued, even if few people knew why. Certainly, local children would never dream of knocking on our door as a joke.

I opened a window and peered down to see who was there. It was winter, and we had no streetlights, so it was impossible to see anything but the dark outline of a man, huddled close to our door. I called out to ask who they were and what was their business, but there was no answer except another loud rapping on the door.

"Go down and find out why they are knocking at this late hour," my master commanded.

To be honest, I did not relish the job. I consider myself an artist, not a man of action. One of the few things I could discern about the person at our door was that they were large—at least two heads taller than I, and I am not a short man. In fact, they were as large as the bear-creature my master created for a client a couple of years ago to add a uniquely exotic touch to his private zoo.

I could not tell if the person was armed, but his stance looked threatening—hulking and bristling, like a dog ready to attack. Still, in the years I had been working here, the worst I had had to deal with was a raised voice when someone did not appreciate my master's humorous additions to their commission.

I lit the oil lamp and carried it with me down the stairs to the workshop. Then, before opening the door, I pulled down and lit the main ceiling lamp so I would have a clear view of our visitor. At present, all I could see was a large looming shadow in the glass, barely differentiated from the darkness behind it. Its clothes were clearly black, or some very dark material, and some kind of scarf covered its face underneath a broad brimmed black hat.

"Who is there?" I asked from our side of the front door.

"A customer," came a gruff voiced reply.

"I'm afraid we are closed," I said. "Our business hours are written on our sign. If you would like to come back tomorrow when we are open, we would be pleased to discuss your commission."

"It's urgent," the person said—a man I thought, by the pitch of the voice— "I need to see your master now."

I was about to turn and go upstairs, to ask if my master would consider seeing the man, when I felt a sharp prick at my neck.

"If you value your life, I would not make too sudden a move," said a female voice. "My stiletto is exceedingly sharp and would spill your life's blood in a second. Reach out and unbar the door, and I will remove it to a safe distance from your throat."

I believed her but also wanted to defend my master. She and her brutish friend outside were clearly not normal customers.

"Why should I open the door?" I asked. "I've told your colleague we are not open."

"Because if you don't, I will kill you and open it myself," she said. "As it is your master we need and not you, I don't care either way. It is your choice."

She was right that I couldn't do anything about the situation with her knife at my throat. If I complied, and she stood away, I would have more options. I reached out and lifted the latch and felt the prick of the blade recede.

I stood away from the door as carefully as I could to avoid a knife in the neck, but allow the man outside to come in. To his credit, he didn't simply barge in, but opened the door slowly and stepped inside with a tread surprisingly light for a man his size. He shut the door behind him quietly, although the only people likely to hear it were already aware of his presence.

"You watch the apprentice, and I'll go and get the Cartomancer," the woman said.

The man grunted assent and drew a long, curved sword from a scabbard at his waist and held it threateningly pointed towards me.

"Sit down at the table," he said, waving the sword at the direction of my work desk. I turned and stepped towards it, looking round to see the woman heading for the ladder that led to our bedroom. In contrast to the massive man, she was small and slim with long black hair tied in a ponytail. She was also dressed completely in black with a scarf covering her face. She moved with the soft tread of a cat as she advanced cautiously up the ladder.

As I said, I am not by nature a physically brave man, but I did look round our shop to see if there was anything I could use as a weapon. Nothing immediately occurred to me, unless I could turn my pens to deadly use. I did not think they would fare well against a big man with a sword. The old saying has no validity in a combat situation.

I heard soft voices from upstairs, and after a minute or so saw my master's feet stepping down, followed by his body and the woman. He was smiling, but knowing him, I wasn't sure if it was because he was happy, being ironic, or because he had a plan which he found amusing. I was hoping it was the last of those.

"Good evening again William," he said. "This young lady seems to think we can help her and her companion with a very special map. I've told her we are simple craftsmen who can prepare all kinds of charts, but this particular request is somewhat out of our normal range of work."

"Cut the lies, old man," she said. "I know you make magical maps. A former colleague told me, after Blane here persuaded him to talk."

"Always good to get a recommendation from a previous client," my master said. "Can you tell me his name so I can thank him?"

"His name wouldn't be useful for you, as he is past caring about thanks," she said. "You can find his body if you want—it's buried a mile or so outside your town, by the side of the road. What's left of him is, anyway. If you fail to do what we ask, we can bury you next to him, if you like."

"If you explain again what you want, William and I can try to help," he said.

"I've told you once," she said.

"Yes, but William needs to hear as well. I need him to assist me, as my eyes are not what they were, and my hands are less agile."

She was clearly not keen on sharing her request but must have decided she would be killing us both anyway, so it didn't matter.

"Very well," she said. "Blane and I need to disappear for a while. There are some people who want to harm us, and the law are the least of them. They have a very long reach, so we need to be somewhere they can't find us, but it also needs to be somewhere where our talents are appreciated and rewarded. I don't want to be stuck hiding out in some backwater scraping a living from the soil. So you and William here need to make us a map to such a place."

"You do appreciate that we can only allow the map of another world to exist for a finite amount of time, to avoid danger to both planes of existence," my master said.

"So your former client said," she said. She was obviously not happy about it, but confirmation left her with little choice. "All the more reason to make it exactly what we need. We also have to be able to get there tonight so the entrance has to be close at hand."

"That is a very great challenge," he said. "The closer to populated areas the junction is, the greater the potential for damage to the world."

"Frankly, we don't really care what damage you do to this world, as we will be leaving it." Her smile was full of disdain and spite.

"I don't suppose there is a fee for this?" he said.

"You get to keep your life," she said.

"That is a given," my master said. "Otherwise, there would be no-one to close the link at this end and your new home would be destroyed as well. And that work needs both of us, as does the map's creation, so don't even think about killing or hurting either of us if you want me to do this successfully."

She considered this for a second. That had obviously been her plan, as she wouldn't want to leave any chance of another map being made to allow her enemies to follow her. We could leave that antinomy for her to work out. However it was clear if we didn't make the map for her—or rather if my master didn't—she would have no reason to keep us alive.

"William," my master said. "Can you open the store cupboard—you will find the key in its usual place under the cushion on my chair—and bring out the partly completed map you find there. It is the one which includes our own front door at the extreme right-hand side of the parchment, leading into a grand pleasure dome."

I had never been allowed to go into the cupboard before. He had always told me it was too dangerous until I was fully initiated in his craft. I trusted him with my life—after all, he had rescued me from my abusive father and treated me with nothing but kindness and respect—so I had never tried to find its key, and it was a bit of a surprise it was in so accessible a place. He obviously trusted me as much as I did him.

The key moved easily in the lock, and, as it opened, I saw the inside was full of pigeonholes filled with parchments. It seemed to be a lot deeper than it appeared from the outside. I took each out in turn until I found the one I needed at the fifth attempt. All the while, the woman was muttering at me to hurry up, while her companion may as well have been carved from stone for all the sound or movement he made.

"Is this it?" I asked my master as I unfurled it for him to see.

"It is indeed William," he said. "If you could spread it out on your worktable and fetch the special ink and pens from the back room, we can make a start."

"I want to see it first," the woman said. "To make sure you are not attempting to trick me."

"By all means," said my master, waving her towards my desk and the unrolled map. "As you will see there is a shared door between this house and the large pleasure palace which will be yours once you cross over. The scale is a bit tricky, working with individual buildings as well as the wider landscape, but you can see there are rich farmlands surrounding the palace, a sea full of fish nearby, and a short distance away is a city which will be full of your servants. Whoever occupies the palace is lord of all the land."

"And what about other lands?" she asked. "Are they full of enemies who will attempt to take my kingdom from me? I do not trust you old man."

"I can assure you there will be no enemies to worry about. No monsters to threaten you, no schemers within your own court—assuming you can trust Blane. I created it a number of years ago, but could not have made a more perfect place for you if I had been told then of your requirements."

"And why did you create it?" she asked. "Come to think of it, why are you not making a new map especially for me?"

"It takes many, many, days to create one of my special maps," he said. "You told me you were in a hurry, so I thought it best to use one I had already part-prepared for just such an exigency."

She grunted. Blane still stood impassively by the door. At first glance, he would seem the more dangerous, as he filled the doorway with his over-muscled physique and a sword he was obviously skilled in the use of. However, it was the woman I was more afraid of. She was on edge and clearly wanted to hurt someone to ease her frustration. That made her unpredictable and therefore far more deadly.

I examined the map I had spread on the desk. It was unlike any I had seen before. Even my master's magical maps looked like ordinary charts, if you did not notice the unknown features and names. This was more like the drawing of an artist than a map. Perhaps it was one of my master's early creations, before he had developed his art fully. As he said, the scale was inconsistent, with the pleasure palace being larger than it would be, given the size of the area covered by the rest of the landscape. Still, I was sure he knew what he was doing, so I went into our back room to get the inks, brushes, and pens, having explained my movements so the woman knew what I was doing and would not try to interfere.

My master was sitting at my desk and had pulled over a stool for me to occupy at his side. The woman stood behind us so she could observe everything, while Blane still stood unblinkingly at the door. I placed the drawing tools on the table and awaited instructions.

For the next few hours, I was concentrating too hard on the work to even think about the woman and the danger she posed. My master instructed me to colour in sections of the map as if it were an ordinary chart, but, as soon as the brush touched the parchment, I could feel the power in the paint and paper. A tingling ran up through my fingers and arm, and travelled up my shoulders and neck to blossom in a golden light behind my eyes that illuminated the map with an inner luminescence. The lines seemed to dance, except where I was working. However, as I coloured each section, it became fixed and certain. Although the scale was still different on different areas, this seemed less and less strange as we progressed, and it was more and more like a mundane map of our world. Even though the features did not exist in our universe, they seemed to be every bit as real as those that did. My master used his pen to thicken lines and add new details, as if this anchored the place in reality by chains of ink.

All at once I knew it was finished. Though there would be little change a non-initiate could discern, having worked on the map, I could sense its completion. My master sat back in the seat and turned to look at the woman who had been standing impatiently behind us, tapping her stiletto against the fingers of her other hand.

"Everything is prepared," my master said. "As soon as you open the front door, the pleasure palace will be on the other side. When you close the door, you can spend ten minutes looking round and come back if it does not meet your needs. After that I will have to destroy the map to close the connection and prevent both worlds being destroyed."

"And how do I know that will not destroy the world on the other side of the door?" she asked.

"It is not a world I can create and destroy," he said. "What the maps do is to create a link between another world which exists and ours. There are an infinite number of universes—everything we can imagine exists somewhere, and there are philosophers who have speculated what we think is imagination is simply our unconscious minds visiting those worlds. By destroying the map, I simply close the temporary link between our world and that one."

She did not look convinced, but she realised she had little choice but to take my master at his word.

"Blane, open the door and step through to the other side," she commanded. "When you are there check that everything is as the Cartomancer described and is safe and then come back and report. I can then feel safe to follow."

My master's face fell. She was more clever and cautious than he had expected, clearly. She saw this, too, and smiled.

"You were not expecting that, were you?" she said. "In fact, I think we will send your apprentice through first to be doubly sure there are no traps.

I looked at my master for reassurance. He nodded.

"There is nothing on the other side of the door that can harm you," he said. "It is all exactly as I described and as you can see on the map. But by all means test it out."

Blane opened the door, and he indicated with a wave of his sword that I was to get up and go through.

There was no feeling of transition as I walked through the door, and, as I looked back, I could see our shop with no distortion, so I felt assured I would be able to re-enter our world if I needed to.

I stepped further into the new world and looked around in amazement. There was a broad marble floor stretching away on all side. The space was empty for a dozen yards apart from the doorway, which seemed to stand free on the floor. There was nothing behind the portal if I moved around it. The vast space was covered with a glass dome at least 100 feet above my head. At intervals on the marble floor there were trees reaching up towards the glass, and further away were brightly coloured gardens. A river snaked its way through the building.

"Go further in," the woman commanded. "Walk to where you can see outside and tell me what is there."

I walked across the floor past some of the clumps of trees towards the gardens. After five minutes progress I found the floor fell away from a viewing platform overlooking the profusion of plants, where the river dropped in a waterfall and presumably fed a fountain that sprayed rain and mist across the flowers and bushes.

There was a heady scent rising from the blossoms, which was almost intoxicating. I could now see further across a plain, which stretched outside the pleasure palace, and looked over rich fields leading down to a sea which seemed to stretch onwards forever. Exactly as it had shown on the map.

By the side of the viewing platform, there were comfortable seats and tables laden with exotic foodstuffs, as well as goblets of wine and other delicious drinks fit for a monarch.

I walked back to the door, which I was pleased to see still opened into our workshop with my master, the woman, and Blane standing on the other side.

"It's exactly as expected," I said.

The woman told Blane to come through the door and check on my report. He waved the sword at me and indicated I was to walk ahead of him. He was obviously a man of few words.

We retraced my earlier journey and also walked round other areas of the floor before returning to the doorway.

"Seems all right," Blane said. "The apprentice was telling the truth, as far as I can see."

"I don't wish to hurry you," said my master, "but it has now been more than quarter of an hour since the doorway was opened, and I cannot guarantee the safety of the worlds if it stays open for much longer. I don't mind if you go through it, but it needs to be closed fairly soon."

"Are you sure you are telling me the truth?" the woman in black asked. "Your former client said he had been in the magic country for two weeks."

"As I said," said my master, "the danger increases the closer the gateway is to populated areas. I normally draw the bridge between the worlds in places that are seldom visited and where dangerous changes would happen more slowly. As I said, you can trust me or not, but I cannot allow a dangerous link to persist—even at the risk of my own life."

This seemed to make up her mind, and she walked to the door, pulling me back into our world and stepping through into the pleasure palace. As she closed the door, she took something from her bag and threw it into our workshop. I recognised it as a grenade.

Heedless of my own safety I leapt at the grenade as it bounced across the floor and ran with it to our front door. As I opened it, the street was beyond as it always had been. I threw the grenade out, slammed the door, and waited for the explosion.

Which didn't come.

"The portal ensures nothing dangerous can travel through it," my master said. "The grenade was disabled as soon as she went through the door."

"Thank you for saving me," I said. "I know you could very well have completed the map by yourself, and you included me so they wouldn't harm me."

"It was also a good opportunity for you to learn," he said. "I felt you were ready."

"Thank you for that, too," I said. "I am only sorry they have escaped whatever justice or retribution they were fleeing. I am sure it would have been well deserved."

"Do not assume because I gave them what they asked for, they got what they wanted," he said. "I assume you noticed the irregularities with the scale on the map?"

"Of course," I said. "I had no idea you could do that."

"You cannot," he said. "The scale was exactly correct. Everything outside the pleasure palace was exactly to the same scale as it appeared on the map. The fields and the sea are all tiny, although perspective meant you could not tell the difference between something big, but far away, and something small and close. I created the drawing for a poet, to help him realise a vision he had, without intending to turn it into a magic map. That was why we had to spend those hours adapting and finishing it.

"I am not a petty man, but I would have enjoyed watching their discovery of just how small a world they now inhabit. The food will soon be eaten and the tiny plants that exist in the fields outside will never sustain them, even if they can communicate with the miniature farmers."

I smiled. This had been a very good day after all. I could not wait to start the next phase of my apprenticeship.

I have been a map maker, but soon I would be a Cartomancer.

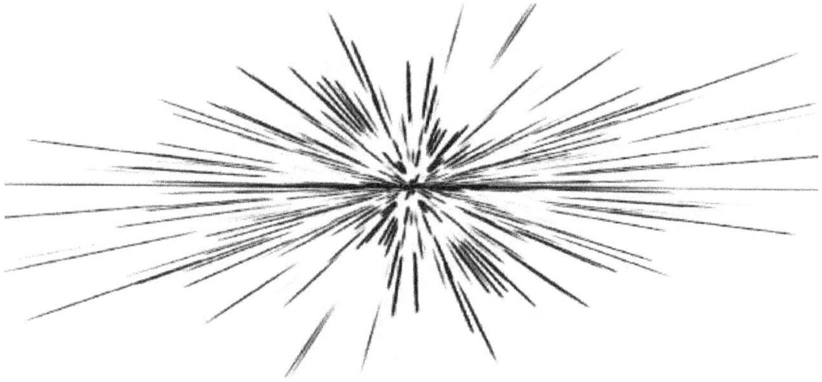

About the Author

Tim Newton Anderson is a former senior daily newspaper journalist and PR executive who recently started writing, including a self-challenge to write at least one story a week during lockdown. So far 15 of these have been accepted for publication. When not writing he plays guitar, blues harmonica and sings.

Angels and Apnea

by

David Boop

Angels and Apnea

I die for two minutes every night, and I wake one step closer to hell each time.

At thirty-seven years old, I'm still scared of the dark. Not because of some imagined boogie man in the closet. My fear doesn't come from bad dreams brought on by spicy food or all-night horror-thons. You see, after I start breathing again…

I'm no longer alone.

<u>Cam</u>

"I look like Darth Vader—without the helmet."

The sleep study center lab tech smiled politely. I'm sure it wasn't the first time he'd heard the joke, or some variation of it. I've got electrodes on my temples, under my nose, at the sides of my mouth, and all over my chest, arms and legs. Every step I take, every twitch I make, they are recording me.

Their instructions suggested I get up early and said not to take any naps. Not a problem considering my job keeps me on my feet all day. I stock and merchandise kiosks for a big-name battery manufacturer. Glamorous, I know. Even have a replica of their never-ending mascot on my desk at home.

"Okay, Mr. Hagadon. I need you to lie back and get comfortable. I'll be talking to you from the other room. If you need anything, just call out, and I'll come in."

I gave my best puppy dog eyes. "Will you read me a story? I can't sleep without a story." That should've have cracked him up. If there's one thing I no longer am, it's cute. My raccoon-like eye sockets are dark from decades of poor sleep.

My joke wrought the polite smile again. Maybe he'd heard that one too many times, as well. Guess calling out for a glass of water after the lights went down would be in bad form.

It wasn't until I got married that my wife noticed that I occasionally stopped breathing throughout the night. Freaked her out the first time. Always the wanna-be doctor, she brought home pamphlets labeled things like "Sleep Apnea and You!" Five years and a divorce later, I'd only recently read them.

"You need to radically change your lifestyle, Cam," my doctor lamented. "Apnea weakens the heart. Remember that football player, Reggie White? That's what he died of."

That meant no more white bread, cutting down on salt, and going to see a sleep specialist. Now, feeling like an extra for the Matrix, I laid down to try to sleep on command and...

Ensar

Ensar studied his partner Altros, who stared at his own reflection in the demon blood pooling below his feet. The archangel's long blond hair had matted flat with the same liquid. His chest, loincloth, and sandals were similarly stained. The only things not covered in gore were his black wings, tucked in tight against his back as was common during a ground assault, which also kept them free from being struck by an arrow or sword. Ensar had positioned his the same.

Stepping over the last slain demon, Altros approached the Vault of Souls doorway tentatively. Ensar quietly motioned him to stop and then took two cautious steps forward himself.

Altros whispered, "I believe this was a diversion."

"You think they're already to the vault?" Ensar asked.

Altros nodded.

"Then why are we whispering?"

Ensar had a way of pointing out the obvious that made him the perfect "wingman" for Altros. He had Altros's back even when all the other angels wrote him off ages ago.

Altros was Heaven's version of a human conspiracy nut, making him a pariah amongst their brethren. Any peculiar or odd happening must be a sign of the ever-impending final war.

Archangels, while serious in the execution of their jobs, preferred to spend their off-hours in the pursuit of pleasure and relaxation. Ensar, known for his cherub-like demeanor, had been legendary in that regard. But then he was re-assigned to Altros, and free time became an ancient thing. Whenever they were off duty, Altros wanted to follow up on some portent or sign of the rapture.

At first, Ensar questioned even the attempt.

"Don't you recall? 'No man should know the day of my returning?' "

"We're not men," Altros replied.

Resigned to his fate, Ensar came to understand that Altros, while seemingly an angel short of a heavenly host, had keen intuition. Several of their unofficial investigations did bear further looking into. Despite this, the Apostles had questioned his decision to stay with Altros, knowing how hard it'd been for anyone to work with the rogue angel. Ensar replied that if no human soul was to be abandoned, then no angel should be either. He joined Altros's apocalyptic theories, taking them in stride, following his partner down each loose thread.

Ensar swallowed hard. If the demons were actually in the Spirit Vault, maybe "The End" had begun.

Demons knocked at the vault on a regular basis, although they never made it through the door. The best archangels were always there to protect it. Altros, his instincts predicting something big coming on the horizon, brought the two of them there that day. Outside the vault, they found several dead Guardians and a legion of living demons. A bloody onslaught left the two archangels victorious, but Ensar had to agree with his partner: they'd been patsies from the get-go.

As they moved to the door, they found the anti-demon seal broken. Somehow, while the guardian angels battled a horde of lesser demons, something had gotten through.

The interior hallway held no torches, no lights, yet the ethereals could see perfectly. A warrior's senses were gifted to each archangel upon their creation, yet none had more wisdom than what they earned in the service of God. Covering each other, Ensar and Altros leap-frogged their way down into the depths of the vault. They passed many witness rooms. As Ensar had never been in the vault before, he looked in to see if the rumors were true.

Cloudlike eternal souls of the previously departed hovered over a glowing orb, making them look like the atmosphere covering a planet. They sung praises to the Creator and ministered to a spirit within the sphere. The spirit pulsed and shone brighter.

Altros tapped Ensar's shoulder, bringing the guardian's attention back to the mission.

"They won't be holed up in any of the witness rooms. These spirits are active."

"But why would they seek the inactive spirits room?"

Ensar didn't see any benefit to stealing souls that were so jaded they served no allegiance to the Holy Father nor to the demon kind.

"Depends on who the spirit belongs to. In demon hands, what might be an inactive spirit to us could be corrupted into a soul for Satan's army."

Ensar shuddered. Inactive souls drifted through life, until such time they died. But to take an inactive soul and corrupt it, well…that took their free will away. Some poor human might wake up one day and not understand why he suddenly had an urge to kill an office full of people or run for political office.

After passing many witness rooms, the duo descended to the inactive spirits level. The supposedly impenetrable door to the storeroom was ajar, barely hanging upright by its hinges.

As they stepped through the opening, no rumor could have prepared them for what they found.

Faintly glowing soul orbs sat abandoned on miles of shelves. Millions of orbs. One for each lost soul, and too many to search through.

A moan leaked from an alcove just inside the warehouse. Well, less of a moan and more a strangled hymn. Rushing over, they found the broken form of Odtasear, the storeroom's guardian. Blood burbled in his throat as he tried to keep singing with a sucking chest wound.

Altros dropped to the floor and cradled the angel who couldn't stop singing long enough to tell what had happened. It didn't matter. They knew who their enemy sought. So many signs and only Altros had seen what they meant. Now, another of their brothers lay dying.

Ensar knelt next to them. "If Odtasear stops singing, we lose all the inactives, don't we?"

The inactive souls storeroom guardian was an angel chosen to minister to all the lost souls alone. It was a singular honor and once chosen, they could never stop.

His partner nodded. "All these spirits will feel, in that moment, that God has abandoned them. There'll be mass suicides, murders, even genocide. The song keeps them connected to Heaven, regardless if they hear it or not. If that were to stop…"

Tears forming at the edges of his eyes, Ensar looked to the dying angel. "Was that their plan?"

Altros shook his head. "No, this is another distraction while they find the soul they're looking for."

Ensar wiped away his tears and began to sing, matching his voice and words to that of Odtasear. Altros grabbed his shoulders.

"Ensar, no! They'll send someone down to replace him. I can't do this without you."

Ensar didn't break his growing song, but within his eyes, he told Altros he believed in him. The hymn faded from Odtasear's throat, and Ensar carried it onward. Transforming from an archangel into a seraphim, Ensar smiled sadly and nodded a goodbye to his friend.

Altros

Determination welled up in Altros as he moved through the racks. He'd never admit it, but Ensar's friendship is what had reined him in all these centuries, kept him from going overboard. A friend will make you choose carefully what you say or do. With that limiter gone, Altros freely went into full avenging angel mode.

He leapt into the air, unfurled his wings and drew his sword. The blade ignited with a *woosh,* and the flames echoed his rage.

Cam

When I opened my eyes, I floated in midair.

Actually, "floated" didn't quite capture the experience. I bounced, as if I were being carried under someone's arm. Someone who ran as if Satan was on his tail. I looked to the left to see a forearm and the inside of an elbow. I tried to look at myself, and found nothing, no body to gaze at.

Shit! I'd died and been reincarnated as a football! Damn those Buddhist bastards! Spiked in the end zone of eternity! I took a moment to consider my situation. Maybe I would be the game winning ball of a Superbowl? That'd give my life meaning.

I found I could move some and spun around until I could see who was carrying me.

If I'd still had a bladder, I would have unloaded it.

The creature embodied every evil trope Dante dreamed up in a nightmare. It had eyes where eyes shouldn't be—not that its eyes looked human. They were bisected and yellow, peering at everything and nothing. Its body oozed puss and bile from orifices like miniature volcanoes. On its massive head, a razor-toothed maw filled the entire space where a face should be, and ram horns sat on either side.

I wanted to vomit. I wanted to break free of its grasp. I squirmed, rolled and twisted. I was in some sort of orb; escape was impossible.

The demon slid to a stop when a golden beam of light struck the ground in front of us, causing it to fall back on its haunches. Prone, I could tell my demon running back had four cloven hooves, and it held me under one of its six massive arms.

Its eyes rolled up to see what attacked us.

I had a sudden rush of relief and a weird burst of adoration that I feel must be akin to what Jimmy Olsen felt when he saw Superman soaring to the rescue.

An angel, with large, glorious, black wings, swooped down at heroic speed while brandishing a flaming sword that caused extreme trembling and panic in the demon-like thing holding me. I thought it might drop me and flee. Instead, it dove forward at the last moment, ducking under the sword. I thought I smelled singed flesh.

You know…if I had a nose.

When the demon hit the floor, it did, indeed, drop me. Ever wonder what it's like to be a bowling ball? Yeah, you try not to puke.

Suddenly, I stopped rolling and I opened my eyes to the real world once more.

The funny-bone lacking sleep study tech pressed repeatedly on my chest—hard—panic evident in his eyes.

Wait. Was he giving me CPR?

"What the…" I croaked out. In hindsight, maybe croak wasn't the best choice of words.

An EMT stood on the other side of my bed. She placed a stethoscope on my now rising and falling chest. She smiled, looking relieved, and nodded to the tech.

I sat up woozily. "What happened?"

"Something went wrong," my tech said apologetically. "We lost you for almost two minutes."

I blinked, confused. "That's why I'm here. The apnea. I know this already."

The EMT shook her head. "No, Mr. Hagadon. I don't think you understand. Yes, apnea causes you to stop breathing, but the body's own self-preservation instinct will normally cause you to roll over or wake up, whatever to get you breathing again."

The tech looked at me solemnly. "You didn't just stop breathing. Your heart stopped beating. You were clinically dead."

While I digested that, the EMT ran battery of tests and, when everything checked out as normal, I was given the choice of going to the ER or going home. It was strongly recommended that I go to the ER, but I chose to go home.

I showered twice as long as I normally did; water bill be damned. Gel globs lingered on me in a dozen places from those electrodes, and I'd never get back to sleep feeling sticky. Once I felt clean, I changed the sheets on my bed for no explicable reason.

I also went commando. Full commando. Not my normal modus operandi, I assure you. I hadn't gone to bed naked since my first year of marriage.

Something inside me was off. If I hadn't been exhausted to the point of collapse, I might've done some serious soul searching to find out what it was. Instead, I chose to let the black take me again.

Altros

Altros swung around for another pass. The demon dropped the orb-bound soul. It rolled down the aisle and the angel caught wind of a full, conscious soul inside.

That shouldn't have been possible.

All spirits were connected to their orb until time of death when they either crossed into the Kingdom of Heaven or descended into Hell. Inactive souls have only the smallest of tethers and certainly wouldn't contain a full soul. The Lamb's Book stated that Cameron Hagadon wouldn't be judged for nearly a dozen years yet.

So it was written and couldn't be changed.

What had the evil spawn done to wake an inactive soul?

Then, as quickly as it had been activated, Hagadon returned to his previous state.

Altros deduced that the soul's dirt shell must have suffered some sort of trauma, dying briefly, and then had been resuscitated. Those types of events didn't end up in the Book of Life; only births, deaths, and status at time of death were scrawled within its pages. The events in-between were listed in a human's personal Book of Days, and angels were never allowed access to that.

The demon scooped up the orb and resumed its escape.

Why? Why risk a fight with an archangel over one tragic soul?

When Hagadon returned to active status a few moments later, Altros finally understood.

Cam

Laying on my side, I planned to forget the sleep lab folly with the bliss of slumber. It seemed I lay there for an hour, however, when I rolled over to look at the clock, barely five minutes had passed.

I tried emptying my mind, only to find the space filled with a dozen eclectic images. I focused on one; that angel I'd dreamt about. Majestic, he was reminiscent of Angel from the X-Men, only with black hair and wings. The original Angel, not the blue one with silver wings. The flaming sword the angel had wielded added a nice touch to the dream.

I considered my years in Campus Crusade. The bibles they handed out were big on imagery with lots of illustrations. Guess they were trying to reach the comic book generation. After college, I can't remember ever opening that bible again, yet there in my undead state, was an image straight out of it.

But the creature? I'd never seen anything like that before. Not even in a Del Toro film.

I yawned.

What a hideous,

disgusting

demon.

And in a flash, I saw the creature again. Both it and the angel.

Fighting.

Slashing.

Clawing.

Bleeding.

One of the demon's severed arms lay on the ground near my orb. That left five to grapple with the angel and doing a fair job of it. The stump where its arm had been was cauterized thanks to the flaming sword, which was keeping the creature from bleeding out.

But like most evil things, it cheated. In three of its massive paws it held other orbs, similar to the one I was in, and threw the occasional one into the air, forcing the angel to react.

With amazing aerial acrobatics, the angel would have to catch the orb less it hit the ground, which left his side open for the creature to attack. It rent the angel's flesh in such an efficient manner that I thought it must have been designed just to kill angels.

However, my angel flipped upside down at the next orb toss, catching the sphere with his feet, and slashing the midriff of the demon as he spun. The creature's unholy scream shook the whole room and gore spilled from the wound.

And then the demon glanced over and saw me looking at it. We locked eyes.

Me, just two. It with all of them.

"No!" the angel cried out, having obviously miscalculated the fatality of his disemboweling.

The demon became translucent, hollow, almost the same as the mist form I'd become, only darker, like storm clouds.

I scanned for my warrior angel, and he'd become an outline, almost like a pencil sketch.

Both cartoon and evil mist launched at me. I couldn't tell which one of them would reach me first, so I closed my eyes…

And drew in a breath again.

I spilled over the side of my bed and grabbed a trashcan under my nightstand. I vomited. I emptied more food than I could remember eating. My throat burned as the puking turned to dry heaves. I pulled myself and stumbled into to the bathroom, lapping at sink water from cupped hand. My skin had blanched, and my eyes were more deep-set and darker than normal. After taking a handful of Tums, I returned to my room.

Just as the demon from my nightmare climbed out from my puke-filled trashcan.

Altros

Altros squirmed. The sensation of being a passenger in someone else's body unnerved him, the control freak that he had become. He attempted to move his arms and legs, with no luck at all.

Angels inherently knew how to possess a human vessel, but it was rarely done these days and was frowned upon from up on high. Human free will was the second of God's gifts, after life itself, and thus could not be compromised without serious repercussions.

It was only by grace that the archangel made it to Hagadon's soul first, allowing him to expel the demon from the vessel's body. However, this presented a different problem. A corporeal monster could kill Cameron Hagadon, thus killing Altros. The demon already showed a propensity for killing angels and wouldn't hesitate to kill a human.

The Earthbound demon had already reverted back to its original size, crushing the vessel's bed, knocking over lamps and pictures on shelves. It also grew back its severed arm.

Altros needed control over Hagadon. For the moment, he could only give instruction.

"Dodge left, NOW!"

Without thinking, the vessel dove to the left. He didn't have the ability of an angel, though, and the demon claw-raked Hagadon near his hip. Hagadon screamed, nerves on fire, and pain shooting through Altros, as well.

"Vessel, Run! Get out of the house! I need room to fight."

Hagadon stopped.

Altros guessed the vessel misinterpreted the first command to be his conscience telling him what to do. He was unprepared for that inner voice to be sentient.

"Who?"

"Run! Just run! We'll discuss the rest later!"

The demon couldn't easily maneuver around the room. It got its back legs tangled in the vessel's pile of dirty clothes and fell forward. Hagadon bolted, barely dodging another attempt to slice him open, but then he stumbled down the steps; blunt pain came with each tumble.

Hagadon, as a vessel, would be inadequate for Altros.

"You are overweight! How do you expect to evade a demon if you cannot evade stuffed crust pizzas every other night? You're clumsy and already winded."

Hagadon scanned in a circle, then looked up to the ceiling. "Who gave you the right to judge my lifestyle? For that matter, who gave you permission to be in my head?"

"God, the Almighty. The Creator."

The vessel froze again, jaw agape.

He started running again when the demon busted out of his room and, hunched over, moved down the stairs. Hagadon got through the front door before the creature reached the bottom floor.

Once outside, he picked up the pace, but Altros could tell he only had a block or two in him before he'd collapse.

"I need control. Your heart will give out at this rate."

"Who. Are. You?" Hagadon asked between huffed breaths.

"For now, I am your guardian. I came through your spirit portal with the demon. Only, I'm stuck in your body."

"Why. Me?"

"That's a much longer story than we have time for. Will you let me fight for you?"

Hagadon limped now, holding his side and hip. The breathing became gasping lungfuls that would do nothing to save either of them.

"What. Do. You. Mean?"

"Let me have control of your dirt shell."

"My WHAT???"

If the angel could have shaken his head, he would have. Instead, Altros lost his calm. "Listen you bag of meat, hear that demon pounding asphalt behind us? It'll be here in seven seconds. Now, repeat after me!"

Cam

I was going to die, painfully, naked in the middle of the street, ripped to shreds by a demon I'd apparently brought to the real world. Even more unbelievable than that, I knelt down in the middle of the street and prayed right before it reached me.

Ironically, I can't think of a better time to pray.

"Lord, let ministering angels protect me in my time of need. I give you my will to see yours done."

I couldn't move. I no longer had any control of my body, much as I'd been in that frickin' celestial Poké Ball. I'd taken a back seat to the angel I'd been fascinated with earlier.

And I got real sexy, real quick.

I could see my arms had buffed out and my hair, long and blond draped over my ripped chest.

Oh, and I could fly. So, there were benefits to this arrangement, given.

The angel wove a mystic incantation and my new, superhuman body manifested the sword I'd seen him wield in my dream. Once the hilt touched my hand—er, his hand? Our hand? Well, the sword burst into flames, regardless.

We hovered high above the road, and the tips of our black wings peeked in and out of the corners of our eyes. We dove at the creature like eagles hunting prey, making me want to puke again. We skimmed inches over the street, and he, the angel, drug the sword into it, melting blacktop, and sending a cascade of sparks in our wake.

Remembering his mistake from before, where he cauterized the demon, the angel turned off the flames right before an upward swing. I knew the angel's thoughts as we shared one mind.

The demon now had arms only on the right side of its body, thanks to us. It howled, and I thought the whole neighborhood would wake up.

The angel answered as if I'd spoken aloud.

"I have created a shield of the Holy Spirit around the area. No one will see or hear our battle."

The voice didn't sound like mine. I didn't sound so Vin Diesel-ly when I talked.

The lopped-off stumps gushed fountains of gray blood. Or, a blood-like substance. Sort of like molten ash. I figured that stuff would be a bitch to clean off your shoes.

"It is," the angel responded, matter-of-factly.

The monstrosity hadn't given up yet. It circled around, bouncing off the invisible barrier my puppeteer had erected. Once it gauged the circumference, it charged at us, barely slipping under the sword's arc. It slid on its own blood and crashed against the shield. It kept at us, challenging us, dodging at the last moment.

"The loss of blood must be making it mad. It doesn't seem to be making any sense. Can't we just put it down and I get my body back?"

"Agreed."

The archangel climbed skyward until it reached the top of his dome. I instinctively knew he wanted to find the best approach to avoid the demon's still deadly right side. When we looked down, we discovered this monster wasn't as crazed as we thought.

It had made a pentagram in its own blood.

"It's trying to break the seal. If it does, it'll escape into the world."

I calmly said, "Stop it. Kill it anyway you can. Don't worry about me."

The notion of dying to save the world didn't come easily, but upon making it, a peace flowed through me. Maybe because there was an archangel using my body. Who knows?

Conversely, the decision to sacrifice my body wasn't even a consideration for my pilot. We swooped in, fangs bared for the kill.

"Thank you, vessel."

"It's Cameron. And you?"

"Altros."

We flew parallel to the ground once more. The creature, sensing our approach, turned from his devil's work to face us.

"Not so close to the ground! We're still naked!"

We rammed the creature at full speed, sword running through its chest, our shoulder smashing against its pustulous skin. Its claws dug into our back as we lifted it up and flattened it against the barrier. There was a resounding splat as it liquefied all over our flesh. It burned us in places, like the acid when you killed a xenomorph from Aliens.

Dozens of eyes flittered to the ground, one projecting a last menacing glare before it, too, dissolved into goo.

We knelt on one knee, breathing hard, pain lancing up and down our spine. The sword, no longer aflame, kept us propped up.

"You are injured." Altros sounded nervous.

"Tell me about it."

"You were injured while doing God's work, while not in control of your body."

"Now you're worried about that?"

"It's forbidden to let you die. We need to get you medical attention."

I laughed.

"And tell them what? See that mess of a house? How do I explain a demon came out of my nightmare, destroyed my place, and did this to me?"

Altros, stood, aimed the sword at my house, and a giant fireball leapt from it.

My house was incinerated.

"What the fuck, man!"

He walked my body over to the opposite side of the road, ignoring the debris as it fell.

All, but one, which we could see coming right at us, but he just turned our back to. The chunk of wall slammed into us, sprawling us out naked on the neighbor's lawn.

"Fuck! You did that on purpose!"

"You have no idea what just happened," he narrated. "You were asleep and woke up here."

I whimpered. "My house. You black-winged asshole! That was my house!"

"What's more important? Material possessions or a believable cover story?"

I would've punched him if he was in anybody else's body but mine.

Fire trucks and ambulances wound their way toward us. My neighbors came out of their houses to find out what the explosion was all about. Someone noticed me on the lawn and yelled for help.

"And you couldn't think of anything else?"

"No."

Luckily, I was face down. An EMT arrived and checked my pulse. I moaned, the pain hitting every cell in my body. Top to bottom.

Wait?

I moaned?

Shit, I was back in control.

"I have to return you to the 'driver's seat.' The wings would have been much harder to explain than the gouges in your side and back."

A blanket was draped over me as EMTs worked on me for the second time that evening.

I wouldn't be getting any sleep anytime soon.

<u>Altros</u>

Humans, Altros reflected, excelled at lying when their backs were against the wall. Torture them, and they'll still tell you only their name, rank, and I.D. number. From Adam's, "She made me do it!" to Nixon's, "I am not a crook!" there were countless examples of really good liars.

Cameron Hagadon's lies would have ranked right up there with the best. He completely convinced the investigators that he knew of nothing that would cause the contained explosion that destroyed his house. The Fire Investigators had already begun a search for the methamphetamine lab they believed to be there, but Cameron didn't have to lie about that. He stuck with his claim that he'd taken some sleeping pills after his shake up at the sleep study center and woke up in his neighbor's yard.

The ER doc backed him up by saying that his drugged state probably saved his life. Unconscious as he was, Cameron would've tensed up causing grievous bodily harm to a person thrown through the air in such a way.

Well, in most cases, she said.

Cameron wondered how many cases there were like that.

Altros answered him, "More than you could conceive."

"So how long are you staying in my head?"

"Because I came way as the demon did, it seems I'm stuck here until you die."

"What?"

Cameron shouted and nurses came running to his side. Seasoned liar that he was, Cameron assured them that he just had a PTSD moment.

"When will that be?"

"Hopefully, no time soon. I need you. There's a war starting, of which you are the first soldier."

"Great. And you can just take over anytime?"

"No," Altros admitted. "Only when you give me control. Or possibly when you die, which seems to happen quite regularly, I take it."

"Yeah. For about two minutes every night."

"I will have to test my limitations and control when that happens. This is uncharted territory. I've never shared a body before."

"Like I have?"

Visibly relaxing, though dreading the answer, Cameron asked, "So, the demon? He came over because of my apnea?"

"No," Altros corrected, "you don't have sleep apnea in the basic sense of the condition. You don't stop breathing because of a small air passage or chest cavity, nor from being too fat."

"Hey!"

"Your condition is something different, unique. Your heart stops. You brain shuts down. Your entire body goes into shock. You are technically dead. Otherwise, your soul wouldn't enter the spirit vault as it does."

That scared Cameron more than the apnea did.

"Will I always wake up? You know, come back to life?"

Altros didn't have an answer to give him. "Until we find out the cause of your regular deaths, I cannot say."

"But you can leave then, right? And I can have my body back?"

"Now that Hell's demons know of your situation, I cannot leave you. You'll be in danger every time you go to sleep."

"What?" This Cameron shouted out loud again. Altros sighed. The vessel had to learn how to take bad news better.

"Sorry," he told the nurses. "Just remembered I have, had, a cat."

The nurses gave him "Oh, no's" and pity and hugged him. He basked in it.

Altros continued explaining, but he was not sure Cameron even listened anymore. "It is rare enough for a demon to actually posses a human. Most demon possessions you read about are fabrications, delusions of the mind. People seeking attention…like you are now."

Cameron straightened up in his bed and tried to wipe the smile from his face after the nurses left.

"What's even rarer is for demons to find a portal in which to cross over physically. That's not been heard of for millennia. That makes your spirit orb desirable to them. If they have it, then they could send whole armies over to this realm through you. And nothing on this plain of existence could stop them."

Altros felt relief when vessel finally showed some concern for the bigger picture. "Holy sh—I mean, that can't be good. Can I do anything to help?"

Altros considered. "You could die…for good, and thus depriving them of the portal." He should have considered his words longer.

Nothing.

"Vessel? Cameron?"

"You're not a real people person, are you?"

"I am not a person at all. I am an ethereal being. I can speak only truth. Lying is what you do."

Ignoring the unintentional jab, Cameron smiled. "So then, God, and angels, and demons; they all exist." A statement, not a question.

"You once believed that readily. You find that so hard to believe now?"

Cameron shrugged. "Well, it's just, well, life happened, and shit happened, and well, it just didn't seem to matter anymore."

The archangel sighed. "It's because of that lukewarm faith that you ended up in the inactive spirits vault."

"The place with all the orbs?"

"Yes. If you had been an active spirit, you would have been monitored closer. As it was, the inactive souls are sung to by a single special angel, who waits for spirits to either become active or souls to go to their final judgment."

The thought of Ensar gave Altros a sharp pain of loss.

"What was that?" Cameron asked, feeling his chest. "I felt an emotion from you. First one, actually."

"My partner, Ensar, gave up his freedom as an archangel when the previous singer died at the hands of the demon you and I just killed. He will have that position now until the apocalypse."

"And he was also your friend." Again, not a question. Cameron was more observant than Altros initially gave him credit for.

"As close to one as we can have. He kept my inner, how would you say it, 'demons' in check. Before him, I had not thought I even needed a partner. Now, I am not sure I know how to go on without him."

"Dude. I'm real sorry for your loss. That bites." The angel knew Cameron's empathy was true. But why should this temporary vessel care about him, especially after all that happened up to that point?

Altros started to understand why the Creator had set humans above ethereals.

"You have a great capacity for compassion, Cameron Hagadon. Even toward someone who has been blunt the point of rudeness. Who put your life in danger and blew up your house."

Cameron crossed his arms and scowled. "You did that, and thanks for the reminder." He lightened up. "Seriously though, you're right. I lost a house, but you lost a friend. And I can tell from your sparkling personality, you probably don't have many of those."

Altros chuckled, which caught him by surprise. He'd seen other angels laugh and considered it such a waste of emotion when so many bad things waited to happen. Now that he tried it, he found it cathartic. The chuckle grew into a good laugh.

Cameron joined him, caught up in the mirth.

When Altros finished, he accepted the thought that Ensar, if he could've seen him laugh, would have been very happy.

Cameron called for a nurse. "Ma'am? I'm going to try and sleep. If for some reason all my lights and bells go off saying I'm flatlining, tell your trauma team not to worry until the two-minute mark. Then, if I don't wake up then, you can do those paddle things on me until I fart lightning."

She stared at him dumbfounded.

"You'll see."

To Altros he said, "Catch you on the other side?"

"Yes, Cameron. It will be a pleasure fighting demons with you."

"You, too, Altros."

Cam

I wished I could see that nurse's face when I flatlined, but I had other concerns at that moment. My orb was no longer in the inactive soul's vault. I was under an arm again, this time hoofing it across a rocky field of despair. Another demon, a female one I surmised by the three breasts she had me tucked next to, had escaped the vault with me. Somewhere, far behind me, I could hear Altros calling out my name.

This was going to be a long two minutes.

About the Author

David Boop is a Denver-based speculative fiction author & editor. He's also an award-winning essayist, and screenwriter. Before turning to fiction, David worked as a DJ, film critic, journalist, and actor. As Editor-in-Chief at IntraDenver.net, David's team was on the ground at Columbine making them the first internet only newspaper to cover such an event. That year, they won an award for excellence from the Colorado Press Association for their design and coverage.

David's debut novel, the sci-fi/noir *She Murdered Me with Science*, returned to print in 2017 from WordFire Press. (Simultaneously, he self-published a prequel novella, *A Whisper to a Scheme*.) His second novel, *The Soul Changers*, is a serialized Victorian Horror novel set in Pinnacle Entertainment's world of *Rippers Resurrected*. David edited the bestselling weird western anthology, *Straight Outta Tombstone*, for Baen, and has followed with *Straight Outta Deadwood* and *Straight Outta Dodge City*. David is prolific in short fiction with many short stories and two short films to his credit. Additionally, he does a flash fiction mystery series on Gumshoereview.com called *The Trace Walker Temporary Mysteries* (the first collection is available now.) He's published across several genres including media tie-ins for Predator (nominated for the 2018 Scribe Award), The Green Hornet, The Black Bat, and Veronica Mars.

David works in game design, as well. He's written for the Savage Worlds RPG for their Flash Gordon (nominated for an Origins Award) and Deadlands: Noir titles. He owns Longshot Productions, a multimedia company specializing in books, games, and short animated videos.

His third go at a "real" degree landed him Summa Cum Laude in the Creative Writing program at UC-Denver. He also is part-time temp worker and believer. His hobbies include film noir, anime, the Blues and Mayan History.

You can find out more at:
Davidboop.com
Facebook.com/dboop.updates
or Twitter @david_boop

Mists of Time

by

Robinne Weiss

Mists of Time

Ow! Turn your brights off." I squinted into the lights of the oncoming car and sipped the tepid coffee I'd picked up in the airport. I didn't really expect the caffeine to keep me awake, but the act of drinking helped.

It had been an exhausting visit. Dad held up well, all things considered. Of course, Mom hadn't really been there for years. For both Dad and me, it had been a bit of a relief when the hospital had called to say she'd passed away.

Relief or not, it had been a crazy week, with relatives coming and going, and all her stuff to deal with, and a funeral to arrange. On top of it, Dad needed to talk. As an only child, guilty of growing up and moving far from home, I felt obliged to sit up late with him, listening to stories of Mom before she got sick.

Not that I didn't enjoy it. I never really knew her before her illness. I was only ten when it started.

Ten. My own kids were nine and eleven. How would they manage if I...?

I sighed. Why was I thinking depressing thoughts? I was in great shape. Besides, even if something *did* happen to me, they'd manage. Lane was great with the kids, just like my dad had been great with me. I imagined how their bedtime ritual had gone this evening and hoped Lane would be waiting up for me with a cup of tea when I got home. Exhausted or not, it would be good to decompress a bit.

I turned off the main road and breathed a sigh of relief. There would be no more idiots with their high beams on, now that I was on the back roads. Few people came this way—Google Maps never suggested it, and its remote feel made city dwellers nervous. I found it relaxing. I rolled down the window and let the cool night air in.

The road snaked among the willows beside the river, and my view narrowed to a green tunnel. The landscape opened up again when I reached the lake, spreading wide in front of me. The moon, high and bright, glinted off the water and lit the open fields to muted grays. I smiled as I passed my favorite farm, with its mixed herd of highland cattle and colored sheep. Most of the animals were grazing in the moonlight. I wondered whether we had room for a couple of those pretty black sheep on our property.

I slowed down as I drove through a patch of fog. These little fog patches were common along the lake edge at night. Someone had once explained to me why they occurred—something about cool air and warm water. I couldn't remember now. The headlights seemed to flicker as the car passed through ropy tendrils of mist.

The fog patches made the drive more challenging. Probably a good thing; a little challenge would keep me awake. I took another sip of coffee and grimaced. It was completely cold.

I rounded a bend, passing through a long patch of fog before making a left turn. The sound under the tires changed to gravel.

That wasn't right.

The way home was paved.

I slowed to a stop, shook my head to clear it, and turned the car around. I must have taken the wrong turn. How had I managed that? Must be the jet lag. I took another swig of cold coffee.

Back at the intersection, I frowned. It *was* the right turn—Lakeside Road. Why was the road gravel? Were they resurfacing it? But there were no construction signs or road cones. I sighed and turned around again. I couldn't wait to get home.

I moved more slowly on the gravel. Dust billowed up in my wake, and soon I had to close the window to keep it out.

I passed through another patch of fog, and the car gave a lurch as it hit a pothole.

"Geeze!" They might be fixing the road, but they'd made a mess of it doing so. I crept forward over the rough and rutted road. Why hadn't Lane warned me not to come this way?

The fog patches grew thicker. I passed through one that seemed to go on forever. When I came out the other side, a tree trunk loomed in front of me. I swore and slammed on the brakes, lurching to a halt.

Turning the car off, I closed my eyes and took a deep breath to stop my shaking. How had I gone off the road? I took another breath.

I was too tired to be driving. I should take a break, text Lane to let him know I'd be a little late.

I opened the car door and stepped out, stretching my neck and swinging my arms. As I looked around, I frowned. Where was I?

Dense trees blocked most of the moonlight. The lake glittered between their trunks.

Trees?

If I'd gone the right way, I should have been driving through pastureland, not a forest. I rubbed my eyes and groaned. I just wanted to be home. I pulled out my phone to check where I was, but the app couldn't identify my location. Figured. Just when I needed it. I sighed. Nothing for it but to turn around. I typed a text to Lane, but it didn't send.

"No service. Really?" I huffed. Fine. I'd just turn around and go back the way I came.

Using my phone as a torch, I scouted the way, a sense of dread creeping up my spine. I seemed to be in a small clearing, but how on Earth had I gotten here? I followed the car's tracks, but they disappeared after about ten yards. The only break in the vegetation around the clearing was a vague path leading away from the lake.

"What is going on?" The trees muffled my voice, making me feel small and alone. A knot began to form in my stomach.

As far as I could tell, there was no way to get my car out, and maybe it was better if I didn't get behind the wheel again. Maybe I should walk back to the road and flag someone down. I regretted my decision to take the back roads—it could be morning before another motorist came by. Even so, it was the sensible thing to do. Maybe there would be cell phone reception at the road.

I picked my way along the narrow path, lifting the beam of my light every few steps, expecting to see the road up ahead. With each sweep of the light, the knot in my stomach grew tighter. Where, exactly, was I? And how had I gotten here? My heart pounded and my palms were clammy. I stopped walking and took a steadying breath. My thoughts flashed briefly to my mother, and I shoved them away. I was not my mother.

"Okay, don't panic." There was comfort in the sound of my own voice. "Think logically. Somehow, you've driven off the road. You probably fell asleep, and you're lucky you didn't hit something. That's good. You have no idea where you are. That's bad. But, you know you're still near the lake, so you're not far from home, and there are plenty of farms nearby. That's good."

I shone my light up the path. "Do I follow this? It must go somewhere." I chewed my lower lip and considered it. The first thing you were supposed to do when you got lost was stay put.

Yes. Stay with the car. That was the most logical thing. Lane knew I was on my way from the airport. When I didn't arrive home, he'd worry. He'd call the police. They'd search for me along my probable route and find where my car had left the road. All I had to do was wait.

I turned back toward the car, feeling more calm now. Exhaustion washed over me, and I thought I'd crawl into the back seat for a nap.

Tendrils of fog wafted through my torch beam. The air felt damp. Had it rained while I was gone? I trudged on.

A rustle in the undergrowth made me jump.

"Hello? Anyone there?" I strained my ears but was met with silence. "Hello?"

Nothing.

I took a deep breath and peered into the fog ahead. The clearing couldn't be too much further. I pushed forward along the path.

A minute later, the fog cleared, and my foot splashed into a puddle. I stopped and looked up.

"You're kidding." I stood at the edge of the lake. Somehow, I'd missed the car. "This is ridiculous."

Was this how Mom felt that first time she'd wandered off, confused? My pulse throbbed in my ears, every whoosh of blood hissing *crazy, crazy*.

No. I was simply tired and lost. I would *not* panic. I just had to think logically. I was at the edge of a lake I knew, not far from home. Lane expected me home soon, and within an hour, he'd be out searching for me.

I shone my light up the path, wishing for the familiar comfort of the car. Should I try to find it again? What if I missed it a second time? It was probably better to stay here by the lake. I rubbed my face. If I could only take a nap.

Well, the night was warm. Unusually warm, now I thought about it. I would find a comfortable spot and sleep for a bit. In the morning, I'd go back to the car. Everything would be easier in daylight, after a sleep. I'd find my way back to the road then.

I curled up in the shelter of a bush with my head pillowed on my arm. Maybe Lane would find me before morning. With that comforting thought, I fell asleep.

I awoke confused and sore. As the events of the night came back to me, I groaned and sat up. The sky glowed magenta with the sunrise. The fog was gone, and the day promised to be bright and warm. I checked my phone. Still no service. Strange. The area felt remote, but it wasn't really that far from town.

They'd be looking for me by now. I stood and cupped my hands to my mouth. "Hello! I'm over here! Anybody hear me?"

Where those voices I heard? Maybe they'd found the car. I hurried up the path. "Hello! I'm here!" I increased my pace to a trot.

The next sound brought me to a halt. I held my breath and heard it again—a long bugling sound, rising in pitch, followed by three squawks. Some sort of animal, but not one I'd heard before. "Hello?"

There were no voices now.

Voices. That's how it had started with Mom, too. Voices that had led her out into the woods. But this wasn't the same. I was simply lost, not sick. I shook my head and continued on.

Ten minutes later, I still hadn't come across the car or any rescuers. Fear settled into the pit of my stomach. How far had I wandered last night? A twig snapped in the undergrowth. I jumped.

"Hello?" My voice quavered. My car, the road, people searching for me… They all had to be close, right?

Even though I couldn't remember trees along the lake, this little bit of forest had to be real, right?

Logic had to be the way out of this situation. Logically, I was perfectly sane. Logically, this patch of trees must be small—the area around the lake was heavily farmed. No matter which way I went, I would come out of the trees before long, and then I'd see where I was.

"And I'm on a path," I reasoned aloud. "It must go somewhere." I straightened my shoulders and walked on.

An hour later, the day had warmed up. Sweat soaked my shirt, and my stomach was tight with anxiety and hunger. I should have come out of the trees a long time ago. Every time I heard a noise, I called out, hoping to hear a shout in response. But the forest fell silent at the sound of my voice.

When I saw light between the trees ahead of me, I broke into a jog. That must be the road. I could flag down a vehicle and be home in no time.

I broke out of the woods and faltered to a stop. "The lake again?"

Had I been walking in circles? I looked out in dismay at a dense bed of reeds rising from the water, blocking my view of any landmarks that might help me orient.

The strange cry I'd heard earlier sounded again. At the noise, there was a splash among the reeds, and five scaly heads poked up on sinuous necks taller than me.

I sucked in a breath and staggered backward. "What the…?"

Ten amber eyes turned toward me, curiosity in the curve of necks and the tilt of heads. The strange call rang out again, and one of the animals in the lake grunted. With a great surge of water, the elephant-sized animals heaved, hurling themselves further into the lake. Their long necks stayed above the surface. The humps of their hindquarters moved rhythmically, and I imagined pedaling feet underwater. Long tails trailed behind.

The cry sounded again, closer now. The hair on the back of my neck stood up, and I felt a sudden need to hide. I fell to the ground and crawled under the arching fronds of a large fern. Trembling, I peeked out from between the leaves.

A heavy tread vibrated through my hands and knees. When the monster making it stepped into view, I slapped a hand over my mouth to keep from screaming.

It walked on two legs, with an odd, lurching gait. A yard-long snout, narrow and toothy like a crocodile's, extended out over tiny arms set on a body the size of a motor home. It had a thick neck, and a yellow crest ran down its back. Long claws and teeth promised swift death to its prey.

It lurched to the edge of the lake and stopped, lifting its head, nostrils twitching. It gave a low growl, then waded into the shallows. Beyond the reeds, it slid chest-first into the water, like some giant duck.

My body shook, and even my thoughts were jittery. I'd seen this animal before. A sketch in my mother's journal. The one I'd found shoved under her pillow when I was clearing out her stuff. But that couldn't possibly be true. It would mean I was… I clutched at my hair and began to hum a tune in my head, to drive out the thoughts.

I know an old lady who swallowed a fly. It was a song I sang to the kids. The vision of the predatory old lady struck me as funny, under the circumstances, and I hiccupped a hysterical laugh before clamping a hand over my mouth to stop it.

I crouched in my hiding spot, studiously humming *I Know an Old Lady* and checking my phone for a signal, until mid-afternoon when thirst, hunger, and a dead phone battery drove me out. I had seen nothing but insects since the toothy…no, I would not call it what Mom had…since that *thing* had come out of the forest and swum away.

My throat was dry, and I felt light-headed as I stood. My vision darkened for a moment before clearing again. I eyed the cool wet ripples of the lake, imagining the green taste of the water. No. The lake regularly failed water quality tests. I'd have to be a lot thirstier to drink from it. There must be a stream somewhere. Or better yet, a house with running water and a phone so I could call Lane.

I reviewed my options, clinging to logic as though it could magically teleport me home. I could follow the path back to where my car must be, but I'd done that this morning and hadn't found the car. I could skirt the edge of the lake.

At least I wouldn't get lost doing that. There was a boat launch at Minnow Point. From there, I could follow the road home on foot. I eyed the water with distrust. Those huge animals were in the lake. And that toothy one had the face of a crocodile. What if it hunted like a croc, at the water's edge? I shuddered.

No. Those animals could *not* be real. But if they weren't real, it would mean they were all in my head, like the monsters in Mom's head.

Darn it! My car had to be nearby. It was shelter. It was transport. *And* there was a water bottle in my carry-on bag. *That's* why I was hallucinating—dehydration.

I should look for the car. *Stop wasting time; the day's half over.* I started up the path, away from the lake.

After an hour, I had to admit I was completely lost. I couldn't find my car, and I seemed to have veered far from the lake. The sky clouded over and it began to rain.

Rain was water, and I had a screaming dehydration headache by now. I opened my mouth wide and tried to catch the drops that made it through the canopy of trees. It barely wet my tongue. I gave up and trudged on, still following a path.

I told myself it was a fisherman's trail and would come out at a road somewhere. *It was definitely not made by something non-human, something as long as a bus, with teeth like kitchen knives.* I refused to believe I had even seen that thing. I was thinking clearly now. That was what mattered.

The light began to fade. The rain stopped. I had seen nothing but vegetation since I'd left the lake. My thoughts were sluggish, and I hummed *I Know an Old Lady* aloud now, my only comfort, the familiar tune reminding me of home, Lane, and the kids.

And Mom.

A rhythmic thudding sound from behind made me turn. Was someone running along the path? Someone looking for me?

"Hello?" I called out.

In response, I heard a sort of growl. The thudding changed cadence for a moment, and then resumed. I didn't know what the growl was, but whoever was coming had heard me.

"Hello! It's me, Tori!" I took a few steps toward the sound, squinting into the gloom.

A form appeared around a bend in the path, and my next shout died in my throat. A second, third, and fourth form appeared. They were vaguely the size of a person and running on two legs, but that's where the similarity ended.

Reptilian heads, long necks, and scaly tails set my pulse racing. When a massive creature with snapping jaws appeared behind them, I turned and ran.

Wobbly and dehydrated, hungry and confused, I tripped on a root and fell, hitting my head on a rock and rolling into the ferny undergrowth to the side of the path. The animals behind me thundered past.

When I came to, it was dark. My head hurt, and my hair was sticky and matted with blood. My clothes were still damp from the rain, and I shivered. Sitting up left me feeling dizzy and nauseated. I stuck my head between my drawn-up knees and wrapped my arms around myself. I rocked back and forth in time with the word my brain repeated over and over. *Crazy. Crazy. Crazy. Crazy.*

Logic eluded me. Even if I *could* think straight, there was no logic to what I'd seen. The animals by the lake, the animals on the path... They'd gone extinct millions of years ago. I knew that for a fact. My son had been crazy about dinosaurs when he was six, and I'd learned all about them as I read him book after book about them.

They didn't exist. They *couldn't* exist.

Your mother thought they existed.

"Yes, but mother was insane. I'm not!" I growled aloud. Then I whimpered. "This can't be happening. I'm overtired. I'm jet lagged. I fell asleep. The dinosaurs were a dream." That made sense—I'd been thinking so much of my mother. I touched my head again. "That's it. I fell asleep at the wheel and have had an accident." It made sense when I spoke it aloud. It was logical. I took a breath and tried to calm my racing heart.

"I've had an accident. I should call the ambulance." I pulled my phone from my pocket. The screen was shattered. Shit. I'd just upgraded, too. I tried to turn it on, but nothing happened.

I shoved the phone away. "Okay. I guess I just wait. Someone will come looking for me when I don't make it home." I frowned. Hadn't I done this already? No. That was in the dream, along with the dinosaurs. I shivered and wrapped my arms around my knees.

I remembered Mom, when they finally found her, her bathrobe torn and filthy, her eyes wide with terror. I'd cried at the sight of her. Would my kids do the same?

Morning found me still curled among the ferns. My head had stopped bleeding, but I woke with sticky eyes, a parched throat and a stomach that felt hollow and caved in. I blinked and rubbed my eyes, trying to make sense of my surroundings, my memories.

"An accident. You had an accident." My cracked voice was swallowed up by the dense vegetation. I stood, and the world swam and dimmed around me. I bent forward until my vision cleared, and then slowly raised my head.

"Find the road. Find the car." Talking aloud made me feel more in control. I started walking on the path nearby. After a few yards, my steps slowed. "Wait. I've done this already."

I stopped walking and clutched my head. What was real and what was a dream? Big scaly animals, strange plants, and memories of crouching under ferns crowded into my head. Were they all hallucinations? "What is wrong with me? Why hasn't anyone come for me? Lane?" My eyes stung, but my body had no extra water for tears.

I closed my eyes and drew in a long breath to the count of five. I held it for five, then let it out slowly. Mindfulness techniques had always helped when I was upset. Another slow breath, and I felt my pulse slowing. I opened my eyes.

I screamed.

The toothy head was as long as my arm. It seemed to grin at me—the grin of a hungry diner presented with a steak.

I ran.

I ducked into the undergrowth, dodging around tree ferns and leaping over clumps of reeds, hoping the huge animal would have trouble following. I didn't dare look back for fear of tripping, but the crashing behind me told me the animal was keeping pace.

I passed a clump of ferns, and two creatures about the size of chickens burst out of it. I screamed again, but the little animals sprinted away. I glanced back just in time to hurl myself away from the giant predator's snapping jaws. I dove at a clump of ferns, and then scrambled to my feet again as the animal lunged for another bite.

I ran, zigging and zagging through the trees. The ground turned to swampy mud, and I lost a shoe. I didn't dare stop to retrieve it.

I realized the creature had fallen back and risked another glance at it. It was sniffing my shoe.

I stopped, and in the pause, had a moment of clarity.

This was a hallucination. Mental illness ran in families; I had to accept this. And if it was a hallucination, it was all in my head. My own brain was making this up. So, my own brain could make it stop.

"Hey, Toothy!" I yelled. "Go away!" The beast looked up.

Something grabbed me from behind. A limb wound around my waist, and another slapped across my mouth. I struggled and twisted, trying to get away, but whatever had me pulled me backward into a mass of tall reeds. The mud gave way to water, and I struggled even harder. It was going to drag me into the lake!

"What the hell do you think you're doing? Stop struggling." More than the words, the fact it was a man who had me, and not the tentacled monster I envisioned, made me go still.

The man continued in a fierce whisper. "It hunts by smell and sight. In the water, it can't follow your scent. But if you're making the reeds thrash around, it'll know exactly where we are. Now shut up and hold still."

He pulled me deeper and deeper into the water, until it was up to my shoulders. The reeds closed in around us. He didn't loosen his grip on me, nor did he take his hand off my mouth, but I didn't fight him. I was too confused and frightened to do anything except obey.

The animal stomped along the shore, crashing noisily through ferns and reeds. Then it held still for a long time. The man whispered in my ear. "It's trying to catch your scent."

I felt myself trembling against the man's grip. The creature's footsteps retreated, but the man held me silent and still. His grip only relaxed after the shore had been quiet for a long time.

"What is going on?" were my first words. I turned to see a young man in the blue coveralls popular among the local dairy farmers. His sandy hair was long and unkempt, and his beard reached the middle of his chest. Relief flooded through me. "Are you part of the search team? I must have fallen asleep at the wheel. I—oh my god, I've been hallucinating, and—"

The man held up a hand. He took a deep breath. "You haven't been hallucinating. Trust me. You'd better come with me." He took my arm and drew me behind him as we waded out of the lake. I followed in confused silence, just like my Mom had when the police had found her.

We followed a route that wasn't quite a path. It snaked through the forest, and I couldn't tell which way we were going. The presence of another person who seemed to know what he was doing calmed me, but I was still thirsty, hungry and confused. As we walked on, I added hot to my discomforts. I was about to ask where we were headed when we emerged from the undergrowth into a clearing.

Three people sat around a small fire, an unidentifiable animal turning on a spit above the flames.

"Found another," said the man. He drew me toward the fire. A woman in a filthy pink dress straight out of the 1950s, and a man in a ripped t-shirt and shorts looked up at me.

An older man with matted white hair and a dirty beard stood. He wore wrinkled pin-striped trousers and a dingy button-down shirt. A paisley tie was threaded through his belt loops and knotted to cinch the overly-large waist of the trousers. He held out his hand.

"Welcome to the Cretaceous."

About the Author

Robinne Weiss is an author, educator and entomologist writing fantasy, science fiction, poetry and non-fiction for children and adults. Her short stories have most recently appeared in *Andromeda Spaceways Magazine* and the anthologies *Alternative Deathiness*, and Te *Kōrero Ahi Kā*, and have won multiple awards. She's published eleven books, including a series of middle grade fantasy novels infested with dragons, a lighthearted urban fantasy, an epic YA fantasy, a book of poetry, and some rather more serious non-fiction about insects.

Robinne lives in rural New Zealand. Visit her online at

https://robinneweiss.com

or follow her at

https://www.facebook.com/AuthorRobinneWeiss.

Deep Cleaning

by

Edward J. Knight

Deep Cleaning

Molly opened the portal hatch and shoved the turkey carcass down. As always, she leaned against the cool Formica counter and listened to hear it land. And, as always, the refrigerator hum and the tick of the wall clock drowned out any sound of a splat or a thud. Still, she started to count, like she always had. Grams had said it could take a full five seconds for the trash to land. Being little, Molly hadn't thought anything of it at the time. It wasn't until high school science that she'd realized how long a full five seconds was to fall.

She sighed. After ten-Mississippi, she closed the hatch, latched it, and turned back to the mess of a kitchen. She sighed. Some days she wished she could push it all into the trash portal, but buying new dishes was no fun. She'd lost a good stainless fork once, by not being careful enough. That's what came from cleaning when she was too tired. One had to be meticulous, because once it went into the portal, it was gone.

She stared at the disaster that had become her kitchen. It wasn't the usual Thanksgiving mess. Not with them eating it on Black Friday, thanks to that last-minute emergency job in Vegas. And not with it only being her and Ron, thanks to that stupid COVID-19. Ron had thought it'd be fine if Charlie came home from college, even if they couldn't have the rest of the family over. He'd argued that it wasn't like he and Charlie had any pre-existing conditions, and Molly couldn't get it at all. But she'd put her foot down. People were too sloppy and too messy out there, and the coming mutations were nasty. Charlie flying home was just out. And Charlie driving all the way from New York City to Nevada, with all the stops for gas and food and sleep?

No, no, no. Just no.

She knew how bad this pandemic was going to get. No way she was going to risk her own flesh and blood for a holiday meal.

Still, it was nice for them both to suggest it. She'd been truly touched. Family was family, after all. And if you didn't have family, what exactly did you have?

But without them and Ron's sister's family and all the rest, well, there were far too many leftovers in the freezer and no one to help tackle the spectacularly dirty kitchen with her. It would take hours to get everything clean, and Ron had gone back to Vegas to finish cleaning up from the job, and that would keep him there all day. She was fine with him going, since she knew he'd be careful and keep outside, but it would've been nice to get the help. It didn't matter. By god, she'd get the kitchen sparkling clean if it took all day.

She looked around the kitchen once more and sighed. Pots and pans and spilled food everywhere. Perhaps she should've tried harder to cut back on the cooking. She just wanted to make it as normal as possible. Even if Charlie was only there thanks to Zoom. As it was, she'd cooked the turkey too long and it'd been dry. Worse, she'd run out of onions for the green bean casserole and had to use fried onions from a can. Ron hadn't said anything, but she knew he'd been less than impressed.

But the new pumpkin pie recipe had been heavenly. That pie had been worth savoring. She could still taste the spices on her lips if she stood still long enough. But why would anyone want to stand still?

She shook herself out of her reverie and started collecting the plates and glasses and putting them by the sink. She'd barely gotten one counter cleared when her phone chirped. She pulled it out of her pocket, and noted it was her niece, who rarely called.

"Aunt Molly? It's Kelsey."

"Kelsey." Molly couldn't avoid a frown. "What's wrong?"

"Oh, Aunt Molly. I screwed up. I screwed up bad. You gotta help me!"

"You hurt?"

"He busted my lip. But I gotta cold washcloth on it."

"He?"

"Brett. He's— Well, it's— Could you just come get me?"

Molly pursed her lips in frustration. She glanced around the mess in her kitchen. Most years, Kelsey would've been here, helping. Even as a little girl, she'd loved wiping down the refrigerator door. Of course, that was before the virus.

"Where are you?" Molly asked.

"Sundown Motel. By the highway."

"I know it. Which room?"

"110. It's such a mess!" Her voice broke. "I—"

"Where's this Brett?" Molly was already trying to figure out who Brett was.

"Passed out in the bathtub. I, uh, well, he's still breathing…"

"He busted your lip first?" Molly couldn't keep the impatience out of her voice.

"Yes." Kelsey started to softly cry.

"Okay. Then stay inside where you can keep an eye on him. I'll be there in fifteen minutes." Molly looked around her kitchen. Kelsey had said the room was a mess. "No, make it twenty. I'll bring my cleaning supplies."

The Sundown Motel had never lived up to the glory its original owners had imagined back in the fifties. The interstate hadn't come to Cave Creek like they'd expected, and so they'd been stuck with a two story, thirty room squat pile of bricks. People who actually came to visit Cave Creek stayed at The Golden Dream Hotel. People who were passing through… Well, there were no people just passing through.

Still, the current owners had kept it up and they kept it clean. Not quite up to Molly's standards, but enough for her to appreciate the effort. They'd added a pool and offered free drinks at happy hour and so drawn a steady clientele of Vegas refugees trying to live cheap while they figured out their next move. It was a place you could wash the dust off while you turned out your pockets looking for that last missing dime.

Which made it a strange place for Kelsey, Molly mused. Even though Kelsey and her mom fought like cats with their tails tied together, home was home and Kelsey had been staying there since her roommate had tested positive way back in March.

Still, Molly pulled up in front of room 110 and turned the Cherokee's ignition off. She looked around for security cameras but didn't spot any. As she slid out of the driver's seat, the curtain in the window moved and a moment later the door cracked open.

"Just a minute," Molly called. "Let me get my supplies." She walked around to the hatchback without looking back at the room. After she opened it, she paused to get her mask in place, since she needed to set an example. Once she had her carrying bucket, mop, and special bag, she headed to the hotel door.

Kelsey swung it open and then quickly stepped back to let Molly in. Molly frowned.

"Where's your mask?" she asked.

Panic appeared in Kelsey's eyes. She darted back inside. By the time Molly shut the door behind her, Kelly had the fabric over her face.

The room was trashed—the lamp knocked over, pillows and clothes tossed everywhere. Small streaks of what looked like blood ran across the sheets. Several bottles of booze covered the small nightstand, one of which lay on its side, empty.

Kelsey wasn't much better. At twenty, with a physique and curves that mimicked Molly's, Kelsey usually looked like a model, but not today. The mask covered her fat lip, but she also sported a black eye. Her normal black braids were half undone, which, combined with her pale face, made her look less like Pocahontas and more like Wednesday from the Addams Family. Worse, she was barely dressed, in just some panties and a flimsy chemise.

"What were you thinking?" Molly chided. "You know what the virus can do."

"He said he'd been tested." Kelsey hung her head.

Molly opened her special cleaning bag and found the cotton swabs and a test bottle.

"Here," she said, thrusting them at Kelsey. "Stick one of these up your nose and then put it in the bottle. Give it five minutes and tell me if it changes color."

With a sniffle, Kelsey took the test kit.

Molly poked her head in the bathroom. A naked man, about thirty with a black Van Dyke beard, sprawled in the tub. Blood from his nose had dried in his beard and on his chest. His head lolled to one side, but his chest rose and fell rhythmically. Molly snorted in resignation and returned to the main room.

Kelsey'd had the sense to find her skirt and was tugging it into place. The bottle stood on the little round table by the door with the thin stick of the swab sticking out.

Molly crossed her arms and gave her niece the parental glare. "I think you better tell me what happened."

"Brett…" Kelsey shuddered. "He was so nice! I thought— And then he— And I said, no, Aunt Molly!" She was on the verge of crying again. "I said no! But then he hit me and—" The tears began to flow.

"I think you'd better start at the beginning." Molly lowered her arms but only softened her stare a notch.

Kelsey nodded and took moment to compose herself.

"We met online," Kelsey said. "He was so nice. He made me laugh. A lot." She snorted softly. "I was so tired of being stuck at Mom and Dad's."

"You were safe there."

"I dunno," Kelsey said with a shrug. "Britni says the quarantine's an overreaction."

"Britni's wrong. I *know*."

Kelsey shirked at her tone, and Molly's glare went back to daggers.

"So you met online," Molly prompted.

"He made me laugh," Kelsey repeated. "We started FaceTiming. We started doing…more. And then he suggested getting together. We met at a bar in town— He was so nice, Aunt Molly! We had a lot of fun, so…we came here."

"You went to a motel with a guy you'd just met."

Kelsey nodded. "I'm sorry, Aunt Molly. I know it was stupid. I was just, so— I've been stuck at Mom and Dad's for months! No job, no going out, no dating, *no privacy*—"

"You got horny."

Kelsey hung her head.

"Well, a young woman like you, it's understandable. But this was a bad choice. So, then what happened?"

"He…uh…he'd been drinking. A lot. He started again this morning, and he wanted… I said no… I said no!"

"And then he hit you."

She nodded. "I hit him back, and then he went to wash his face…" She gestured toward the bathroom.

"Well, you didn't kill him, if that's what you were worried about. You've gotten yourself in a bit of a mess. Now we have to figure out how to fix it."

Kelsey looked up, her eyes filling with hope.

"You won't tell Mom?" she asked.

"We'll see." Molly gestured toward the bathroom. "Tell me more about Brett. Where's he from?"

"D.C. He flew out yesterday."

"What else?"

"He's single," Kelsey's shoulders sagged. "He works in politics. Mostly we talked about music."

Molly fought back a smirk. Ah, to be young and carefree, even when the world was barreling straight to hell.

"I never thought he'd hit me," Kelsey repeated. "He was a fun guy online…"

"Do you care about him?"

Kelsey vehemently shook her head.

"Well, you finish getting dressed and gather your things. Put them in the Cherokee." Molly tossed her the keys. "I'll attend to your friend."

Kelsey nodded. She touched her mask—blood from her lip had started to soak through.

"If that's turned blue," Molly nodded toward the vial, "you can take the mask off." Then she gave Kelsey an "it'll be all right" smile and went into the bathroom.

Brett had turned his head while she'd been gone. He snored now, and his breath stank so badly of booze that Molly wondered if she could light the fumes on fire. He had a large knot on the back of his skull. Not one bad enough to have knocked him out by itself, but combined with the alcohol?

Molly pulled a pair of latex gloves out of her pocket, slipped them on, and then checked his pulse in his neck. It was steady enough that he wasn't going to die right away. She looked over the rest of his body. He had scratches all over his forearms and a new bruise on his thigh.

Kelsey'd fought back, Molly realized. At least the girl had had some sense. Come to think of it, she usually did. Meeting a guy—that must've been the COVID crazies. Molly started a COVID test on Brett. She hated touching him, but it had to be done. She washed her hands after but kept the gloves on.

Back in the main room, she looked around until she spotted a pair of men's pants in a heap against the wall. Kelsey looked up from packing a duffle bag as Molly extracted Brett's wallet from the back pocket. The young woman had taken her mask off, so the test results must've been good. Now she moved like someone with a purpose.

"Where's your car?" Molly asked as she flipped through the wallet.

"Um…we left it at the bar. His is out front."

Well, the car was a complication. Molly found his driver's license and pulled it out. Brett McGuire of Virginia. He was thirty-two. She set the license on the bed, unlocked her phone, and searched for his name. Since she had his date of birth, it didn't take long to find him.

Her eyebrows rose. She checked the phone again, the picked up the license and made sure she'd entered everything correctly.

"All right," she said to Kelsey. "We can't stay here, and we can't leave him. We'll have to get him into the Cherokee."

"Why? Why can't we just leave him?"

"Because he has friends you do not want to meet. Come on. The faster we get out of here, the better."

Kelsey started at that and, despite the panic in her eyes, she picked up her pace. After she had all of her things in the Cherokee, Molly had her gather up Brett's clothes and put them in one of the Hefty garbage bags from Molly's regular supplies.

Molly watched her niece with growing appreciation. Kelsey had realized the seriousness of the situation without being told. Brett's friends wouldn't care that she'd hit him in self-defense. They wouldn't care one bit. And now that Kelsey had direction, she was moving fast and efficiently. Like when she helped clean after the holidays. It was good to see.

Brett stirred when Molly went back into the bathroom. He didn't open his eyes, so she looked at him and frowned. The fact that he associated with bad people didn't necessarily make him unredeemable. A quick check of his COVID test showed he was negative. That was good. Still, she wanted to talk to Grams. In the meantime…

She retrieved her special cleaning bag while Kelsey continued gathering up the detritus of the night before. Molly closed the bathroom door and opened the bag on the counter. She twisted the vials so she could read all the labels at once. She hated when they were turned the wrong way. But the one she wanted was in the third spot, just as she'd expected. She slotted it into the hypodermic and returned to Brett.

Now it'd be hours before he woke.

Which left Kelsey. Molly sighed. Kelsey was going to be the real problem. The girl was bright, except when it came to men. Then she was downright dumb. What was she thinking? In the middle of a pandemic?

Obviously, she wasn't thinking. At least not with her brain. This was worse than that talent agent she'd gotten mixed up with in Vegas. At least he'd only taken her money.

Still, she'd kept her wits about her after Brett had punched her. She'd been smart enough to call Molly instead of her parents. Did not panicking under pressure make up for a bad decision or two?

Kelsey had floated as a teenager until she discovered theater. Then she'd been driven. She was still young, though. Oh, so young.

But Molly needed her. At least for this mess. She'd need Kelsey's help with the car. Molly looked over the snoring Brett. She'd need help with him, too. Two petite women could get him into the Cherokee much faster than one, and if they were going to get caught, that'd be the time.

Kelsey knocked on the bathroom door. "Uh...Aunt Molly? The room's picked up now."

"Good," Molly replied. "Bring me one of the blankets to wrap Brett in."

To her credit, Kelsey didn't fall apart as they pulled the man out of the tub and wrestled him into the blanket. She helped fold the cloth like a burrito with feet and then helped lift him up. She seemed steadier and calmer the more they worked. She glanced at the vials on the counter but didn't ask.

Molly had Kelsey hold him against the wall while she herself hustled out to turn the car around and open the back gate. She silently chided herself for getting sloppy. She should've done that first. But no one was out, and no one saw her, and a few minutes later the two women successfully wrestled Brett into the Cherokee and covered him with another blanket. Molly checked carefully to be sure nothing showed that could make it clear what he was. The long lumpy bundle was suspicious enough.

"Now what?" Kelsey asked as they shut the gate.

"Who checked in?" Molly asked as they walked back into the room. "To the motel?"

"Uh, we both did. He paid though."

"So the desk clerk saw you both." Molly waited for Kelsey's nod before continuing. "So here's what you do. You go check out, and you ask if they've seen Brett. He snuck out while you were asleep and abandoned you. Give them the whole teary-eyed thing. Think you can do it?"

"I *am* an actress." For the first time, fire shone in Kelsey's eyes.

"Good. Go win an Oscar."

"Tony."

"Fine." Molly shooed her on. "I've got some deep cleaning to do."

Kelsey actually broke into a jog toward the motel lobby.

Molly packed up her vials and briefly considered her regular cleaning supplies. It'd be too obvious to the maid, which was a shame. They didn't need her wondering why someone had scrubbed the bathroom. So she reached into her special bag and extracted the UV Cube and her protective goggles. She set the cube on the counter and pulled the shower curtain all the way open. It didn't bunch up, though, and still blocked the end of the tub.

She sighed. She'd have to flash the tub separately as well.

With her goggles on, she set the timer and quickly retreated from the bathroom. She closed the door and waited. After the flash, which leaked through the crack under the door, she went back in and moved the cube to the middle of the tub. Once again, she retreated to the main room, closed the door, and waited for the flash. This time it smelled of ozone.

She frowned. She'd have to get a new one.

With a grumble, she opened the door, retrieved the cube, and pulled the spare from her bag. She looked around the room for a suitable spot and frowned again. The only place that made sense was stuck to the ceiling. She climbed on the bed and was standing there when Kelsey returned.

"All set Aunt Mol—" Kelsey's eyes went wide.

"That was quick." Molly raised her goggles.

"What…what are you doing?"

"Cleaning." Well, it was time to see what her niece was made of. Molly held up the cube. "This is a blood cleaning cube. It destroys hemoglobin. It turns blood into just a dark smear."

"You can *do* that?"

"Yes, but it's dangerous. Wait for me outside. No—see if you can find Brett's keys. We have deal with his car. It's a rental, I presume?"

Distracted by the change of subject, Kelsey nodded, but didn't take her eyes off the UV Cube. Molly stuck it in place and clambered off the bed.

"Go." She shooed Kelsey out the door. "It's not safe to be in here when it goes off."

Reluctantly, Kelsey stepped back outside.

"Car keys?" Molly prompted.

Kelsey snapped out of it and hurried to the side door of the Cherokee. Molly closed the motel door and waited for the flash. After it finished, she headed back in, and Kelsey drifted behind her. The girl did have the sense to pull the door closed.

Kelsey stared at the UV Cube as Molly climbed on the bed and retrieved it. Various emotions warred on Kelsey's face, and her mouth moved as if she was trying to work out the words. Her lip split open a bit, but the blood only oozed instead of flowed.

"That… You… Where did you get that?" Kelsey asked.

"It's part of my cleaning supplies." Molly jumped off the bed. "Did you get the keys?"

Kelsey held them up. "Enterprise."

"Good. You drive and follow me."

Molly led the way out of town and up the back dirt roads into the hills. At a suitably scenic overlook, she pulled over and waited for Kelsey to ease the rental in behind her. Both women got out of their cars at the same time.

"Now what?" Kelsey asked. She put her hands on her hips. Her eyes flicked toward the back of the Cherokee where Brett was.

Molly ignored the hint. "We clean the old-fashioned way. Wipe down everything you touched. Use the rags and bleach in my grey bag in the back seat."

As Kelsey headed for the Cherokee, Molly strolled to the edge of the overlook. She couldn't see the portal at the bottom, but the rock formations told her she was in the right spot. Anyone who knew about the portals would assume Brett had gone through it. Anyone who didn't would think he'd wandered into the desert.

Assuming he disappeared. She wasn't completely sure about that.

She returned to the rental car, where Kelsey had already wiped down the steering wheel and was working on the seat. She'd pulled her hair back and loosely bound it with a hair band while she scrubbed. She only gave Molly a quick glance as she focused on her work. Molly smiled when she saw her wiping down the seams of the seat and all the knobs on the dash. The girl paid attention to detail. That was good.

Molly returned to the Cherokee and extracted the black film from her special bag. Then she opened the hatch and lifted the blanket. She fished around until she found Brett's hands.

"Uh, Aunt Molly," Kelsey said as she walked up from behind, "I finished the front. Do you want me to clean the back seat? I was never in it."

"No." Molly pressed Brett's fingers against the film. "They'll expect to find some of your DNA. We just don't want any in the driver's seat."

"What are you doing?" Kelsey had reached her side.

"Collecting his fingerprints. It'll be suspicious if they can't find any of his."

Kelsey swallowed and nodded. Her eyes were wide, but she refrained from saying anything.

Instead, she watched as Molly took the film to the rental and pressed it against the steering wheel, the gear knob, and the outside door. Then they walked back to the Cherokee, scuffing up their footprints behind them. Molly gestured for Kelsey to get in the passenger's seat while she got behind the wheel.

They drove in silence back to town. When Molly glanced at Kelsey, the young woman seemed lost in thought. As they entered Cave Creek, Kelsey sat up and took a deep breath.

"Are…are you going to kill him?"

Molly blinked. That was a bold question. Her opinion of Kelsey rose even more.

"Do you want the answer to that?" Molly asked.

"I…I think I do."

"Well, the answer is maybe. I want to talk to my grandma first."

"But…your grandma's dead."

"Oh no," Molly chuckled. "She's very much alive. She's just not here."

Kelsey's mouth fell open, and she stared at Molly for a moment. Then she closed it and turned to face the road.

Molly parked the Cherokee next to Kelsey's Honda in front of Murphy's Irish Pub, which was owned by a Korean couple. The front was festooned with all the usual harps, four-leaf clovers, and green and gold. More importantly, the bar owners had commandeered a good swath of sidewalk, roped it off, and added tables with column heaters nearby. They weren't quite warranted in the Nevada November, but Molly imagined they gave some comfort to the drinkers. Just as the outside seating might let them think they were safe from the pandemic.

She shook her head. That attitude wasn't fatal. Yet.

Fortunately, the Pub's door was open. Molly checked the clock in the Cherokee's dash. She wondered how much lunch business the Pub actually got. She turned to Kelsey.

"So," Molly said, "you need to go in and ask if they've seen Brett. Give them the same story you told the clerk. Then go home and pack a bag. You're going to stay with us for a while."

"Why?" Whatever misgivings Kelsey'd had earlier no longer showed on her face. Her lip had started to scab.

"So," Molly said, "when the police come by, I'll be the one in the room instead of your parents." Hopefully Sheriff West would be with them. That'd make the questioning easier. He'd believe Brett had gone through the portal.

Kelsey slowly nodded. Then she set her jaw.

"A Tony," Molly said. "Best Actress in a Dramatic Role."

"That's an Emmy." But Kelsey still cracked a smile. Then she took a deep breath, put her mask on, and got out of the car.

Molly managed to wrestle Brett out of the Cherokee, through the garage, and into the kitchen. She sat him in the old chair at the breakfast table and pulled the blanket off. His face had gone pale, but he still breathed. He'd even managed to drool a little on his chin. It looked like the blood he'd left on Kelsey's.

She sighed. What was she going to do with him? He'd beaten her niece and possibly done worse. Kelsey hadn't said so, and Molly certainly hoped not. Since Kelsey was holding up pretty well, she figured he hadn't. In fact, Kelsey had pulled herself together quite well. But she was so young. Only twenty.

They could always leave Brett in the desert, drunk and delirious, with no memory of how he'd gotten there. Sometimes that was enough. It just wasn't…tidy. It left nagging loose ends.

She needed to talk to Grams.

Molly knelt in front of the cabinet next to the refrigerator. She pressed her thumb against the lock and sat back on her haunches as the door sprung open. She smiled when she saw the new message cube. She'd watch that later. She reached into the little plastic storage bin and pulled out a new one. Then she stood and went to the clean kitchen counter. She didn't want any of the mess in the background.

Molly held the cube at arm's length. She smiled and squeezed the sides. When the recording light flashed on, she began.

"Hi Grams!" She said, with the same girlish tone she'd had at sixteen. "I've got one I need to know more about. A Brett McGuire." She turned to cube to take some holos of Brett. "I'll send his driver's license through, too."

She paused and took a breath.

"He attacked Kelsey," she continued. "He could've just been drunk, but I'm worried about his friends." She briefly described what she'd already learned and what she'd done to cover their tracks.

"I'm also wondering about bringing Kelsey inside. I think she deserves to know, and she *is* family. Let me know what you think."

She released the button and the light faded. Then she went to the cabinet, set the new cube against the back wall along with Brett's driver's license, and pushed. They disappeared the same way they always did.

While she waited, she emptied the dishwasher she'd run the night before. She frowned. A couple of the glasses had come out spotty.

She needed to find a new rinse aid. Still, it didn't take her long to get everything neatly where it belonged.

She checked on Brett. He was glassy-eyed and still, other than the rise and fall of his chest. When she knelt by the cabinet again, a new cube sat there, as well as a thick file folder.

Molly climbed back to her feet with a groan. Getting older was hard on her knees. She set the cube on the counter and pressed the top.

Grams's face appeared in the air above it. Her expression was serious, but with that hint of amusement that always peeked from the corners of her mouth.

"How's my favorite granddaughter?" Grandma began. Being her only granddaughter, Molly couldn't help but roll her eyes.

"I hope you're doing well," Grandma continued. "Do please send more about your life when you can. Your father's getting antsy. That boy!" She rolled her eyes. "Our most recent comings and goings are on the cube we already sent, including a message from Hal. Your brother's determined to find that cure. We keep telling him he's wasting his time, but..." she huffed.

"In answer to your questions, we'd be happy to have Kelsey inside. We spent a few days looking at all the timelines we could, and she does wonderfully in all but two. Just keep her from going to Hong Kong if you can."

Molly nodded. That would be easy to remember.

"As for your Brett McGuire, we've sent the full file we've been able to build. But—what's the phrase in your era? Too long, didn't read?—whatever. The world is better off without Brett McGuire. Good luck, and record a cube for your father!"

The hologram faded and the cube turned off.

Molly opened the folder and skimmed through the first several pages. As she did, she couldn't help but shake her head.

"Oh, Mr. McGuire," Molly murmured. "You've been a bad, bad man. Or, at least, you will be a bad, bad man. We can't have that. It's down the portal for you." She set the papers down, went to the portal she used for trash disposal, and unlatched it. She looked at its size and sighed. She'd have to get the bone saw again.

Kelsey arrived just before dinner. Ron had called and said the job was running long and he'd be back closer to midnight, so Molly had taken some shrimp out of the freezer. Ron hated shellfish, but with some scallions and some garlic, she and Kelsey could enjoy a nice stir fry. She had just started cooking when Kelsey entered the kitchen.

Kelsey sniffed the air. She couldn't help a small smile as she looked around.

"This place is spotless," Kelsey said. "As always."

"It's what I do." Molly shrugged. She stirred the garlic as the oil sizzled.

"Yeah…um…it's not all you do, is it?"

"Well, in a way it is." Molly couldn't help a small chuckle. "Get the plates down, will you?"

Kelsey moved to the cabinet, but quietly, with a studious expression.

"Go ahead and ask," Molly prompted.

"So, what are you cleaning?"

"The timelines."

"The timelines?" Kelsey pulled two glasses out of the cabinet as well.

"I'll explain over dinner. If you want."

"I want, Aunt Molly," Kelsey said. "I want to know it all. What happened to Brett. Where you got that thing you sterilized the hotel room with. How you know things. I want to know."

"Your life will never be the same," Molly warned. After all, hers hadn't been the same since she'd picked Grandma's cabinet as the perfect spot for hide and seek all those years ago. Or all those years from now?

"My life hasn't been the same since COVID closed the theaters," Kelsey said morosely. "I need something to do. Something meaningful. Something better than flirting with guys online." She shuddered. "I can't believe I wanted to meet Brett."

Molly threw the shrimp into the sizzling pan and stirred.

"And thank you," Kelsey said. "Thank you for coming to get me, and thank you for making Brett go away."

Molly shrugged. "You're family." And nothing was more important than family.

Especially when they helped her clean.

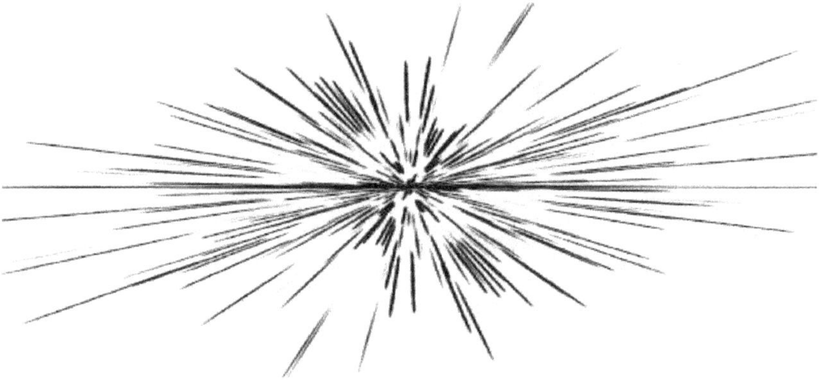

About the Author

A fourth generation Coloradoan, Edward J. Knight only left the Denver area long enough to learn how to put a satellite into orbit. Four satellites (and counting) later, he's returned to both the mountains and writing fantastical fiction. Along the way, he met the love of his life and became the father of two amazingly curious kids. He's a huge fan of tightly constructed universes and smart plots. He hopes his own Mythic West stories hold up to those standards. More of his work can be found at www.edwardjknight.com.

Doors Out of the Dark

by

Ken Hoover

Doors Out of the Dark

The day my brother disappeared was in another time, another world. It was the eighties, and music, pop culture, and fashion were optimistically colored. Back then, we lived in Old Mesilla, a small historic town with no shortage of ghosts, weirdness, and legends. Its centerpiece was the plaza, where mariachis blared their festive music in the shade of a large gazebo, and colorful *carruchas* drove past, thumping bass.

The plaza had two sentries. At the north end was the famous San Albino Catholic church, and to the south was El Patio, the local bar, where our mom worked. Cars parked in front of the church. Harleys and choppers lined up in a row near the bar.

As the older brother, I was always stuck with Mike, so I dragged him along the ditch banks, our own little roads across the village, fearful of *La Migra* as much as *La Llorona.* One afternoon, years before Mike vanished, my friends invited me to drink stolen beer at the cemetery, but Mike refused to step a single Reebok into the cemetery.

"There is a bad door," he said.

I didn't know what that meant, not back then, so I sat him in the shade of a juniper tree, rocking back and forth, and humming a Johnny Cash tune. Always Cash. I made sure his Tigers baseball cap was shading his face, then caught up to my friends.

They didn't understand why Mike's head never pointed straight, why he knew every Crayola color ever made, or why he had to touch every door or window. Words like *Asperger's* and *the spectrum* didn't exist back then, but uglier words did. They called him a *retard* as we walked between graves, sipping warm beers. They knew I hated that word more than anything, and so we fought. It wasn't our first time or our last. I gave *chingasos* as good as I got, but I was outnumbered two-to-one, and they left me in the dirt of the cemetery, covered in dust, scrapes, and stickers.

Later, as Mike and I shuffled back into town, I wiped blood off my face and plucked goat heads and crab grass burrs from my Magic Johnson tank top. He was oblivious I'd suffered on his behalf. As always.

In autumn, evening came quickly, and the temperature dropped with the sun. Pecan trees were silhouetted against the pumpkin orange sky. The air stank of burning plastic or Styrofoam, coming from someone's backyard, where tongues of flames flickered through the rusted holes of steel drums. The houses, galleries, and storefronts were built right up to the edge of the sidewalks, which meant Mike had to touch them all.

"Closed," said Mike, tapping a blue door.

"Who cares, Mike? I just got my ass kicked."

"Closed," he said, touching a storefront window.

"I was defending you. Again."

"Closed."

"And what do I get for it? Nothing. Do you know what I go through? Do you even care?"

I wanted to grab him by the shoulders and make him look me in the eyes, but that would only send him into a screaming fit that could last minutes or an hour. So, I restrained myself, pushing all that anger down, compacting it, until its only expression was a stiff-limbed teenaged pout.

He stopped and raised a single finger, as if to make a point. "That door was open."

With a growl of frustration, I stormed up the sidewalk. I wanted to punch through the doors and windows and let him sort that out by himself.

We were raised on tips. Our mom divorced our deadbeat dad when we were too young to understand. She worked long hours at El Patio, waiting tables and serving drinks to pay the bills. She told us to stay away from the bar unless it was an emergency.

The steady oompa-oompa Chicano music wafted through the adobe walls of El Patio before we rounded the corner, and I wanted to bust through the flimsy screen door and scream about my unfair life, but that would only end badly for me. Not Mike. Just me.

Reeling away from the bar, I aimed toward home, but the neat row of motorcycles stood in my way. There must have been eight or nine of them, all vibrant colors, flame jobs, and gleaming chrome. They were beautiful, and I hated them.

I threw myself at the nearest one, shoving it hard with both hands into the next motorcycle. One by one, they toppled, crunching and crashing into each other. A mirror snapped off a long handlebar.

Chrome exhaust pipes were crushed. Bits of plastic skittered across the brick road. They were powerful machines, and I had destroyed them in seconds.

For a moment, I stood wide-eyed in amazement, my mouth open. Then, realizing what I'd done, I grabbed Mike by the wrist and ran as fast as I could drag him, past the church toward our small house, not looking back.

To this day, I don't think he understood the hell we could've caught for that, and I didn't know what to feel. I was angry, thrilled, terrified.

No one saw us. We lived a block away from the church, and we were at our tiny three-bedroom house in thirty seconds. As I fumbled with my key, Mike reached out and touched the doorknob.

"Closed," he said.

Mike's fascination with doors and windows continued throughout our childhood. Not only were they opened or closed, but some could be inherently good or bad. I couldn't tell the difference—a door was a door—but Mike's brown eyes saw everything differently, and I began to realize his strangeness was a unique form of genius.

He picked up other obsessions. He could match every color in the world to a Crayola crayon. He knew the Dewey Decimal System and the Periodic Table. After one listen, he could sing a song perfectly and knew every Johnny Cash song forward and back. And he was a neat freak. The term *OCD* didn't exist back then, either. His room was immaculate. He kept his colored pencils in a shoebox, all facing the same direction, always perfectly sharpened, and he kept his clothes expertly folded. His loose change was sorted, always heads up. If there was a smudge by the light switch, he would wipe it off and then continue to clean the entire wall.

Years later, when I was in college, and Mike had been in and out of Special Ed, I was working part-time at the Life Center. I had gotten the job because I delivered my brother there every day, and the boss liked how I treated him and thought I might be a good fit for the members. The job saved my life. While my friends were overdosing or in shootouts with the cops, I was working. The Life Center was the only place in the state with a rec center for the challenged. It hosted a small library, a TV room, a cafeteria, and a rec room. It even had a grass lawn in the back for games and picnics. The developmentally disabled were allowed to be as quirky and happy with themselves as they wanted to be. You could see it in their beautiful faces. They had fun, laughed, socialized with their peers, and sometimes even fell in love.

Mike befriended a woman named Crystal, who wore thick glasses and had a warm, kindhearted smile. Soon, the two of them became inseparable. It was magical, but for the parents of developmentally disabled, love was a complicated and frightening thing.

It was Movie Night when our mom learned that Mike was in a relationship. When she shambled into the Life Center, she wore her usual work clothes, jeans and a t-shirt, both a little too tight so she could make better tips. She'd worked a ten-hour shift on her feet and was wincing with every step.

"Where's your brother?" she asked.

"Hi, Mom," I said. "Good to see you, too."

She pinched the bridge of her nose. "I'm tired, okay? Let's not do this."

Although she'd trained me to sling smartass with the best of them, I knew when to lay off. "He's watching a movie with everybody else. Why don't you get off your feet? I'll get him."

Mondays were always movie nights, and the members were watching *Back to the Future* for the seventh time this year.

When I peeked into the dark TV room, everything was running smoothly. The members were laughing at Christopher Lloyd's antics, showing their wide-toothed smiles and awkward grins.

Mike was sitting on one of the couches, holding hands with Crystal, smiling happily. I hadn't known that kind of love yet. My relationships, all three of them, had been short-lived and meaningless. I'd just been dumped, in fact, and the wounds were still fresh.

I quickly crossed the room, ignoring the irritated puffs of air and frustrated groans from the members who didn't like distractions and weren't afraid to say so.

"Down in front!"

"You're in the way."

"I know that guy. I know that guy. Hey guy."

"Shhht!" hissed several members at once.

I squatted down beside Mike and Crystal and kept my voice low and calm. "Mike. Mom's here."

"Time to make like a tree," said Crystal, quoting the movie.

"That's right," I said. "Exactly."

Mike was filled with longing. I had never seen such a complex emotion on his face before. But there it was. Longing. And I felt my first pang of jealousy, for I hadn't known that kind of emotion for anyone, and I worried I never would.

Mike leaned in for an awkward smooch goodbye. I didn't stick around to watch. I exited the room to more exaggerated sighs.

When I stepped into the bright hallway, Mom grabbed my arm. "I saw what was going on in there."

"What do you mean? We always watch *Back to the Future*."

She leaned in, keeping her voice soft. "Mike is holding a girl's hand. Is there any funny business between them?"

"Funny business, Mom? Really? They don't even know what that means. I barely know what that means."

She stood with her hands on her hips, frowning. "Well, I don't like it."

"He's never been this social, Mom. Ever. I'll make sure it stays G-rated. I promise."

Our mom sighed, touched me on the cheek. She smelled like cigarette smoke and stale beer. "I know you will, mijo. I'm just tired, that's all."

Mike shielded his eyes with his hands when he stepped into the hallway. He didn't like fluorescent lights, and the hallway had a hospital's antiseptic brightness. He touched the doorknob with one hand, announced that the door was open, then he held up a single finger. "I am going to wipe this mark off the floor. It is Cornflower Blue." With the tip of his white sneaker, he carefully removed the scuff mark.

When Crystal came out a minute later, we watched my mom and brother walk with their arms around each other like they were old pals.

"Mike left," she said, her voice tinged with sadness.

After that, Mike was absent for several days. I finally went to check on them that Thursday. It was Mom's day off, and she was busy around the house. She worked six days a week yet spent her free time cooking and cleaning. She was wearing an apron over her jeans and red t-shirt, and she wore her usual white orthopedic nurse shoes.

The air smelled like hot cooking oil. Flour dusted the countertops white. A stack of fresh tortillas sat on the kitchen table as if waiting just for me.

I grabbed a tortilla and buttered one side. As I chewed, I noticed Mike's bedroom door was closed.

"Shouldn't you be in school?" she asked, slapping a fresh tortilla onto the stack.

"Thood be," I answered, mouth stuffed with warm tortilla.

"Samuel, college is a privilege. You're the first in our family to go. Don't waste this opportunity." She told me this in Spanish, which was reserved for the most important conversations.

I held up my hands defensively. "I'm in between classes, Mom. I just wanted to check on you. Can't a son check on his only mother?"

She muttered in Spanish and went back to rolling dough.

"Is Mike okay?" I asked. "He hasn't been at the Life Center in a few days."

"We had an argument," she said, as if that explained everything. "He's in his room. I can't get him out of there."

"Why didn't you call me?"

"I should be able to handle this. I'm his mom."

"Is this about Crystal?"

"A little. I told him I didn't think he was ready for a relationship."

"Mom, this has been really good for him. Why would you take that away?"

She turned to look at me. Flour dusted one cheek, and it made her look old and tired. "Michael is my baby boy. I look at him, and I see a toddler."

"He's almost twenty years old," I said. "You've got to let him grow up a little. What do you see when you look at me?"

"A pain in the ass," she said. She turned back to her dough.

"I'll see what I can do," I said. "Make me some tortillas to-go, would you?"

She threatened me with her rolling pin.

I knocked on Mike's door. He'd carefully taped a note to the door that read, "Keep Out! Top Secret." The block letters were meticulously drawn and colored. I knocked again.

"Mike? It's me, Sam. I'm coming in."

The doorknob was locked, but I knew how to get past its high-tech security. I lifted on the handle and shouldered it open.

"That door was closed. Now it is open," said Mike, sitting on the floor, rocking back and forth. Spread all around him on the carpet were markers, colored pencils, and crayons, arranged by color and size. They were fanned in neat arcs, all pointing outward in rainbows.

The walls had been stripped of their science posters. Instead, Mike had drawn large rectangles on each wall, each in a different color and design. Some were colored sky-blue with white clouds, while others were colored with zigzags, polka dots, or stripes like something right out of Dr. Seuss.

"Dude, you've been busy. How long did this take?"

"These doors are closed. They will not open."

"None of them have doorknobs," I said. "Listen. I'll talk to mom. See if we can get you back to the Life Center."

"There is a good door at the Life Center," he said, eyes rolling to look at one of the walls. "I know it is there."

I nodded absently, still taking in the scope of his room. "Hey, I get it. It's a good place for you."

"There are science doors and lawyer doors and mechanic doors. I want to become a country music star like Johnny Cash."

"I've always wanted to be stunt man. Isn't that crazy, the direction life takes you?"

"The door will open."

He was staring directly at me, then, which he almost never did. He was telling me something important, and I didn't understand.

If only I'd been listening.

"We'll get you back to the Life Center. I promise," I said. "Do you want me to shut this behind me?"

"It is closed," he said, "but I will open it soon."

I kept my promise. He was back the next day for Karaoke Night. I organized the music and ran the boombox, but the show belonged to the members. Rows of tables were lined up near the front of the cafeteria, and the benches were filled with the members who were waiting their turn to sing. The back half of the cafeteria was cleared for dancing. Around the perimeter, the chairs and tables were filled with members or family and friends.

Mike was always the first to go. Maybe I had a little bias there, but he was always insistent, and the other members had no objections. He always sang Johnny Cash tunes. That night he sang "Ring of Fire." He had a flair for the stage, standing boldly, flicking the microphone at the right moments, and he knew every word. His lower octave wasn't half bad.

When he was finished, he took a seat at the end of the line for another turn. Crystal sat beside him, leaning her head against his shoulder, and he put his arm around her.

Next, Donny Palmer sang "Sweet Dreams." He sang every word to his own beat and then stopped singing to wave at another member. "Look! There's Sharon. Hi Sharon!"

"Sharon is wearing a Dandelion Yellow shirt," said Mike.

"Shoot. My parents are here. I have to go," said Crystal.

I popped in "I Wanna Dance with Somebody" and queued up the next song. When I looked up, Mike and Crystal were crossing the room. Mike was deftly avoiding every person on the dance floor while holding on to Crystal's hand. I saw Crystal's parents in the doorway, and they looked *pissed.*

The room grew feverishly hot, and the disco lights whirled around me, making me feel submerged in water.

I had about three minutes before the song ended. I hurried across the dancefloor, ignoring the calls and grabby hands to dance with one member or another, and raced into the hallway.

I was too late. I got there just in time to see the doors close behind them. Her mom glared over her shoulder disapprovingly at Mike. When she saw me staring back, she turned and continued marching down the sidewalk. She took one of Crystal's hands in her own while her father took the other, as if she was a little girl.

"Closed," said Mike. He stomped into the TV room, pouting. When he got like that, he shut down completely. He needed time and space.

The song was ending, so I raced into the cafeteria, announced the next song, "Wild Thing," and went back to work, making everything groovy.

Our mom arrived a few songs later. When I was able to break away, I found her leaning against the doorframe, watching Mike as he organized the art supplies, facing the paint brushes in the same direction and sorting them by size.

"He doesn't even know I'm here," she said.

"Crystal's parents were upset that she was holding hands with Mike. It didn't go well. Now he's focused on something familiar and comforting," I said, giving her a reassuring squeeze on the arm. "Go home and rest, Mom."

She finally conceded with a kiss on my cheek. "Thank you, Samuel," she said. She leaned into the room. "Michael, your brother is going to bring you home tonight."

Mike said nothing.

With a sigh, she walked down the hallway to the exit, looking exhausted and sad, her tennis shoes squeaking on the linoleum. "Okay, Mom. Thanks, Mom," she muttered.

I took the chair next to Mike, purposefully making as much noise as I could, hoping to catch his attention, but he didn't react. Instead, he began lining up the paints in order of the spectrum.

"Are you going to be in here a while?" I asked him.

"I need to find the right colors."

"Which one are you looking for?"

"I'm going to be a country music rock star like Johnny Cash."

I wanted to ruffle his hair, but I knew better than to touch him right now. "You're already a rock star, bro. I'll be running the boombox. Come back when you're ready to sing your next song. Maybe 'Hey Porter.' What do you think of that?"

"This door is closed," he said.

He didn't come back to sing. I checked on him periodically, hoping he'd pull himself out of his funk, but he didn't. Toward the end of the night, he had moved into the TV room and was scrubbing a section of wall with a sponge and soapy water. He'd pushed a Ficus tree out of his way, and it now stood in the middle of the room.

"Whatcha doing, Mike?"

"I am cleaning this wall."

"I kind of figured. Why?"

"It's got to be perfect." He took several deliberate steps back to admire his work. "I don't want to get lost in the dark."

My next shift was Bingo Night. Everything seemed to be back to normal. I was sitting at the front of the cafeteria, drawing numbers from a tumbler and calling them out with my best game-show host voice. All eyes were fixed on me.

"G-57," I called out.

"I got it," said Donny Palmer in his teenage sing-song voice.

"Me too. This piece is Yellow Orange," said Mike.

The members grinned eagerly, waiting for the next number. I paused dramatically, then leaned into the microphone. "I-24."

"Bingo!" shouted Mike mischievously, raising an arm.

Several members groaned and rolled their eyes, since this was only the second letter I'd called.

"Do you really have Bingo?" asked Crystal.

"No. I'm just joking," said Mike, chuckling to himself. "I am a comedian."

I had never seen him so happy. He was brimming with joy. I'd never known such happiness. The closest I'd ever come was on nights like this, while helping the members.

Later, as everyone was packing up to leave, I saw our mom, waiting with Crystal's parents, arms crossed. Crystal stood with them, and it was clear she'd been crying. By the conflicted body language, I knew this was about Crystal and Mike being a couple. I looked for Mike but didn't see him anywhere. I'd have to deal with him next.

"Hey, Crystal. What's wrong?" I asked, entering the room, pretending to be clueless. "You were so happy playing Bingo tonight."

"Her parents don't approve," said our mom, and I flashed her a look that said, *You're not helping.*

"I'm leaving," said Crystal.

"That's okay. You'll be back, right?" I turned to her parents, full of infectious hope and certainty. *Right?*

But her mom wasn't playing. She ignored me, her eyes stern and downcast. "Time to go, Crystal. Get your things. Be quick."

"When will we come back?" asked Crystal, wiping tears from her cheeks.

"I don't know. Maybe never. I don't like this, Crystal. You know that. We talked about it."

"Time to hit the road, sweetheart," said her dad.

"Roads? Where we're going, we don't need roads," said Mike, quoting *Back to the Future*. He shuffled into the room. His hands were stained with dark paint.

"What were you painting?" I asked, thinking of the large sketchpads and easels.

"I painted a door for me and Crystal."

I was about to comment when I understood what he meant. I remembered his Seussian bedroom, the colorful collage of rectangles, and the empty canvas he'd just cleaned a couple days ago. "You didn't."

"The door is open."

I wasn't listening. I was thinking about how long it would take to repaint the wall. Maybe the Ficus tree could hide it. "We'll have to clean that wall. You know that, right?"

"I'm going to be a country star like Johnny Cash."

"He really is, you know," said Crystal.

I saw that he meant what he said, believed it with all his heart. Crystal did, too. Her smile was joyous and proud, and for a moment I imagined them happily married, living out their days together, their own version of Johnny and June. It came to me in a vivid, jarring flash that made me stagger. I leaned against the wall.

Mike and Crystal hurried away together in a clumsy sort of speed-walk toward the TV room, giggling.

Mike passed several scuff marks without stopping to clean them.

"Did you see that?" asked Mom.

"I did."

I was filled with an instinctual fear. I wanted to keep Mike in this room with me. He was my baby brother, and I didn't want him to leave my sight.

"They can't be alone together," said Crystal's mom.

"Yeah, they might hold hands or something," said our mom, and I heard the eyeroll in her tone.

If I hadn't been so distracted, I would have been proud of her. Instead, my mind was connecting all the dots, and they came together with the click of an opening door.

"The door," I said.

Mom said something else to me, but I didn't hear her. I was already striding toward the TV room, as if pulled toward its orbit. The TVs blue light flickered on the walls. The short hallway felt impossibly long.

A sharp headache fissured through my brain, and I grimaced, having to close one eye to ward off the pain.

In the distance, I heard what sounded like country music and the roar of applause coming from the TV. When I turned the corner, the TV was dark and silent. I expected to see Mike and Crystal in there somewhere, but the room was empty.

There was no other way in or out, and I spun in a circle, as if I'd missed them. The TV room was sparse, containing two couches, several chairs, and potted plants. I spun in another circle, and that's when I noticed the Ficus tree in the middle of the room. Behind it, one of Mike's rectangles was painted on the wall with something oily and black. The door was tall and narrow, and he'd glued thick, pearly ribbons along the top edge. The ribbons fluttered slightly from a draft, flaring like rhinestones.

I caught one and lifted it. The wall behind was the black of space. If I stuck my hand through it, I had the sense I'd be reaching into emptiness. From the darkness, I heard a steady drumbeat and a twangy guitar. I pulled my hand back with a gasp.

"Samuel?" asked our mom from the doorway. Behind her stood Crystal's parents, arms folded angrily.

I plucked the ribbon off the wall.

It snapped free and a tight pressure release all around me. As the ribbon fluttered to the floor, I touched the space where it had been, but the wall was solid and dry. I removed the ribbons one at a time, letting them gather at my feet. When I was finished, I was looking at a child's drawing of a door, scribbled in black Sharpie, along with a circular doorknob.

I faced my mom, her face furrowed in concern, demanding answers.

"They're gone," I said. "The door is closed."

It is late August now, and I feel the heat emanating from the black tar and concrete like warm coals, even though it's the middle of the night. This part of the city is hushed and still, and my worn Sketchers make almost no sound. I am little more than a ghost, someone between worlds.

I hang the straps of my duffel bag on the wiry top of the chain-link fence and haul myself over, careful not to snag my clothing or skin. I land and roll on the dead grass, as smooth as any stunt man. The doors and windows are boarded up. It has been decades since Mike and Crystal went missing. The Life Center is closed, and the empty building is up for sale.

With a short crowbar, I pry open the plywood at the bottom corner, crawl through the open space where a glass pane used to be. I smashed it months ago, and I've been coming here regularly since then. Nine years ago, my mom lost a short battle with lung cancer. I'm living in our old house by myself now. I listen to a lot of Cash these days. I work three jobs to pay the bills.

Inside the empty Life Center, doors and windows are painted in every room and hallway. Spider webs darken the ceiling corners. Roaches scurry away from my small flashlight. It smells dusty in here, but familiar. It still has a good vibe. I pass through the activity room, where Mike used to sing karaoke, and down the hallway to the TV room.

I step over to the space where Mike's doorway had been. I've painted it a few dozen times already, trying to get the exact size and shape, the precise color.

I open my duffel bag and set my supplies out in front of me. Every brush is facing the same way, and my paints are arranged in the spectral order. I think I finally got the black paint right. It has the proper oily color and texture, the right toxic smell. The ribbon was harder to find, but I found it at a fabric store on a clearance endcap. I bought every roll they had.

Call it a gut feeling, but I think tonight I will get it right. A door will open for me, and I will walk through.

And then it will be my turn at last.

About the Author

Nearly every morning, Ken Hoover wakes up at an ungodly hour to gulp down several cups of coffee and write before he goes to work at his day job. He's never been more disciplined and productive...and tired.

He lives in New Mexico with his wonderful family. Ages ago, he received a Master of Arts degree in Creative Writing from NMSU, and he's an alumnus of Superstars Writing Seminars.

His short fiction has appeared in magazines and anthologies, and he has published two weird western novels. Visit his website for more—short fiction, deleted scenes, musings, and merchandise.

https://kenahoover.wixsite.com/website

http://www.facebook.com/ken.hoover.52

https://www.instagram.com/kenhoover7/

https://twitter.com/KenHoopster

https://www.goodreads.com/author/show/7043785.Ken_Hoover

From the Editor

WHEN I WAS YOUNG, but older than I would every really want to admit, my sister and I made a pact: if one of us ever found a way into another world, we would immediately come get the other. No messing around and being gone for ten years, like in Narnia. Nope. We were both going! Promise!

I held up my end of the deal, at least in as far as I never found the backway into Xanth. I can't say the same for my sister for sure, but, at the very least, I think she'd eventually gloat a bit…

Magic Portals have been at the heart of our stories for generations. From fairy rings of mushrooms that transport you to the fairy realm to caves that lead to the center of the Earth—or worse.

Many peoples' myths and legends are centered around ways and places to travel between worlds and realms. Some are places lost to us, and some are places we hope will stay sealed. Either way, like ghosts, the legends of them are ubiquitous.

Which leaves me with the eternal hope that I'll still bumble my way into a magic land, even if I have to ask the princess on the unicorn to please wait a moment while I call my sister, who never answers her phone, and is likely over an hour drive away from me.

And what do we do about the kids?

Well…cross that bridge when we come to it, I guess.

If it's a bridge you're looking for, I hope you find it. If you do, send me an email before you go, so I know there's one out there somewhere. Meanwhile, I hope our collection of stories hold you over.

Sam Knight
5/8/2022
(The third year of "we really need a portal to somewhere else…")

Additional Copyright Information

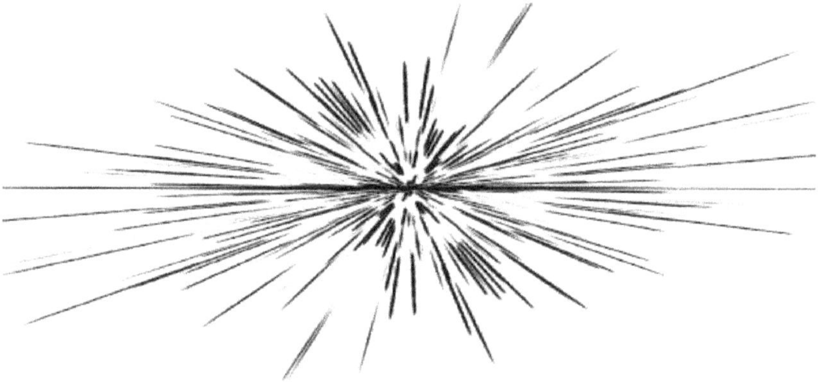

CPSIA information can be obtained
at www.ICGtesting.com
Printed in the USA
JSHW020354100622
26909JS00001B/4

9 781628 690491